SCANDAL
IN THE SUN

Yvonne Purves

*First published in Great Britain 1992
by Mills & Boon Limited*

© Yvonne Purves 1992

*Australian copyright 1992
Philippine copyright 1992
This edition 1992*

ISBN 0 263 77818 5

*Masquerade is a trademark published by
Mills & Boon Limited, Eton House,
18–24 Paradise Road, Richmond, Surrey, TW9 1SR.*

*Set in 10 on 11½ pt Linotron Times
04-9208-75094*

*Typeset in Great Britain by Centracet, Cambridge
Made and printed in Great Britain*

CHAPTER ONE

Goa, India, 1784

'IT IS wise for you to see Lopez Sahib. Assuredly he can help you. He looks after the affairs of this house, is it not?' Ramona's ayah said while dusting the volumes in the study.

Worriedly Ramona stood her quill in the inkstand on her desk and brushed back a strand of silver-gold hair on her wide sweat-dampened brow. 'Hmm, he is the family lawyer paid by my father. Or should I say, a *split*-family lawyer?' she stressed on a dry note. 'Anyway, I have far too much work to do and can't spare time to visit him today.' And as an afterthought, 'I must try to do so tomorrow.'

The clanging of a bell in the front veranda heralded a caller.

'I wonder who that could be?' Ramona asked the room at large, standing up and pushing back from the escritoire.

'I shall go and see, Ramona *baba*.'

'Very well, Ayah, I'll be in the parlour.' Smoothing the muslin frill round the neck of her yellow-print day gown, she moved to the reception chamber. Sending a quick glance round the large, high-ceilinged room, taking in its faded brocaded hangings and matching upholstered suite, she felt satisfied that it was clean and tidy, and seated herself in a high-backed chair, neatly arranging her skirt with its wide flounce at the hem.

She felt uneasy; she was rarely visited by anyone at

this time of morning. Something of importance must have occurred, and she sensed it boded ill.

'Lopez Sahib to see you, missahib,' Ayah announced formally, lifting aside the split-bamboo curtain in the doorway to allow the visitor to enter.

Ramona sensed that her fear was not unfounded. Even so, she rose, smiled and held out her hand as befitted a lady of breeding. '*Bom dia, senhor.*' She always conversed with him in Portuguese and her ayah in Urdu, the only language the latter spoke, though she understood both Portuguese and English. With her eyes Ramona motioned the older woman to stay.

The aged but dignified Senhor Lopez took Ramona's dainty hand and bowed over it. '*Bom dia, menina.*'

'Pray be seated, *senhor*. To what do I owe the pleasure of this visit?' Her apprehension increased; she knew that he had not come on a social call.

Senhor Lopez sighed and plucked at the wide lapels of his dark blue cutaway coat before parting the tails and ponderously depositing his frame on a chair beside Ramona. His faded grey eyes viewed her sadly, the grooves on his forehead beneath the ill-fitting periwig deepening. 'I fear, *menina*, that I am the harbinger of joyless tidings.' He took her slim, trembling fingers in his podgy ones, staring abstractedly at the perfection of her immaculate nails. 'And not long after poor Senhora Dominic's demise. Four months, is it?'

Ramona nodded. She still suffered the pain of her mother's death, but now that the grief had subsided she was able to concentrate on how best she, her beloved ayah and the servants could survive in moderate comfort. Since her mother had died her father had cut off the allowance that had helped to maintain this villa.

'Is it something to do with—with my father?'

Gravely the elderly man nodded.

'Is he—is he. . .?'

'*Sim*, I fear he is dead, Ramona.'

Gently she withdrew her hand, her blue-green eyes growing dark, her cheeks empty of their usual colour, the pallor drawing attention to the attractive mole above and to the left of her upper lip.

'When? How?' Shock made her voice shake.

The lawyer's tone softened with sympathy. 'A month past. He probably caught the same plague that beset your mother and thousands of others.'

'Thank you for telling me, but why have you taken so long to do so?'

Senhor Lopez lifted his shoulders in an apologetic shrug. 'There was legal business to attend to and until it was settled I did not think it advisable for you to know. Now that he is safely buried I feel the time is right.'

'I—I suppose I should visit his grave. Where is it?'

'In Bombay. But I do not think you will go, after what I have to say, *menina*.' Lopez paused and mopped his brow with a large white handkerchief. He sighed. 'I find it difficult to tell. But it must be told.'

She refused to make any guesses. 'Pray continue, *senhor*.'

'Your father made a will.'

She tensed.

Senhor Lopez opened a document case and extracted a sheet of paper with a large seal on it. He examined it as if making sure that he had not been mistaken by its contents. Clearing his throat, he forced himself to sound as professional as he could. 'I will leave out the legal terms and simplify the matter for you. Senhor Dominic has decreed that the villa be sold and——'

Ramona interrupted, staring at Senhor Lopez, her

heart slipping in dismay. 'But he said——' She swallowed. 'He said Mama and I could live here till——'

'Till your Mama died and you had completed your schooling or you married. You are how old now? Twenty-two? Alas, he was well within his rights to do as he has said. He also knew that your work is lucrative.'

Yes, she supposed her career as a translator brought her generous fees, considering she had supported her mother and employed six servants to maintain the villa on her earnings with help from her father's allowance till her mother's death. Moreover, she had been able to save a small sum. Except that money would not be sufficient to buy her another house, even a small one. She glanced in alarm at her ayah, who stood in a corner of the room, her immaculate sari blending with the whitewashed walls, and received a look that said, Courage, my child. Everything will work out for you.

She smiled bravely, squared her slim shoulders and asked the lawyer, 'When did he make this will?'

'Two months past.'

'When will I be required to vacate this place?'

'Within a month—that is, by the beginning of March, when the new owner moves in.'

'You mean the villa has already been sold?' Her voice squeaked in alarm.

'*Sim.*'

'But surely I have some say in the matter? It was my father who was at fault. He created the most appalling scandal by eloping with Madame Fontaine.'

Twelve years ago the heirarchy of Goa's staunch Catholicism had been gravely breached by two of its wealthy merchant families who had enjoyed the respect of the citizens in this close-knit enclave.

Unhappily Senhor Lopez scanned the will again and

shook his head. 'No, *menina*. Perhaps Senhor Dominic assumed you earned enough to support yourself.'

She rubbed her forehead. 'I-it's unbelievable! Do I inherit some of the money from the sale?'

'I'm sorry, *menina*, you have been cut out of the will. He has left everything to his wife and children.'

Her head reeled like a spinning wheel. She glanced at her ayah for her reaction and was appalled to notice how ill she looked. She quickly returned her attention to Senhor Lopez. 'I—I do not understand, *senhor*.'

'I thought you knew that your father had married again, soon after your mother died.'

A low roar sounded in her ears. '*What*?'

'Then I have been remiss. He kept me informed from his—er——'

'His hideout?'

'*Sim*.'

'And whom did he marry, *senhor*?' She noticed the disapproval on his face.

'Why, none other than Madame Fontaine. He had two sons by her. They and their mother are the sole beneficiaries of his will.'

Ramona felt sick with disgust. She closed her eyes for a moment, swallowed and tried hard to control her dizziness. 'But what of Madame Fontaine's husband—is he not alive?' She could barely get the words past her choked throat. 'He left Goa with his fifteen-year-old son soon after his wife deserted them.'

Senhor Lopez's voice sounded muffled through the noise in her ears. 'Monsieur Fontaine died six months past in the vicinity of the French settlement of Pondicherry. I received the news by special runners. I am in the pay of both families and act as mediator. It was my duty to inform Madame of her husband's death. That would make Madame's marriage to Senhor Dominic legal.'

'And what has become of Monsieur Fontaine's son?' She could not imagine what caused her to ask the question.

Senhor Lopez shrugged his ample shoulders. 'Gerard has made his own way in life. I am not at liberty to tell you, Ramona.'

'So. . .so I have just one month to find alternative accommodation?'

Senhor Lopez looked with compassion on her. 'You could contest the will, but I fear you are unlikely to win the case, as Senhor Dominic has sons and they have first claim to the estate.'

Ramona clenched her hands tight in her lap and stared at them, while blood pounded in her head. 'Y-yes, but they were born out of wedlock, which means they are not the legal heirs!'

The old lawyer shook his head. 'If you contest the will it'll be exceedingly expensive, and might drag on for years, I fear. Alas, *menina*, I must impress upon you that this document is legal and your father's widow has the means to fight the case. Do you?'

Fury surged in Ramona's veins. How could her father have done this to her? As if she were the illegitimate child to be cut off and forgotten. 'No. What money I've earned I must live on.' Her voice rose. 'And I have nowhere to go!'

'I'll speak to my wife, and see if she can lodge you till you can find. . .'

Ramona stood up. 'Oh, I couldn't impose on you and Senhora Lopez. But I thank you kindly. I might go to my mother's people in Bombay.'

'Ah, yes, she was English! It was in Bombay while your father was on one of his trade missions that he met your mother. Yes, yes, that is a good idea.' He seemed relieved that she had rejected his offer. Ramona smiled wryly. No doubt Lopez thought that she might taint his family, since she was the daughter of a scandalous father.

She did not mention that her mother had never been close to her family. Her grandfather had been a compulsive gambler and wagered away his fortune, which he had accrued as an East India Company trader. When he'd died he left a few pieces of jewellery, some of which had come down to her. There was an aunt married to a Company officer, but whether she was still in Bombay or not, Ramona did not know.

Senhor Lopez rose to go. 'I will be in touch, *menina*.' He hesitated. 'Oh, forgive me, I meant to commiserate with you on the death of your father. I know how attached to him you were before. . .'

Not now am I fond of him, *senhor*, she said to herself. He destroyed my mother's life and broke my faith in men. Calmly she held out her hand. '*Adeus*, Senhor Lopez.' Earlier when her ayah had suggested she visit him she had meant to ask him to enquire of her father whether she could rent half this large villa to help with its maintenance, since he had stopped the allowance. She could have sacked the servants, but they depended on her. She occupied only three rooms, while her mother's suite and the guest chambers lay empty. Now there was no point in discussing it with Lopez.

After she heard his carriage rumble out of the courtyard she glanced round at her ayah, her face as pale as the moon. The older woman hurried swiftly to her side and, heaving a sob, Ramona buried her head against the only person in the world who loved her and whom she loved. 'It is all right, Ramona *baba*. Do not

fret, child. The gods will help you. Come, lie down and
I will bring you milk.'

Ramona gently disentangled herself from Ayah's
embrace. 'No, no. I must do those translations. If I
finish as many as I can before the month is out we
might be able to find a decent place to rent.'

She ignored the ayah's entreaty to rest, and with
single-minded purpose made for her study. Here she
tried to steep her mind in work.

'You would do well to marry, missahib,' the old ayah
advised, slipping into the room and taking up her
dusting where she had left off when the lawyer had
called. She flicked a cloth over the neat rows of books
on the shelves of the beeswax-scented study, where
Ramona concentrated at her escritoire to translate a
document scheduled for collection late in the
afternoon.

If it had been another servant—apart from the
punkah wallah who pulled the rope attached to the
screen fan suspended from the ceiling—Ramona would
have expressed annoyance at being disturbed from the
intricate work in hand, though she was having considerable trouble in stopping her mind from worrying over
the bleak future. Her ayah was an exception, considering her important role in Ramona's life.

The woman was more of a mother to her than her
own mother had been, even to the extent of being wet-
nurse. Whatever knowledge of life Ramona possessed
she owed to the wisdom of her ayah, on whose advice
she more often than not acted. However, in one area
the nursemaid had failed: Ramona refused to be persuaded into marriage.

She sighed and let the gaze of her blue-green eyes
fasten on the ayah, marvelling that the pale-skinned
north Indian held herself as she had always done, with

imposing dignity. It was not difficult to believe that she was descended from nobility. On her husband's death, to escape the widow-burning rite of suttee, she had fled to Goa with her infant, who had later died. She had taken the humble occupation of ayah and wet-nurse in the prosperous Dominic household. As she had said, better to remain alive in obscurity than die in agony to attain renown. But lately Ramona had noticed that the older woman stooped slightly and that her breathing was laboured. All her enquiries about Ayah's health had met with polite rebuffs or the time-honoured 'I'm getting old'.

'You know my views on marriage, Ayah. Look what it did to my mother. It killed her!'

The nurse laid her duster on a volume and turned to look at the girl, whom she regarded as her 'foreign' daughter. Fondly she studied her beautiful charge, whose hair, taken up in a heavy knot on the crown of her head, shone like silver-gold satin in the rays of the February sun pouring through the open window. The mole near her lip called attention to the faint colour in her cheeks and the redness of her wide and slightly full lips.

'It was not marriage that killed the memsahib, Ramona *baba*, it was the plague.'

'My dear Ayah, you are in no position to encourage marriage. The outcome of it very nearly destroyed you: *you* would have burned to death on your husband's pyre.'

Ayah's dark eyes gleamed with admiration. '*Hah*, that is so. But you are a Christian and such is not permitted by your religion. If you marry, your man will take care of you. You have had many rich foreign suitors, Ramona *baba*. Why do you not marry one of them instead of doing all this hard work?'

Ramona grimaced. 'Stop! I'm surprised you remember all these so-called suitors. I've made up my mind. I intend to remain single. I'm not chancing what happened to my poor mother.' She sighed. Dear Ayah believed that these men had offered her the respectability of marriage. She did not know that they wanted her for a mistress till such times as they found the right bride. They could not ask her to wed them, considering she was smeared with her father's scandal. Fools! They did not realise that she had no intention of marrying, let alone being a mistress. Ramona had heard gossip via the servants that her father was not the only one who led an adulterous life; other merchants in Goa did so too—except they kept their affairs discreet.

'It's true I have trouble maintaining this villa since my father's allowance for its upkeep ceased. Now, ironically, I am free of the place. And if I had somewhere smaller to go I would feel happy to leave. There was never much joy here. Alas, there's the matter of the servants. What will they do? I must ask Senhor Lopez if they can remain on to work for the next owner.'

'You feel too much about others, Ramona *baba*. What of yourself? We must think on that.'

Ramona gave a dry laugh. She had been sure her father would have left her the villa, since she had made no claims on him. Now Senhor Lopez had put her right. Worried questions swam in her head like restless fish in a small pond.

The ayah finished her dusting and left to supervise the other servants. For the rest of the morning Ramona forced herself to work on a document due for collection at four o'clock, and finished it shortly before lunch. The merchant who called for the translation paid her generously and brought more work.

She stayed awake all night, wondering what she could do to help the people who depended on her for their livelihood.

Most of the time she spent walking around the villa like a haunted wraith, fluttering a hand fan to cool herself in the heat of the night, despite its being the mild month of February.

Before dawn she took a bath behind the wall dividing the bathroom where the floor sloped to a drain that carried away the water. She slipped into a muslin dress of pale blue draped over a full, printed underskirt.

Ramona stepped out into the front courtyard to greet the scarlet orb emerging from the mists of a pleasant dawn. Her day usually started with her taking a ride along the riverbank, on Midnight Grandeur, but this morning she felt too tense for exercise. What would become of her Arab horse? she wondered wretchedly. Would he have to be destroyed? Oh, God, save us all, she prayed fervently.

She hardly touched breakfast, eating only a piece of papaya to satisfy Ayah, though she drank a full pot of China tea.

At eight o'clock the six servants began their chores. Today, however, no cheerful singing filled the air as the workers went about their duties. Ramona guessed that the ayah had spread the news of what might happen.

She could not bear the agony of her thoughts, so sought the sanctuary of her study to work on the sheaf of papers she had yet to translate. It took all morning and afternoon to do just one document. And Ramona refused refreshment except several glasses of water till she had completed the task in readiness for the client, who came shortly after. Only then did she leave her study to eat some of the lunch she should have had

earlier. Afterwards she retired to her bedchamber and
lay back to rest her tense body and tired eyes.

She felt surprised that she had actually slept when
woken later. Glancing at the ormolu clock at the side
of her bed, she saw it was seven o'clock. 'Dear me!'
Gradually she realised what was missing. She frowned
at the servant. 'Where is Ayah? She usually wakes me
with a cup of tea at four o'clock. Why have I been
allowed to sleep so late?'

'What will I tell, missahib?' the servant said, wring-
ing her hands and wobbling her head. 'Ayahji has
taken bad and she is asking for you.'

Ramona gasped, swung out of bed and threw a
cotton robe over her shift. 'Where is she?'

'In her house, missahib.'

Ramona grabbed an oil lamp, flew down the back
garden courtyard to the little whitewashed building,
specially built for the ayah. She dashed up the veranda
steps and pushed past a group of servants crowding the
bedroom doorway.

In the lamp-lit chamber the ayah lay on a divan, but
her face remained hidden by the shadow of a man
bending over her.

'Ayah!' she called, placing the lamp on the mat.
Immediately the man straightened and stood aside for
Ramona to pass. She knelt beside the divan and stared
in shock at her beloved nurse. Her grey hair lay loose
on an embroidered cushion, her face pale and dry as
yellowing parchment, her eyes half closed in pain.

'You came,' she rasped. 'The gods call me, Ramona
baba.'

'No!' Ramona caught her ayah's face between her
hands. 'No! You cannot leave! We have much to do.
You will get well. Now fight it. F-fight it!' Tears rolled

down her cheeks. She lifted her face to the man standing beside her. 'Please send someone to fetch Dr Pinto.'

'I am a *hakim*, missahib.' Faint indignation laced his voice. 'I have cured many, including white people.'

'What is wrong with Ayah? Can you help her?'

'I have been called too late. She has suffered for some time. Did she not complain?'

'No. I—I did notice she didn't look her usual self. When I asked if she felt well, she always replied that she was getting old.'

'So are we all, missahib. But did she not suffer pain?'

'D-do not question the missahib, *Hakim*. It is my fault I am ill. I—I did not wish to worry her.' A faint smile touched the bloodless lips. 'No one can cure me. It is the heart. It. . . It. . .' She put her hand on her chest and screwed up her face, lifting herself up, gasping for breath. Then she fell back, staring at Ramona, but the eyes were sightless.

'Ayah!' Ramona put her head on her nurse's chest as if willing her to breathe. Then came the huge, racking sobs that went on and on. Behind her the servants had gathered, and wailing filled the small room. She felt gentle hands assist her to her feet and guide her back to the villa. Two women servants helped her to her bed. But she could hardly see what was going on because of the constant blur of tears. She was still sobbing when Dr Pinto came in, accompanied by a Portuguese nun. He prescribed a draught to make her sleep, and vaguely she heard him instruct the nun to stay with her till she felt better. For days Ramona had no will to go on. For hours on end she lay on her bed, staring into space.

A week after Ayah's body was burnt on the pyre Ramona gently dismissed the nun, informing her that she could cope. It was the doctor's enormous bill that

forced her to pull herself together. Already she had
lost income from the documents she had neglected in
the aftermath of Ayah's death. And before she was
sued she must get back to her study. Even so, she ate
little, slept little. Her future seemed a void.

The sister who had been with Ramona assured her
that the convent would give her refuge when the time
came for her to leave the villa. And later Mother
Superior would make arrangements for her to join a
respectable home as a paying guest. Ramona had been
educated in the convent, and she visited the nuns one
morning to find out for herself whether she could stay
with them. The building was in the town square,
dominated by two cathedrals.

Mother Superior greeted her enthusiastically. 'What
a wonderful surprise, Ramona! How are you, dear?
Sister Lucia tells me you lost a valuable servant.'

'She was not a servant. I considered her my foster
mother.'

'I understand, my child. Why have you not come to
see us before? You know you are always welcome.'

'Yes, yes. It's just that I felt ashamed because of the
scandal in my family. Even now my one-time friends
are too embarrassed to acknowledge me when I attend
Mass at the Bom Jesu Cathedral.'

Mother Superior tut-tutted. 'It is indeed sad, seeing
that it is no fault of yours and your departed mother.'
Here she crossed herself. 'God bless her soul. But
despite your friends' callousness you continued to
attend Mass, and for that, my child, you will be blessed.
Come and sit down, Ramona.' She took her into the
stark convent parlour and gestured to a chair. Ramona
arranged her black gown tidily around her. It had been
sewn for her mother's funeral. Now it came in handy
to honour her ayah's death.

She waited till the elderly nun had seated herself, and said, 'I do not know whether Sister Lucia mentioned it, but I am compelled to leave the villa by the end of the month.'

'Yes, she did tell me, Ramona. But why are you forced to leave? Does it not belong to you?'

'No, it belonged to my father. He died over a month ago and in his will ordered it sold and the proceeds to go to his widow and children.'

Mother looked shocked.

Before the good nun could say anything Ramona hastily went on, 'I have no wish to trouble you with details, but the nub of the matter is that I have nowhere to go. Sister Lucia said that you may be able to accommodate me.'

Ramona saw the nun's eyelids flicker uncertainly, and rushed on, 'I know this is a lot to ask of you, Mother, but I am prepared to pay. Unfortunately my money is not enough to buy another villa or any dwelling. Nevertheless, it will enable me to pay rent. But I will also need an office. I do not know whether you still remember, but I'm a linguist and earn my living from translations.'

'Oh, yes, I remember. You are certainly in demand where your work is concerned.' Mother Superior smiled. 'You have done us proud, my dear.' She hesitated. 'I will have to check on what accommodation we have, Ramona, before I can give you an answer. I fear the convent is rather crowded, but we'll find something for you.'

But two weeks later an important occurrence took place, which changed the whole course of Ramona's life.

She was busy in her study one evening when the

visitor's bell tolled and a servant announced that a sahib had arrived and waited in the parlour.

Ramona slipped into her bedroom to glance at her reflection. She no longer wore mourning clothes and had chosen a dress of light amber cotton. Satisfied that she looked presentable, she made for the parlour, wondering whether Senhor Lopez had called.

When she entered the room she felt stunned, as if she had walked into a door.

A tall young man rose with languid grace from the sofa. Impeccably dressed in a fawn cutaway coat, matching breeches and high boots, he approached Ramona. He seemed faintly familiar, yet at the moment she could have sworn that she had never set eyes on any man as compelling as this one, with his dark brown hair tinged with copper, and black opalescent eyes.

His well-shaped mouth curved in a smile, hinting at derision and revealing gleaming white teeth.

She felt too dazed to speak.

'Do I have the pleasure of addressing Mademoiselle Ramona Dominic?'

'Y-yes.' She could not believe that the croak emerging from her throat belonged to her.

He bowed his head slightly. 'Allow me to introduce myself. We met before, *mademoiselle*, many years ago, but I see no recognition in your eyes.' So deep, so alluring his voice.

Ramona blinked rapidly before collecting herself to acknowledge him with a gracious nod of her head. Yet she eyed him warily; she sensed his displeasure. As if he was here against his will. So why should she give him a warm welcome? Coolly she said, 'I fear, sir, you are right; I do not recall who you are.'

He lifted a dark eyebrow in cynical surprise. 'Perhaps my name will nudge your memory.' He sketched her a sweeping bow full of mockery. 'Mademoiselle Ramona—Gerard Fontaine, at your service.'

CHAPTER TWO

GERARD straightened and studied the girl's reaction to him. He found it highly entertaining that, on first meeting him, most women smiled coyly, batting their eyelashes if they had any, or fluttering their fans if they did not. His ego received a blow when Ramona Dominic did none of these. Her face paled and in her wide eyes he spotted an emotion he had not seen in any other woman during all his twenty-seven years— pure dislike.

'Monsieur Fontaine, I thought you were in Pondicherry. What are you doing in Goa?' Her mellow voice, though implying that he was unwelcome, sensually tantalised him.

He did not like that.

The probing gaze of his iridescent black eyes unnerved Ramona. The power that flowed from this superb male overawed her. Her first impulse had been to ask him to leave, as she had demanded of those men who had insulted her by their degrading 'offers'. She held back, believing it fair to hear him out. Had her mother been alive she would not have tolerated a member of the Fontaine family, however innocent, to set foot in this villa. Indeed the very name Fontaine was an obscene word to her. Even so, if Ramona had wanted to order Gerard Fontaine off the premises she lacked the courage to do so, simply because his personality did not allow that sort of humiliation.

'Mademoiselle Ramona, do I have your permission

to sit?' The charm of his voice, despite its trace of sarcasm, sent a series of peculiar shivers along her skin.

She did not like that.

Ramona refused to fall apart. Alas, she felt hard-pressed to control the flush betraying her agitation. 'Pray forgive my manners, sir. Do be seated,' she said with deceptive composure, settling herself sedately on the sofa, gesturing him to sit beside her. Immediately she regretted it; she should have offered him a chair. Her keen awareness of his presence intensified the fear she felt about her odd response to him. Despite her contempt for the Fontaines, she watched every move-ment of Gerard's as he lowered his tall, well-knit frame on to the seat beside her. Resting his left elbow on the arm of the sofa and propping his prominent jaw on his fist, he let his tanned right hand trail lazily along his muscular thigh, tightly encased in breeches, drawing her attention to the length and strength of his limbs just a few inches from her. To Ramona, he resembled the magnificence of a living tiger that one ached to stroke but dared not.

The lamplight picked out the copper glints in his dark hair, taken back in a deep green ribbon to match the silk on his wide lapels.

An invisible force seemed to have invaded the chamber, weaving a cocoon around them. His black gaze scanned Ramona's face and came to rest on the mole at the side of her upper lip. 'Sir? You used to call me Gerard. Twelve years past, was it not?'

Ramona realised how tense she had become, as if on guard from—she knew not what. 'Before then, I believe. Twelve years ago our lives were torn apart when. . .'

'When your father and my mother eloped with each other and created an almighty scandal that Goa had rarely known. *Mon Dieu*! How could either of us forget?' In his voice lurked the suspicion of hatred. And who could blame either of them for nursing this hideous sin? she pondered.

He laughed dismissively. 'However, I would not have recognised you either if I had met you on the off-chance, *mademoiselle*.' He lifted his head, allowing his left hand to drop on the sofa arm and, in a sideways sweep of his thick-lashed eyes, looked her over with glowing admiration. 'Perhaps I'm not the only man to tell you how beautiful you are.'

She inclined her head. 'Thank you—*monsieur*.' Indeed, he himself had grown up exceedingly dashing, and that was an understatement, except to tell him so would brand her outrageous, to say nothing of the vanity it would create in him. His self-confidence was so deep-rooted that he seemed arrogant, but because it was natural it gave no offence; on the contrary, it added to his attraction. Moreover, well-bred women avoided praising men unless closely acquainted with them, which was unlikely between Gerard Fontaine and herself. In the next breath she went on, 'But you will agree that now is not the time for compliments. Perhaps you could tell me why you have come here.'

He stretched lazily, causing a peculiar knot to form in her abdomen. 'I'll answer that in good time. First, you asked what I am doing in Goa. I came to——' a pause, a grim smile '—to kill your father.'

She gaped at him. 'What?'

He narrowed his eyes, clenched his teeth. '*Oui, mademoiselle*.' He lifted his strong hands and to her horror demonstrated, 'With these I yearned to squeeze the life out of him, watch him gasp, turn blue, tongue hanging out——'

Ramona put her palms to her ears. 'Stop! Murder is wrong, sir. You would hang!'

'Then I am saved, am I not? The serpent is already dead. And it could have been my curse.' He breathed out a laugh. 'Do you feel no resentment against my mother?'

She slowly lowered her hands. 'I assure you, sir, I am no saint. I hated Madame Fontaine. But as I grew up I saw the futility and waste of harping back on the past as my poor mother did.' She could not remember the number of nights she had cried herself to sleep, sometimes in heartbreak, sometimes in rage at her father. 'One of us needed to be practical and look ahead. My aim was to make my mother's life as comfortable as I could. Alas, she has gone, and so has my beloved ayah, the two people I loved most in the world. Now I have my faithful servants and myself to support.' She paused, passing a hand across her forehead. 'But my father made a will and in it he gave orders to sell the villa, the proceeds going to his wife, the ex-Madame Fontaine. Did you know they have two children?'

He nodded sardonically. 'I heard everything. My wayward mother and her offspring have sailed for Brazil. It is for the sake of the children that I have spared her life.'

She stared at him in disbelief. 'You mean you planned to murder your mother?'

'*Oui*. You must be wondering why I have taken all this time to seek them out.'

She wasn't, but she would like to know. 'Why?'

'I did try to, the day my father and I discovered that the errant pair had eloped. For three days I went missing, trying to trace them. When I returned home to collect money to travel to Bombay to see if they were there my father was ill. He was more concerned about my disappearance than my mother's. He begged me not to seek vengeance. My father was a man of peace and vowed that God would repay them.' A disbelieving laugh. 'He called me a fool. Said that I was lucky I hadn't committed murder and ended my youth dangling at the end of a rope. He even applied emotional blackmail: said his health would suffer if I went off again.'

He paused for so long that she had to probe. 'Then what happened?'

'I promised I would not search for them during his lifetime. He persuaded me to go with him to Pondicherry. Now he's dead. . .but it's too late.'

Bitterness gnawed at Ramona. 'You and your father took the sensible course, I dare say, leaving Mama and me to bear the full brunt of the scandal.'

'*Mademoiselle*——'

She stood up and glared down at him. 'You were lucky your father was able to sell up and escape what Mama and I had to endure.'

'*Mademoiselle*——'

'I have not finished yet, sir! Perhaps you should know that we received unsigned letters, urging us to leave the Parish, as we shared my father's and your mother's disgrace. We were treated like outcasts.' Her voice began trembling now. 'And, being defenceless women, we had to put up with obscene suggestions from depraved men. Yes, *monsieur*, you were indeed lucky.'

'Sit down, *mademoiselle*!' he rapped out.

She slumped back, not because of his sharp command but because her legs were too weak to support her. She also knew relief from her outburst, which eased the tension built up over the years at the unfairness of fate.

The copper tan faded from Gerard's face. His eyes glittered and a muscle pulsed in his jaw. 'That's better,' he said, leaning towards her. 'You could have avoided all that by joining your mother's people in Bombay.'

Ramona felt too drained to keep up a tirade but her bitterness persisted. 'We didn't know where in Bombay they lived. They might have returned home by now. My mother was determined to stay in the villa, which she said was hers by right. Besides, we couldn't sell it because it belonged to my father.'

His mood softened. 'We'll leave the past for a moment, *mademoiselle*. What have you decided to do about your future?'

She put up her guard. 'Why should that concern you?'

'Perhaps your future lies in my hands, *mademoiselle*.'

She arched a slim eyebrow. 'Really?'

'*Oui*, really! It is about your future that I am here. Now tell me.'

Curiosity to know just what he had in mind for her prompted Ramona to reveal all to him. She lifted her slender shoulders in a helpless shrug. 'In a week the new owners of this villa will move in.'

'And you?'

'Mother Superior of the convent said she may be able to accommodate me temporarily. If not, she will contact a decent family in the hope that I'll be accepted as a paying guest.'

'You have not heard from the nuns?'

'No. I had intended to see them tomorrow after I finished the last of my translations.'

'Ramona, you may know my father died over six months past and his death, along with that of your mother over four months ago, enabled my mother and your father to marry. It was Senhor Lopez who kept them informed of events.'

She nodded. 'Yes, Senhor Lopez told me.'

'*My* father also made a will, *mademoiselle*. Part of it concerns you. I hoped to arrive in Goa earlier except that I had to settle up his estate. Moreover the sea voyage was delayed because of the threat of piracy and sea battles, which forced us to keep close to the coast and shelter in nearly every port.' Interest lit Ramona's eyes, and Gerard thought he had never seen irises of such a superb colour, like that in a peacock's tail feather. *Mon Dieu*! Why could he not keep his mind on the discussion instead of on this girl, whom he considered a sour reminder of his youth?

'According to my father's will, you inherit a small villa and a generous allowance, which will enable you to live comfortably for the rest of your life.'

She drew in her breath and stared at him. 'But why? I meant nothing to Monsieur Fontaine.'

He dropped his head back on the sofa, looking up at the ceiling. Her gaze fell on the fine lace of his jabot and the classical beauty of his profile. 'Oh, he remembered you as a child. Liked you very much. But he also felt sorry for your mother and willed the villa to both of you. Now Madame Dominic has gone and it's entirely yours.'

'I don't understand. You should be the beneficiary of his will, not I.'

He lifted his head, raised a dark brow and looked at her with studied patience. 'Ramona, I own——' He hesitated. 'Shall we say, I am well provided for? The villa is smaller than this one but big enough for your comfort. My father often stayed there.'

'You do not wish to contest the will and claim the

villa?' She found it bewildering that he should submit the property to a hated Dominic without a fight.

'Certainly not. I would not dream of opposing my father's wishes. *Voilà*! You have somewhere to go and you can take your servants if they're willing to be with you. If not, I'll give them money to get on with.'

Ramona marvelled at the swift turn of events. 'I cannot accept all this from you.'

Gerard grimaced and sighed in exasperation as he repeated, '*I'm* not giving you anything, *mademoiselle*. It is the will of my father. His last words were that you and your mother must have the villa.' And, with a touch of irony, 'He probably felt guilty that you both had to bear the effects of the scandal alone while he and I suffered not at all.'

She ignored him. 'And—and where is this villa? How do I get there?'

'The villa is fifteen miles north of Pondicherry. It was my father's wish that I take you there myself.'

Ramona's blue-green eyes, fringed with long dark lashes, gazed at him in a daze. He was respecting his father's dying wish; but he himself found it abhorrent to escort the daughter of his mother's lover. Certainly she had no desire to travel with the son of her father's mistress.

'You appear reluctant, *mademoiselle*. Do you not want to leave Goa after what you have suffered?' This with a faint sneer.

She closed her eyes and shook her head in disbelief. 'It is all so sudden. I—I need time to think. I still have a few days to make up my mind.'

'My time here is limited, lady. There is a long journey ahead and I need to make arrangements to avoid too much discomfort,' he said brusquely, and stood up. 'Can you give me your answer tomorrow night?'

She would visit the convent in the morning and find out what Mother Superior had to say first. If the nun could not help her then she would have to leave Goa. Otherwise she could stay on and continue as translator. It would be preferable to travelling with this near-stranger, who kept alive heartbreaking memories of her early life. Besides, he resented escorting her. 'Yes, I believe I can.'

She rose to see him to the door when he abruptly turned and narrowed his black eyes on her. 'Tell me, *mademoiselle*, are you in any way emotionally involved with a man?'

She smiled wryly and his eyes dropped to her red mouth, white teeth and the mole above her lip.

He would be free of her if she were in love with someone, she thought. So it was a mystery why she said, 'Oh, no!'

'You mean, no man has offered for you?'

Ramona smiled in bitter recall. 'Yes, there have been a few.' She did not add what type of offers they were.

'And you were not attracted to any?'

'Monsieur Fontaine, let me make it plain that I do not intend to marry—ever.'

He smiled, deep grooves appearing at the sides of his mouth, though derision laced his voice. 'Why, *mademoiselle*, we think alike, because I too am opposed to marriage. Oh, by the way, the villa my father left you is not to be sold. He was adamant about that. It's yours for as long as you live in it.'

His bald statement startled her. She had nurtured vague hopes of selling her new-found inheritance and tracing her mother's people, if not in Bombay then in

England; or buying a house for herself here, in Goa. Whatever unhappiness she had endured in this enclave, at least she knew it. Now those hazy plans had been dashed. 'I see. Goodnight, *monsieur*.'

'*Bonne nuit*, Mademoiselle Ramona.'

She followed him out, stood at the top of the veranda steps leading down to the courtyard and watched him untie his horse from the hitching post. A faint ripple of admiration passed through her as she saw him spring with agility into the saddle. She would never have dreamed that the lanky fifteen-year-old youth of twelve years past would grow up into this magnificent man.

Instead of returning the half-mile or so to his friend and compatriot's house, where he stayed when he did business in Goa, Gerard Fontaine decided on a ride in the moonlit night to his favourite childhood haunt, the bank of the wide River Mandovi. It was nearing ten o'clock when he left Ramona, and all was quiet. He skirted the town and reached the deserted bank, where he allowed his horse its head. The gallop along the white sands stirred a breeze, cooling his hot brow, and would have been enjoyable if his mind had not dwelt on the girl.

He could not think why he worried about her, since the blood of the man whom he hated flowed in her veins. Moreover, Gerard felt piqued that his father had been so determined that he himself should escort the girl to the villa. Yet he could not disregard the last words of his dying parent. The mission was proving difficult, because he had expected to escort a plain woman; he remembered Ramona as a skinny, insipid child with blotchy skin. She had grown up beautiful beyond belief and he resented this—this mysterious pull he felt towards her. He had no time for women.

Only his mother had captured his love in all its purity and her betrayal had wounded him deeply, destroyed his faith in her sex. It had taken him years to recover from her absence.

Gerard laughed out loud when he remembered a voluptuous French whore in Pondicherry who had called him a woman-hater because he'd refused to make her his mistress and endow her with a villa. Perhaps she was right, yet he loved women's bodies; from them he had mastered the art of erotic pleasure. He admitted he could not exist as a celibate nor indulge in more than light affairs; he had no desire to be mixed up with women. He had lived without commitments, enjoying an unfettered life. And that was how he intended it to remain.

Which made his concern for Ramona Dominic's welfare all the more puzzling. Perhaps he'd felt guilty when she had pointed out that she and her mother had had to bear the burden of the scandal while he and his father had got off lightly.

He half hoped that she would refuse his offer to escort her to her villa. He did not relish the thought of being with her day and night for months on end. If she refused, that was her look-out. After all, she was not destitute. He had shamelessly enquired about her from her father's lawyer, and had learnt that through her own diligence she had studied to become a skilled linguist and translator. She would not starve.

Shaking the girl out of his head, Gerard concentrated on the ride. The cool breeze with its stench and aromas of the east, rushing into his face, exhilarated him. It was not till he spotted in the radiance of the moon the masts of ships swaying in the silver estuary at Panjim and the flicker of oil lamps, five miles from Velha Goa, that he decided to turn back. He had promised to visit

Ramona again, and cursed himself for a dolt, for he knew he was looking forward to seeing her.

That disturbed him.

The following morning, after a light breakfast, Ramona set out for the convent, within walking distance of the villa. A young nun ushered her into the parlour. While she waited her uneasiness grew when considerable time passed before Mother Superior made her appearance.

'I am sorry, Ramona, I kept you so long, but I have been busy getting the school ready to receive boarders.'

Ramona smiled, though she had an inkling that the nun had bad news for her. 'That's all right, Mother. I came to enquire. . .'

Mother Superior sighed. 'Yes, I know, my child. Unfortunately we are short of accommodation and had to refuse new boarders. If you are desperate, of course, two nuns have agreed to share a cell. . .'

'Thank you, Mother Superior, that's very kind of you, but as it is I have found somewhere to stay outside Goa.'

The elderly nun put her hand on her chest and sighed in relief. 'Oh, I do thank God. Where will you be going?'

'I hope to leave soon for Pondicherry. I have some property around there.' Ramona sensed the nun's eagerness to be rid of her, since she showed no interest in how the girl had come by the property.

Mother Superior blessed her, gave her a wooden rosary, and Ramona left, feeling unwanted.

She crossed the square to the splendid Renaissance cathedral of Bom Jesu, which housed the remains of St Francis Xavier. Here she knelt before the candle-lit high altar and prayed that she had made the right decision.

Back at the villa, Ramona was busy packing her books into trunks in her study late that evening, when a servant entered and announced, 'Missahib, Fontaine Sahib is here. I have shown him into the big room.'

She felt a small flutter in her abdomen and a sudden quickening of her pulses. As calmly as she could she said, 'Order some tea, please. I'll be with him shortly.'

When the servant left, Ramona rested back in her chair and pressed her hands to her temples. She knew what he had come for and knew what her answer would be. Last night she had dreamt about him. And, heaven help her, what a dream! She supposed she should be thankful that it took her mind off her other worries. Except a faint uneasiness warned her that the dream was a foreshadowing of a future that would make her present anxieties laughable.

Since she was expecting him, she had taken pains with her toilet, something she had not done for any other man, she suddenly realised. Instead of the usual knot she wore on the crown of her head, Ramona let her heavy silver-gold hair fall loose to her waist and gathered it back at her nape with a wide green ribbon the same colour as the background of her floral day dress. Sewn from crisp cotton, it fitted her snugly to her slim waist then spread out over a stiff petticoat. She smoothed her hair and skirt, took a deep breath and moved to the parlour.

He was dressed for riding and sat relaxed on the sofa, his booted feet stretched out in front of him. When Ramona entered he rose with lazy strength, and let his dark gaze sweep over her.

She came forward and gave him her hand, inclining her head, and said coolly, 'Good evening, Monsieur Fontaine.'

He caught her fingers and bowed over them, just

brushing the tips lightly with his lips. '*Bonsoir, mademoiselle.*' She disliked the jolt that shot up her arm.

A servant brought in a salver holding tea and home-made biscuits. She asked him to leave the tray on a small table and did the honours of pouring out the brew.

Gerard accepted the delicate china crockery. 'Thank you, *mademoiselle.*' He took a sip and said, 'Can you ride?'

Her eyes sparkled. 'Oh, yes. I have a stallion, Midnight Grandeur. My mother gave him to me on my eighteenth birthday. I rode him this morning, at dawn. I—I woke early.'

'Could you not sleep?'

'I slept well enough. Amazingly so.'

'Why amazingly so?'

'I'm anxious about my future. I fear the nuns do not have sufficient accommodation to offer. And if I am to continue my work of translations then I must have a study.'

'Does that mean you have decided to remain in Goa?'

Her head came up. 'Sir, it is improper for me to travel alone with you. There has been enough scandal in our families, as you are aware. I shall need a chaperon.'

He laughed drily. 'Lady, I can scarce blame you for mistrusting men, but I give you my pledge that all provisions will be made for you.'

'Now, if you were married, and your wife accompanied us, *monsieur*, that would make the whole expedition respectable.'

'I do not think you were listening to me last night, *mademoiselle*. I am not married and never will be.'

'But I need a chaperon.'

His eyes twinkled with humour. 'For sure, I shall not marry to provide you with one.'

'Oh, I did not mean that!'

'If it is any comfort to you, a married lady will be travelling with us. But you are also free to bring your own women servants.'

She shook her head. 'They are not prepared to leave. I shall have to ask Senhor Lopez if the new owner will employ them.'

'I don't think there'll be any difficulty on that score. In any case, I shall give them enough money.'

'Thank you. I will repay you, *monsieur*, as soon as I can.'

He looked her up and down, his eyes lighting up with. . .amusement? Desire? She chose not to know. The effect was spoilt by his faint smile of contempt. 'I'll remind you about that one day.'

She felt a blush threatening to stain her cheeks. 'Are we to sail, *monsieur*?'

'No; there is conflict between the British and French as usual, and battles are raging at sea, as I've mentioned. It took me three months to voyage from Pondicherry to Goa because of the long stays at nearly every port. It will take longer and also be dangerous trekking overland, but there is a mission I must accomplish which I cannot do if we sail. By all this I assume you are willing to take possession of your new property?'

'I have no alternative. I am pleased in a way that I can take Midnight Grandeur. My groom and I are the only ones whom he will allow to mount him.'

She noticed a subtle change in his attitude to her this evening. Despite his couple of attempts at humour, he practised a trace of cool aloofness. Nothing to be offended over. Perhaps he resented having to act as courier and nursemaid to the daughter of the man he hated. She herself felt resentment that she had to entrust herself to the man whose mother had disrupted her life. In effect, their grievances tallied. But that did not help matters.

He drained his cup and stood up. 'I'll be here in two days with the team to collect you, *mademoiselle*. Please be ready at dawn. *Au revoir*.'

In the next couple of days Ramona set about getting rid of her mother's clothes and a variety of odds and ends that had accumulated over the years. She distributed most of them among the servants. Only Midnight Grandeur's groom, a Christian Goan, offered to go with her. And this pleased her very much.

If Gerard and she had been sailing she would have taken all her books, but, since they were trekking overland, possibly with mules and horses, she would have to keep the load to a minimum. So she gave most of her volumes to the convent and took a few she would need for her work. Her entire luggage consisted of two medium-sized portmanteaux and a canvas bag containing a quilt, pillow and cotton mat to sleep on.

On the eve of her departure the servants brought a holy man to bless her. The *sadhu* wore a yellow sheet round him, and a necklace of tulsi seeds, his body and face covered in ashes, long matted hair taken up in a high knot, and the prong of the god Vishnu chalked in white and red on his brow. He squatted in the arcade and lit a silver branch of oil lamps. Then he chanted and smeared a streak of sandalwood and saffron paste on Ramona's forehead. She gave him a purse of *reals*, and he departed. Then the servants placed garlands round her neck and gave her trays of sweetmeats. There were tears in their eyes and hers too. She

presented each servant with the Goan legal tender of a
gold *tanga* and wished them well.

Before dawn the following day she wandered
through the villa, surprised at the nostalgia stirring
within her. This place had moulded her personality. It
was still dark when she visited the cemetery and knelt
before her mother's grave. 'Mama, pray that I have
done the right thing.' She said her rosary on the beads
Mother Superior had given her, then returned to the
villa.

Changing into a riding skirt and cotton blouse, she
headed for the stables, where the groom was saddling
up Midnight Grandeur. 'Are you packed and ready,
José?' she asked him in Konkani.

'Yes, missahib. There!' He pointed to a bundle in
the corner.

'Good. Take Midnight Grandeur to the hitching post
and stay with him. The sahib should be along soon.'

Ramona returned to the arcade and sat in a wicker
chair with her portmanteaux on the floor beside her,
and waited for Gerard. She knew a sudden impulse to
rush to Midnight Grandeur and race away till they both
dropped dead. Ramona controlled it. She was not
given to foolhardiness.

Meanwhile she noticed that not one of the people
who had professed to be her friends had called to say
goodbye. She knew then that she had been successfully
and unkindly cast out from Goan society because of
her father's misdeeds.

As the grey and gold of dawn streaked across the sky
she saw the team trotting into the courtyard, and her
stomach rolled in excitement. But Gerard was not
alone. There was a European man and woman with
him, plus a number of Indians and mules.

CHAPTER THREE

RAMONA'S excitement mounted; she had never ventured beyond the confines of Velha Goa, and the prospect of crossing the vast peninsula summoned in her a spirit of adventure, a trait she had not known existed.

She stood up and settled a straw hat on her head in readiness to join the party. She felt a little baffled when, instead of approaching the villa directly, Gerard dismounted, spoke briefly to his team, who waited at the hitching posts in the centre of the yard, and made his way to the servants' quarters. She remembered then that he had promised to give her people money, and it earned her gratitude. She was beginning to recognise that he was a man of his word, a contrast to his erring mother, who had broken the biggest pledge of all.

The blood-red sun had already made its appearance through the dawn mist when Gerard finished his task and advanced towards the veranda.

As he sprang up the steps he pushed his wide-brimmed hat to the back of his head. '*Bonjour, mademoiselle,*' he said, too briskly, as if he was impatient to be on his way.

'Good morning, Monsieur Fontaine,' she returned coolly, piqued by his brusque manner, as if he had nominated himself her master.

He gave her a brief glance before turning his gaze on her luggage, and frowned. 'Those portmanteaux are too heavy for my mules. You'll have to take the contents out and bundle them into a couple of sheets.'

'I have no sheets, sir. I gave them to the servants.'

He snapped his teeth together in annoyance, and spoke through them. 'If you please, unlock the trunks, *mademoiselle*. Should we fail to find anything to put your clothes into then I fear we'll have to get your sheets back from the servants. Or come as you are, without luggage.'

'You're being uncommonly absurd, sir! I can't wear this riding skirt and blouse for a prolonged trek across the peninsula, unless it's for only a day.' She knew it was longer than that, but wished to rile him as he was riling her.

He laughed cynically, raising his brows. 'One day? Now who's being absurd? *Mademoiselle*, you know full well we'll be travelling for several months. We have nigh on three hundred miles to cover and that's as the crow flies. It will be nearer six or seven hundred, since we'll need to follow the course of one river or another to ensure a constant supply of water.'

Her blue-green eyes grew large. 'Oh, I'm aware of that. Why do you think I've packed two portmanteaux? Certainly not from joy, sir. I'll need plenty of changes in the heat.'

'But not at the expense of my animals and mule-teers,' he said, dry as desert sand and as irritating. 'Now be so good as to open these trunks. The sooner we set out, the sooner we'll reach our destination.'

'And what if we're caught in the monsoon? My clothes will be soaked through without proper protection.'

'You're quibbling over trifles. We'll be too busy trying to survive, lady, to worry about the state of our clothes.'

Although she resented his self-imposed authority, Ramona decided against insisting on taking her portmanteaux. Reason told her that the unfortunate mules would be the ones to suffer; not he or she.

Throwing him a withering look, which appeared to have no effect, she plucked off the keys dangling from a chain round her neck and handed them over.

Gerard opened the leather chests and began tossing her clothes out, looking at each garment as if studying its merit to act as a bag.

His high-handed behaviour added to her ire. 'What do you think you're doing, sir, throwing my things around?'

'Then the devil take it, you do it! Find some shawl or whatever to wrap this lot into. But for sure I'm not breaking the backs of my animals with these damn trunks!'

Wondering what had caused his black mood, she pulled out two of her wide petticoats with drawstrings at the waist, and held them up.

'Those will do, *mademoiselle*. Now come on, I'll help you.'

She watched in horror and anger as he pulled the drawstrings to close one end of the petticoat and with impatient unconcern rammed her neatly folded garments into it as if he were shoving in straw. Still, she hesitated to show resentment, disliking to cause a scene with his team looking on. So Ramona grabbed the other petticoat and followed his example. She was thankful that she had chosen the portmanteau that housed the three translation volumes she used in her work, and she furtively pushed them in among her garments, praying they would not be too heavy for the mule or tear the petticoat.

At last the task was completed, though she had to sacrifice almost half her clothes. Gerard called to one of his men in the team to bring some string to tie up the ends of the makeshift bags and to take the discarded items to the servants' quarters.

Then, hoisting the bundles easily but unceremoniously on his shoulders, he crooked a finger, beckoning her to follow him, which did nothing to improve her vexation. 'Come, *mademoiselle*, we have lost much time already.'

She almost had to run to keep up with his rapid strides. When they reached the hitching posts Gerard handed her things to a muleteer and then introduced her to the two Europeans. 'This is Monsieur Jacques Janvier and his sister, Madame Nadine Harben. Jacques, Nadine, meet Mademoiselle Ramona Dominic.'

Ramona smiled. 'How do you do?' Nadine gave a tired nod, her head elegantly adorned with a fashionable broad-brimmed hat sprouting several ostrich plumes. Jacques Janvier doffed his sun hat and made to dismount to acknowledge the introductions, but Ramona stayed him with, 'Please do not trouble yourself to leave the saddle, *monsieur*, as Monsieur Fontaine insists we must set off as soon as possible.'

'You had better get acquainted with everyone in the group, first, *mademoiselle*,' Gerard said, faintly mocking. 'This is Rabindranath, Rabin for short, our guide, Ahmed, the Mohammedan cook, and the three muleteers, to whom you will not be speaking much. I see your groom has his own pony. Therefore, *mademoiselle*, I urge you to mount Midnight Grandeur. I'll help.'

His strong hands clasped her narrow waist, and the slight jolt of her body responding to his touch sparked the fear she felt at his power. It seemed churlish and prudish to resist his simple act of gallantry, and she made no demur as he perched her on the saddle. After swinging up on a large chestnut stallion, Gerard set out in the rapidly warming morning, leading the team of twelve animals and ten humans. Ramona's former servants and their children ran out to see them off. At the gate she handed the guard the key to the villa, on Senhor Lopez's orders.

Her throat tightened as she watched the people whom she had considered part of her family and whom she was never likely to see again. She wished she had done more for these servants, who had always been there like her shadows. Turning in her saddle, she waved a sad farewell and kept on looking till the team turned left and the walls of the villa blocked the view. I must look forward, she told herself, I must, I must!

As they trotted on the wide path, flanked by towering teak trees, the horses kicking up swirls of dust, Ramona realised that Madame Nadine Harben was riding abreast of her. She glanced stealthily from beneath the wide brim of her hat at the woman, and suddenly noticed her beauty. Her features were regular, and her leaf-green eyes, at present narrowed against the glare, were fringed with long lashes a shade darker than her auburn hair taken in a neat chignon at the base of her neck. Her magnificent figure appeared to advantage in the cool cotton riding habit of buff colour to camouflage the dust of what promised to be an uncomfortable journey. Nadine looked ahead, unbending in her attitude.

There would be plenty of time for conversation, considering they had taken only the first few steps of the six- to seven-hundred-mile journey Gerard had promised, Ramona reflected. She craned her neck to see what he was doing up front. He rode three horse-lengths ahead of them and appeared to be in earnest discussion with the Tamil guide.

'You are Portuguese, Mademoiselle Dominic?'

The unexpected question from Nadine caused Ramona to blink and turn her head to look at her companion. 'Partly. My father was Portuguese and my mother English.'

'They are dead?'

'Yes.'

Nadine inclined her head and glanced at Ramona, faint interest glinting in her eyes. 'So, *mademoiselle*, you have the blood of the English. They mean to take this vast country for themselves. Is it not?'

Ramona felt as if Nadine was blaming her for the turmoil in the south. 'They are certainly in possession of Bengal after Clive's victory at Plassey, and are battling all over the rest of the country. But I am not politically minded, *madame*. I do not take sides.'

'That may be so, but much of the conflict is going on in the Deccan. There is Tipu Sultan, fearlessly fighting the British, whom he hates. He has many French mercenaries helping him; he likes the French.' She smiled in approval. 'It is for this reason I have asked Gerard for help.'

Ramona could not make sense of the conversation and looked quizzically at Nadine. 'I—I'm afraid I do not understand what all this is about, *madame*. Since you say Tipu Sultan likes the French and you and your brother are French, why do you need Monsieur Fontaine's help?'

Nadine gave a dainty version of the Gallic shrug. 'I explain badly, is it not? Gerard knows the ruler and he can speak better for us. You see, *mademoiselle*, my husband, he is English. Did you not notice my name?'

'I thought perhaps it was French.' She wanted to ask Madame where her husband was, but thought it prudent to remain quiet, lest she touch upon a delicate matter. Best to let the French woman do the talking.

'In one of his conquests this Muslim monarch took a whole British contingent captive. They were held in the dungeons of his fort. My Robert—he is one of the prisoners.'

Ramona's eyes softened in sympathy. 'Oh, I'm so sorry, *madame*.'

Nadine nodded and went on woefully, '*Oui*. The force was sent from Bombay under the command of Brigadier Matthew—alas! Gerard has been a friend of Jacques and myself for many years. We met him in Pondicherry. Then Jacques, who is a merchant, had some business to attend to in Bombay and took me along. He preferred Bombay to Pondicherry and we stayed on.' She smiled in remembrance. 'It was here that I met Robert at a private ball. We fell in love and invited Gerard to our wedding. Then my poor Robert was taken prisoner and Jacques wrote to Gerard, asking for his help. He agreed, came to Bombay but said he could not stay long as he had to travel to Goa to fulfil a behest in his father's will. We were shocked to hear of Monsieur Fontaine's death.' Nadine shook her head in sorrow. 'Anyway, Gerard invited us to accompany him to Goa.'

'Then I suppose you know all about me, *madame*.'

Nadine looked scandalised. 'No, *mademoiselle*, of course not. Gerard mentioned that you had inherited some property near Pondicherry and he was escorting you there.'

'I see. Then I suppose he'll be taking me to Pondicherry first?'

'No, *mademoiselle*. Did not Gerard tell you? We are first journeying to Seringapatam to visit Tipu Sultan.'

Ramona sat as if Medusa had petrified her.

Nadine saw nothing amiss and continued, 'Gerard has agreed to ask the monarch to release Robert. He may demand money, but I am not without funds and Jacques and I are prepared for that.'

Seringapatam! Ramona's mind whirled. She knew the outline of its turbulent history. Tipu's father, Hyder Ali, had been a common soldier, an a coup had ousted the Hindu Raja of Mysore, usurping his throne. On his death his son, Tipu, known as the Tiger of Mysore, because of his valour and ferocity, had become ruler.

'Are you all right, *mademoiselle*? You look pale.'

'I'm surprised that Monsieur Fontaine did not mention you and our journey to Seringapatam, *madame*. We shall be in the midst of a war zone.'

'Oh, it is not a war zone now, *mademoiselle*. Some peace treaty was signed in Mangalore between Tipu Sultan and the British, and all prisoners were to have been returned. But the ruler has not honoured the terms, and my husband is among the few he still holds captive.'

'Surely I had a right to know that we were travelling to Seringapatam? Monsieur Fontaine gave me to understand that he was escorting me directly to Pondicherry.'

Nadine raised a fine eyebrow in faint amazement. 'You are angry with Gerard?'

'Yes. He deceived me. But what——?' She was about to say, But what can women expect from men? Especially a Fontaine? Instead she went on, 'Perhaps it explains why he is in so foul a mood. He probably resents having to act as my bodyguard when he has more urgent matters to see to in that his English friend is in danger.'

Nadine laughed softly. 'Do not worry about Gerard's

mood, *mon amie*, he does not wish to offend you, I am certain. No doubt he is troubled over the outcome of this journey. In agreeing to speak on our behalf for my Robert's release, he has taken on a responsibility most grave.'

On a weary release of her breath Ramona said, 'Yes, I dare say. Somehow I sensed that he blames me for his troubles.'

Nadine smiled strangely and slanted Ramona an assessing gaze. 'You are a beautiful woman, *mademoiselle*. Perhaps Gerard is attracted to you and he is angry with himself for being so, for he has vowed never to marry. It is because of his mother. . .' Nadine shrugged. 'There! It is not for me to say.'

Ramona persuaded herself that the idea of Gerard's attraction to her was quite ridiculous; he no doubt found a Dominic female distasteful. It was brought to her mind that Nadine was not aware of the scandal linking Gerard and herself, and she felt no compulsion to offer an explanation.

Gerard led the team into a canter till they reached the right bank of the River Mandovi where it widened out into a lake. He called a halt, and urged everyone to dismount and water their animals. He and Jacques came forward to assist the ladies. It disconcerted Ramona to feel a touch of disappointment when Jacques and not Gerard helped her down. She felt smitten with envy, watching Nadine and Gerard laughing. I must be mad, she mused, to feel as I do; this man hates me for reminding him of his traumatic past, and, of course, the feeling is mutual.

The moment passed and she eventually began enjoying Jacques's company. They sauntered to the edge of the bank and talked of the delightful scenery confronting them. Beyond the shimmering blue, the craggy mountain range of the Western Ghats rose, and a cool breeze wafted over the waters, creating pleasantness. On the lake itself a variety of waterbirds kept up a noisy chatter. 'It is idyllic, is it not, Monsieur Janvier?'

Jacques's green eyes, so like his sister's, gazed down at her. 'Please call me Jacques, Ramona. We are to be close companions on this long journey, so I pray you do not let us act so formal, no?'

Not far off, Gerard exchanged pleasantries with Nadine, but his mind was not on the conversation. Reluctantly his eyes strayed to where Jacques and Ramona appeared to be enjoying themselves, from the sound of their laughter. He disliked what the girl was unwittingly doing to him. In the last two days when he had not seen her he had not been able to cast her from his mind. Her beautiful face with those extraordinary blue-green eyes and that enchanting mole above her upper lip had seemed to impinge on his brain far too often. It was because of this that he had woken today in a sour mood. He had prided himself on the control of his thoughts. But where Ramona was concerned his restraint was proving difficult. Why her, of all women?

'Shall we stretch our legs a bit, Nadine?' He smiled down at his companion and, taking her elbow, guided her away from the two people who, for no good reason, tended to irritate him by their obvious delight in each other. That woman had no right to enjoy herself, considering what her father had done to his family!

'Oh, I was quite happy watching the muleteers filling up their goatskins,' Nadine remarked, surprised by the hard pressure of his hand.

'You'll see plenty of that on the journey, *madame*. Let us take advantage of this pleasant walk while we can. There might come a time when we'll be in the saddle for hours on end.'

Nadine glanced back at her brother and smiled. 'I see Jacques and Ramona appear to be in good spirits, would you not say, Gerard? I think it is time Jacques found a wife, and Ramona is very beautiful.'

He grunted, and she stared at him.

'I dare say you disapprove of them, *monsieur*!'

He laughed drily. 'Nadine, my love, why should I disapprove? If your brother and Mademoiselle Dominic wish to indulge in droll flirtation that is their business. I have too much on my mind to concern myself with such trifling matters. Now, may I escort you back? I see the horses and mules have all been watered and are refreshed.'

His face grim, Gerard lifted Nadine into the saddle and, without turning round to see Jacques helping Ramona, swung up on his stallion. Gerard yearned to break into a gallop and leave the others far behind— out of earshot of Ramona's melodious laughter. But he had to conserve his mount's and his own energy for the journey; only he and the guide knew of the hazards the party would have to undergo.

The team pushed on at a steady pace so as not to overtax the animals. They stopped at villages to stock up on staple foods of raw rice, flour and vegetables in season. There was also fresh lobster and sea fish to be had from hamlets dotted along the rich Malabar coastal plain, and river fish caught by muleteers from the rivers and their numerous tributaries that flowed from the Ghats.

It was the month of April when the party came to the port of Mangalore. The guide directed them to a caravanserai in a sandalwood and teak forest at the foot of a pass that led inland.

Meanwhile, Ramona had struck up a rapport with Nadine and Jacques. Her excellent command of French endeared her to them. However, it did little to melt the unobtrusive but icy barrier between Gerard and herself. Reason warned Ramona that Gerard and she were incapable of enjoying friendship even if they did try; she was ever-conscious of the knowledge that he was the son of her father's mistress. They were as divided as heaven and hell, but polite to each other when the occasion demanded. Consequently the others in the party seemed to suspect nothing wrong.

Tonight, however, matters changed.

It was late afternoon when the party arrived at the serai, a square precinct with apartments built into the walls, and faced a wide expanse of inner courtyard, where travellers could pitch tents, stake their horses, elephants and camels, and draw water from the central well. It was ideally situated to give those about to journey into the Deccan a few hours' relaxation before they climbed the pass in the Western Ghats.

Servants working in the serai welcomed wayfarers, showing the women to their quarters and the men to theirs. Only Gerard and Ramona could understand the Tamil spoken this far south, and were able to voice their requirements.

Nadine and Ramona shared a large room with simple, clean string beds to sleep on. What delighted both girls was the bathroom attached to the chamber, separated by a bamboo curtain.

Ramona asked a woman attendant to supply bath water. After bathing, the girls slipped into nightshifts. 'I suppose the servant will bring our meal in here,' Ramona remarked. 'There seems no point in dressing fully. Now is the time to relax in something comfortable.'

Nadine yawned. 'I agree with you, *mon amie*. I dare say I am famished and tired. I cannot tell which feeling is the greater.'

A knock on the door heralded the attendant. In Tamil she said, 'Memsahib, the sahibs ask that you join them for dinner outside in the courtyard. It is cooler there. They will come for you.'

Ramona thanked the woman and she left. She grimaced at Nadine. 'I fear we must get into our finery, as Gerard and Jacques have invited us to join them for dinner outside.'

Nadine groaned and flopped on the bed. 'You go, Ramona. I'll fall asleep halfway through the meal.'

'Oh, nonsense! It will give us an opportunity to dress up and treat this as a social event. Think of the hundreds of people who would envy us for enjoying a banquet in the midst of the jungle!' she quipped with a laugh. 'Besides, you have to practise making yourself look beautiful for Robert.'

Nadine sighed and smiled dolefully. 'All right. How can I dampen your cheerfulness?'

Ramona slipped into a lilac gown of silk muslin, and Nadine chose one in pale green. They dried their newly washed hair, and tied back gleaming tresses with matching ribbons. No mirrors graced the whitewashed walls, and neither of the girls had thought to bring one. Hence they had to rely on each other's comments on how they looked.

There was no mistaking the admiration on the faces of the Frenchmen when they came to collect the ladies. Ramona was wont to admit that she did suffer a twinge of envy when Gerard's eyes lit up as he gazed at

Nadine. 'Charming, *madame*,' he said, taking her hand and lifting it to his lips.

She sparkled up at him. '*Merci, monsieur*.'

These French certainly knew the art of charm, Ramona thought sourly. Indeed, she could not find fault with Jacques's compliments, which he heaped on her. Her cheeks began stinging as his green eyes gazed deep into hers and he whispered, 'You look enchanting, *mademoiselle*.' Then he kissed her hand.

Gerard too thought Ramona looked ravishing, and he experienced a mad urge to shove the innocent Jacques to one side and kiss her breathless. He quickly conquered this bizarre feeling. Wishing Ramona a polite '*Bonsoir*', he tucked Nadine's hand into the crook of his arm and led her out into the clear starlit night to a wooden platform, where cushions were placed round a low table. His ears jarred from listening to Jacques and Ramona murmuring together behind him. *Mon Dieu*! Why had he offered to take brother and sister to Seringapatam first, when he could have escorted Ramona Dominic to Pondicherry and then continued to Seringapatam, free of her? Ah! But tonight he would shock her out of her mind. *Mais oui*, that should prove highly entertaining!

The cook had excelled himself with the succulent dish of prawn curry served with a variety of vegetables in season and accompanied by *parathas*, made with wholemeal flour, like rounds of flaky pastry. The meal made Ramona feel mellow, as if she had sipped heady wine, though she had stuck to lime juice, whereas the other three drank fine burgundy. After dinner she enjoyed her first taste of coffee; the commodity was produced here in South India on the slopes of the Ghats.

Nadine broke up the party by stifling a yawn. 'I

confess, I am too weary to keep my eyes open. Perhaps you will escort me back to my chamber, Jacques.' She looked pointedly at her brother, defying him to decline.

Reluctantly he rose. 'Er—yes, of course, dear sister. What about you, Ramona?'

Gerard immediately cut in. 'I wish to speak to Ramona on a matter of importance, Jacques. It is about the situation in Seringapatam, which may have an effect on her.' He sent Nadine a grateful look, while Jacques and Ramona stared at him in bafflement. His manner and determined clenching of his jaws revealed that he was not prepared to go into details.

She watched Jacques and Nadine as they disappeared to her apartment, and felt as if their absence had stripped away her defences, leaving her vulnerable to the mercies of this man, whom she felt certain she despised.

Refusing to meet Gerard's startling black gaze, she toyed with the coffee-cup. 'What did you wish to say, *monsieur*?'

'Not here. As you can see, *mademoiselle*, all the travellers in the serai are sitting outside to enjoy the cool of the night. What I have to say must be said in private.'

Ramona glanced around the courtyard and saw that a number of Indian families squatted in groups. Dressed in printed saris, women cooked over small dung fires and men in shirts, dhotis and turbans dragged on hookahs. Smoke hazed the air, tainted it with its faint acrid smell and no doubt kept the mosquitoes at bay, but Ramona could absently hear the familiar buzz of insects above the loudness of voices.

Finally she brought her gaze back to him and felt the unsettling penetration of his stare. 'Then where do you suggest we go, sir?'

The oil lamp, in the centre of the table, lit up his black eyes, displaying the amusement in their iridescent depths. 'You are the most composed lady I have ever met. Perhaps it is your English blood. Nadine's husband appears to have the same trait.'

'Perhaps. But. . .'

'But what has all this to do with what I am about to tell you? Nothing, *mademoiselle*. Just my personal opinion of your character.' He rose and held out his arm. 'We will go to a private room, which I hired to have a serious talk with you.'

'I'm sorry. If you can't tell me out here then I prefer not to know.'

He came round and, gripping her arm, lifted her to her feet. 'Unless you're prepared to make a scene, I wouldn't resist, if I were you, *mademoiselle*,' he hissed.

Helpless and angry, she allowed him to guide her.

The keeper of the serai himself was waiting at the door of the chamber to bow them in.

Once inside, Gerard discarded his jabot, tossing it on the only divan in the room, rolled up the full sleeves of his white shirt, displaying his muscular arms, and gestured her to be seated. She gingerly perched on the edge of the narrow bed. Her blue-green eyes looked at him warily.

He lowered his tall body with the languor that she had come to associate with him and added to his attraction.

His gaze searched her face and finally rested on the mole above her red lip. 'Ramona, once we arrive in Tipu Sultan's domain after we cross the pass tomorrow, I want you to act as my wife.'

CHAPTER FOUR

FOR a moment or two Ramona remained dumbfounded.

'Have you nothing to say to that, *mademoiselle*?' Gerard lounged back and viewed her with amusement.

Ramona recovered her tongue and her poise, to remark disdainfully, 'I fear, sir, I find you a mystery.'

'Really? How so, *mademoiselle*?'

'You told me nothing of your plans to rescue Nadine's husband from Tipu Sultan—indeed, scarcely spoke a word to me on the journey, treated me as a dumb mule—and now you have the gall to. . .' She passed her fingers distractedly through her silver-gold hair in a vain attempt to withhold her temper. Running her tongue over her red lips, she said, 'I dare say, *monsieur*, you are suffering from loss of memory. Have I not said that marriage for me is out of the question?'

A well-shaped thick eyebrow lifted in mock-surprise. 'Who spoke of marriage, *mademoiselle*? I said it would be in your interest to *act* as my wife.'

'I think you need to do some explaining, Monsieur Fontaine.'

He spread his hands elegantly. '*Mais certainement*, Ramona. Our friend Tipu Sultan has a zenana, and a beautiful unmarried girl like you might be in danger of joining it if he insists on exchanging Robert Harben for you.'

All colour disappeared from Ramona's face when the full impact of his meaning sank in. 'I—I see. And pretending to be your wife will save me from the sultan's harem?'

'Most definitely. Being a good Muslim, Tipu would not dream of taking another man's wife. Unlike your father.'

The heat of anger throbbed in her cheeks. 'There was no need to bring in my father, *monsieur*. You sound as if his misconduct were my fault, and I assure you it was not.'

'Ah, *mademoiselle*, pray do not distress yourself. I meant nothing of the kind. How could I? Considering my mother was at fault too?' He sighed and smiled ruefully. 'Nevertheless, Tipu will not surrender any of his prisoners without some form of payment. It might well be a consignment of arms, which I do not deal in. In lieu he'll want money. I may have enough for his demands, but at my home, not on my person, and that could mean he will take one of the party hostage till I get the gold. He will not agree to bills of exchange.'

'But Nadine told me that she came prepared with enough money to pay for her husband's release.'

He dismissed her words with a toss of his head and flick of his hand. 'Ha! I know how much money Nadine hopes to offer the sultan. It may be a vast amount by her standards, but I assure you, *mademoiselle*, for an Indian monarch who intends to resume the war against his neighbours and the British, all combining to make a formidable enemy, the sum is paltry. If I know Tipu Sultan he will not opt to hold Nadine's husband for ransom, because he is only a friend of mine and I could renege on handing over the gold. Consequently that hostage might well be you, since you'll supposedly be my wife.' On hearing her gasp of horror, he rushed on, 'At least one thing you can be sure of.'

'And that is?' she asked breathlessly.

'And that is, he will not maltreat you.'

She lifted her chin and slanted him a sceptical look, striving to quell her fear. 'How do you know?'

With quiet modesty he replied, 'I know Tipu Sultan.'

It did not have the power to console Ramona. 'So, I am to be a scapegoat to enable your friend to go free? I think this is ill-judged thinking on your part, Monsieur Fontaine. Why cannot Tipu's hostage be Nadine or Jacques? I do not wish them harm, but for the sake of argument, why choose me?'

He laughed cynically. '*Chérie*, is it not obvious? A young and beautiful wife as hostage would ensure that he gets the gold.'

Ramona stood up shakily, her face pale, eyes shedding disdain. 'Perhaps I should applaud you, Monsieur Fontaine, on your clever plan.'

Gerard narrowed his eyes and rose to stand close to her, and she wished she had remained seated. 'I think you need to explain, *mademoiselle*.'

She stepped back and he moved forward. 'Since you cannot take revenge on my father, you are doing so with me.'

He gave a slow, weary smile. 'My dear Ramona, would I ask you to act as my wife if I wanted revenge? No, *chérie*, I would let Tipu add you to his concubines.'

'How kind of you to consider my feelings, *monsieur*.' She bobbed in mock-curtsy. 'Did it occur to you, I wonder, that to masquerade as your wife I will need to know more about you? I doubt whether the sultan will believe we are wed without question. And I do not even know what you do for a living!'

His black eyes gleamed with admiration. 'It seems I have indeed been remiss. I'm a jeweller, as my father was. Towards the middle of this century France discovered a new form of cutting precious stones to bring out their brilliance, especially diamonds. Father and I made use of the art while we were in Pondicherry. Indian monarchs measure their wealth from the amount of jewellery and elephants they own.' He looked down at his hands thoughtfully. 'The Nizam of Hyderabad possesses a diamond mine in Golconda, and Father and I bought the raw stones, which we cut, polished and sold not only for the internal market but for export as well. Now I work to commission only, and one of my clients was Tipu. I designed and crafted his throne of tiger heads. You'll see it for yourself.'

She gazed up at him in awe. 'You must be exceedingly wealthy.'

He shrugged and caught her gently by the upper arms. 'Precious stones are beautiful, and I worship beauty—like yours. I happen to—find you an extremely attractive woman.' The soft allure of his deep voice silenced her protests. As his powerful arms circled her body like bands of smouldering steel, drawing her close to his strong frame, she could feel the heat of his body and the steady thud of his heart. Unable to subdue the vibrations shooting through her, Ramona stared helplessly at him.

Her rapid breath stopped for a couple of heartbeats; his eyes, so densely black, shot iridescent shards of desire, his nostrils quivered, and a ruddiness suffused his copper tan. His breath, emerging from slightly parted lips, spread an aroma of wine and warmth on her face. 'If we are to act as husband and wife, *chérie*, perhaps we should indulge in a little practice. Hmm?'

Ramona was incapable of thinking. Her body, enthralled in his embrace, seemed to have taken control of her mind. In a daze she watched his mouth lowering. At first it gently kissed the mole on her face, then lightly brushed the parted fullness of her red lips.

'*Chérie*, enjoy this,' he murmured. Moving his hand up, he untied the ribbon confining her hair, combing his fingers through her bright tresses, and holding her head steady while his mouth came down with sensual pressure on hers.

His taste, his male scent of sandalwood soap and freshly laundered clothes and, most telling, his closeness, made Ramona conscious of her erotic arousal, a sensation she had never before experienced. His hands, moving in caressing circles on her back, pressed her closer to his hard chest while he deepened his kiss. It awoke a shocking pleasure that throbbed in her loins and sent tingles in her breasts where they rubbed against him. Was this how Gerard's mother felt in the arms of my father? she asked herself. The thought dispelled the mists of entranced insanity and brought her hurtling down to earth. What surprised Ramona was that both Gerard and she broke away from each other at the same time. Had awareness of their folly suddenly struck him as well?

It surely had.

Mon Dieu! This could not be happening to him, he mused in disbelief. He had always regarded kissing a pretty woman as a brief pleasure and little else. True, Ramona was exceptionally beautiful, and now proving to be dangerous. Why had he allowed this woman in particular, a reminder of his past unhappiness, to create this storm of emotion in him? He had intended to mix his kisses with laughter, as he had done with the others, to impress upon her that he was merely dallying. But it had turned out the opposite: serious, meaningful and earth-shaking.

As he dropped his arms heavily to his sides he knew an ache to take her back again and make love to her all night—in bed. He had given up continually cursing himself for an ass, which had had no effect in calming the tempest within him. Except that he'd be damned if he would apologise for the kiss, which he had never in his life enjoyed so much. And that was all it remained—enjoyment. He hardened his jaw, and refused to think beyond this point. Dragging his gaze away from her bewitching eyes, he abruptly turned and said harshly, 'I'll take you back to your chamber.'

Ramona too felt shaken and furious with herself for giving in weakly to his kiss, considering it had affected him as much as a pinprick an elephant. The hard timbre of his voice implied that he thought her a dolt for taking him seriously. Fine; she would shock him! 'Monsieur Fontaine, I refuse to act as your wife.'

He spun round to face her, the sharpness of his black opalescent eyes making her almost wince. 'What?'

'Do you expect me to fall in with your ideas because of a kiss that you believe will make me your slave? I fear, sir, I am not so naïve.'

A faint smile touched the side of his mouth. Folding his arms across the powerful width of his chest, he gazed at her through narrowed eyes. 'I didn't force that kiss on you, *mademoiselle*. You could have stopped it. Why did you not?'

She tried to hide her shame but the heat in her face betrayed her. 'You gave slight warning, sir. I was too thunderstruck to move.'

His smile deepened. 'I'll wager it was your first kiss, *mademoiselle*.'

Her mouth curved in triumph almost flirtatiously. 'Then I fear your wager is lost, *monsieur*.' Her 'suitors' had kissed only her hand, but he was not to know that.

He looked taken aback and not wholly delighted. 'Really?'

'Indeed, sir.' Inwardly she treasured the tiny victory she had scored. 'Would you now please take me to my chamber?'

He did not move. 'I have not finished yet.'

She sighed. 'Go on.'

'Promise to act as my wife.'

'And if I refuse?'

'Then we all return to Goa.'

For a while she stared at him. 'But what about Nadine's husband?'

He heaved his shoulders in cruel nonchalance. 'Then she must appeal to someone else to help her. But you will not enter the Deccan plateau unless you agree to become my wife.'

'Become your wife? You mean, masquerade as your wife?'

'Precisely, *mademoiselle*,' a mite tetchily. 'Everyone in the team will be informed.'

'Tell me, *monsieur*, why are you so anxious to save me from Tipu Sultan's zenana?'

'Do you want to be part of it? Have you any idea what goes on? There is bitter jealousy among the women, all vying for the favours of their lord. A newcomer suffers the most, unless of course she becomes a firm favourite—then she is given every luxury. Perhaps, having been reared as a Christian, you would like that?'

'No, of course not. . . But why are you concerned about my welfare after what my father did to you?'

'Because on his deathbed my father entrusted me to see you safely to your destination. And I promised him I would.'

She could not understand why his words brought her misery. So it was not out of compassion for her that he was acting so gallantly. Stupid of me to have thought so, she chided herself.

He offered her his arm. 'I'll see you to your room.'

When she entered her chamber she saw that the lamp had been left burning and that Nadine lay propped up in bed, wide awake. 'Oh, Ramona, *mon amie*, I am so relieved to see you back safely.'

'Why were you anxious, Nadine? You knew I was with Monsieur Fontaine. Did you think he would harm me?'

'No, but you could have quarrelled with him and walked out of the serai. I think you dislike him. Why, you barely spoke to him on our journey. La, I pretended not to take the notice, but I did. No matter, I am glad all is well.' She smiled contentedly till her gaze settled on Ramona's head. 'Pray, what have you done to your hair? Your ribbon is missing. It looks as if you and Gerard have been. . .'

Ramona saw comprehension dawn on Nadine's face and said coldly, 'I assure you, *madame*, that what you are thinking did not happen.'

Nadine looked offended. 'I'm sorry, *mademoiselle*, I did not wish to pry. It is none of my business what you do, but as a companion I am concerned for your well-being.'

Ramona relented. 'Forgive me, Nadine.' Nevertheless, she refused to confide in the French girl, afraid of destroying the magic of her first kiss on the lips by sharing the secret. The thought made her impatient with herself for harbouring romantic dreams for a man who had been placed out of her reach by her father's folly.

She remembered the day he had eloped. Early that morning she had woken in terror from hearing piercing screams. Ramona had darted into the main bedroom to see her mother prostrate on the floor, a parchment clutched in her hand. 'Mama, Mama, what is it?' She had tried to lift her parent's stout body on to the bed, but found it too heavy for her ten-year-old strength. As her mother continued to scream Ramona cried and wrung her hands. She dashed out to call her ayah. Together they put the distraught lady to bed. Gently Ayah soothed Senhora Dominic, prised the parchment from her clutching fingers and gave it to Ramona.

'What does that say, *baba*?' she asked the child.

There were only a few words, but they were written by her father and had the effect of a dagger thrust. Ramona let the paper float to the floor and held her stomach as if she was about to be sick.

'What does it say, *baba*?' Ayah repeated, but this time her voice was riven with worry.

'It—it is from my father. He is leaving us. He is not returning.'

Ayah left Senhora Dominic and hurried to Ramona's side, hugging her. 'Your father often leaves for Bombay, my child. Assuredly he will come back.'

Ramona could hardly speak; her throat hurt, tears blinded her. 'No. He—he says he loves Madame Fontaine a-and has. . . He forbids Mama to look for him, or he will not send her any money.' Ramona began sobbing.

For days she had cried, while her mother had taken to her bed, refused all food and prohibited anyone from entering her room. She had not cared whether Ramona went to school or not.

Ramona remembered how the wise ayah had taken her to her house and there told her to return to school and work hard at her lessons. 'A good brain can make one rich, *baba*. So learn as much as the good nuns teach you.'

'I don't want to learn! I don't want riches!' Ramona had rebelled.

'But if you remain ignorant no man will marry you.'

'I—I don't want to marry! I will not marry.'

'Then you must learn! You have to make a living for yourself and your mother.'

And so Ramona had put her mind to her studies. But nothing had completely healed the bitterness in her heart. Now Gerard Fontaine had reappeared in her life to slash open the wound. Not only that, but also to lure and torment. . .

Since she had slept fitfully, Ramona was not disturbed at first light by the excited shouting and bustling of wayfarers coming and going in the serai. She rose quietly, so as not to disturb Nadine. She washed and chose a hardwearing riding skirt and blouse for the tough journey ahead. The serai servant would be in shortly with their breakfast, and until then Ramona decided to see what caused the commotion. She softly pulled the door ajar and peered out. Nothing unusual met her gaze. The scene remained familiar, apart from the noise: trumpeting elephants, harsh cries of camels, neighing of mules and ponies and lowing of cattle, perhaps all calling for nourishment. Groups of humans squatted round cooking fires, whence the appetising smell of food rose and caused Ramona's stomach to protest with hunger.

Then she saw him.

The rapid movements of her heart at the mere sight of the man perturbed Ramona. Faith and charity! What did this mean? Yet she could not drag her gaze from Gerard. He looked stunning, in a cream shirt open at the neck and sleeves rolled up to his elbows, riding breeches and calf-length boots. He was talking with the short, thin Rabin. Behind him the muleteers busily mustered the team animals. Jacques was nowhere in sight and Ramona assumed he still slept, like his sister. As she watched, the guide began introducing Gerard to a tall Indian of light colouring who could have come only from the north. Absently she thought there seemed something vaguely recognisable about him. Her interest in the group was distracted by the arrival of the serai servant with a tray of breakfast.

Though the sun had risen, it was still early when the party set off to climb the pass alongside a turbulent river that flowed through the Western Ghats.

The defile was narrow, forcing the team to ride single file and allow passage for traffic coming in the opposite direction. Ramona noticed that Nadine and Jacques had fallen silent and supposed the reason was that the group would soon enter the state of Mysore, in which Seringapatam was the capital and where Nadine's husband was imprisoned.

Whether by coincidence or unconscious volition, Ramona found herself riding directly behind Gerard, who in turn followed Rabin's mount. The party seemed tense, since they were nearing uncertain ground where short spells of fighting took place, she reflected. Suddenly she felt eyes, almost tangible in their power, boring into her back, causing the hairs on her nape to rise. She had vaguely experienced this feeling from the moment the team had set out from the serai, had tried to shrug it off as fanciful, but it persisted. Moreover, the stare of those invisible eyes told of malevolence born of hatred. She twisted round in her saddle, attempting to catch the culprit, but no one appeared to be interested in anything but their steed's progress over the rough ground. The only person in the team who had reason to hate her was Gerard, because of the scandal in the past; save he rode in front of her, and she felt the evil from behind. Ramona ignored the sensation and blamed it on the strain of the journey.

Though not long, the pass ascended through the gorge. Soon Gerard announced in a triumphant and loud voice that they had arrived on the mountainous Deccan plateau. It was drier than the humid coastal plains and comparatively cooler. The guide led them to a copse of teak trees near the banks of the river, and here the party watered, fed and rested their animals, took refreshments and relaxed. Ramona, Nadine and Jacques ate their light meal together and used a tree trunk for back-rests. Some distance away, Gerard munched while talking to Rabin.

After light conversation Ramona and her companions fell silent, as if by common consent avoiding the question uppermost in everyone's mind: how long to Seringapatam? She saw that brother and sister had closed their eyes, taking a nap. The pleasant air and drone of insects made Ramona drowse also.

'Ramona.' Gerard's voice sounded close to her ear. Her eyes flew open to see him down on one knee, looking at her.

She sat upright. 'Yes, *monsieur*?'

He rolled his eyes up in exasperation. 'We are supposed to be husband and wife, Ramona. No more "*monsieur*" please.'

His presence made her oddly shy, a feeling she had not known with other men. But then, no other man had kissed her the way he had done. Even so, she pulled herself together and said, 'I do not remember agreeing to act as your wife—er—Gerard.'

He smiled. 'I do not think you have any choice, lady. Now let us not argue. Would you walk with me for a while?'

She saw no harm in refusing. What could he do in full view of the party?

He caught her elbow, helped her up and guided her along the bank, out of earshot of the others. Here he brought her to a halt, but did not release her arm. 'As you know, it is customary for a married woman to wear a gold ring. I fear, it did not strike me till we left the serai. Unfortunately I do not possess a ring. In fact, I carry no trinkets when I travel. Do you have any? You did mention that your maternal grandfather left you some jewellery. There might be something suitable there.'

She frowned and bit her lip.

'What's the matter, Ramona?'

'I do have a ring. It's my mother's wedding one. But how can I wear it? You know why.'

'Yes, I know, but we need to be practical if we are to save Robert and ourselves. Now, where is the ring?'

'It's among the jewellery I've concealed in my saddle pouch.'

'Good, let us fetch it, Ramona.'

They walked arm in arm to the tethered animals, being attended to by the muleteers. José had put a nosebag on Midnight Grandeur and was rubbing him down. To one side lay the saddle. She readied herself to kneel and take out the purse, when Gerard stopped her. 'Do not show where you keep your treasures, for God's sake! Dismiss your groom first. When you're sure no one is watching, then take what you want.'

She instructed José to attend to his own pony, and said to Gerard, 'There is someone looking. I've felt eyes on me since we left the serai at dawn.'

He pushed his hat back off his forehead and raised his eyebrows. 'You are sure?'

'Certainly I'm sure, and it's not my imagination, Gerard.'

A spasm of delight passed through him; he had not heard his name spoken with such music, he thought, amused with her melodramatic expression. 'It is nothing to worry about. A beautiful girl like you will naturally cause people to stare. Especially since European women are a rare sight.'

Ramona became suspicious. Gerard seemed too eager to pass off her fears. Did he have anything to do with those 'eyes'?

'This is a stare filled with malice.'

'Can you feel it now?'

'No.'

He shrugged and got down on his haunches near the saddle. 'Tell me where that purse is.'

She felt affronted that he should treat her worry with indifference, but what could she do about it? She lowered herself to kneel beside him, and drew out the pouch. Taking off her hat, she poured the valuables into the upturned crown and blinked in surprise at the dazzling display she had not troubled to look at for months. It took a bit of ferreting for her to locate the ring, a wide gold band that encircled the third finger of her left hand with the right amount of snugness.

'Thankfully it fits,' she said, holding out her hand for him to see. His gaze was not on her but on the gems. He seemed to be frozen. 'Gerard, are you all right?'

He did not answer, but scooped up the jewellery and returned it to its pouch. Thoughtfully he rose and hopped the purse in the palm of his hand. He looked at her, the iridescent colours in his eyes radiating wonder. 'I'll take care of this,' he said. 'Lady, I do not think you are aware of the fortune you hold.'

CHAPTER FIVE

'HAVE you ever worn any of them, Ramona?'

She shook her head and gazed at Gerard quizzically. 'They are not to my taste—too heavy and garish. The stones are dull and poorly cut. Are they really valuable?'

'Yes. They are ancient, hand-made with old-fashioned tools. Most jewellery of this age has had its gold melted down and redesigned and the stones recut.' He took out a brooch, examined it closely and popped it back. 'Yes, this appears to be Inca gold and style. The Incas were an ancient South American race with an advanced civilisation, finally wiped out by the Spanish conquistadors. Which makes the pieces in here near-enough priceless. They probably came to India via the Portuguese.'

Admiration shone in her eyes. 'You are knowledgeable in world history.'

He sketched her a bow. 'I thank thee, lady. My father employed a learned Jesuit to tutor me when we arrived at our property near Pondicherry. And, as you know, the Jesuits travelled where other Europeans feared to tread. My tutor was also skilled in the history of jewellery. He taught me well.'

'He certainly did, sir.'

His gaze flicked to her. 'How much sentimental value do you attach to these trinkets?'

She turned the corners of her mouth down and shrugged. 'Not a great deal, I fear. They belonged to my grandfather and I scarce knew him. I dare say he

won them in a wager; he died leaving little else. I
regard them as an heirloom, some reminder of my
mother's family.'

'Your *grand-père* has left enough to buy a kingdom,
chérie.'

Speechlessly she gaped at him and then at the purse
he coolly hopped up and down in his hand. She had
not seen him look so gravely handsome as he stared in
contemplation at the pouch.

'If I could give you the money in lieu of these I
would have traded them to Tipu for Robert.'

Ramona thought about that. She needed the money
to buy a villa, perhaps in Bombay in the British
settlement, and set herself up as translator or inter-
preter. If she had but known the value of these jewels
in Goa she would not be on this gruelling journey with
the son of her worst enemy. She could even have
contested the will! Fate had played a cruel joke on her.
Still, it was not too late; she could——

He sliced through her thoughts like a knife through
fruit. 'If you think you can return to Goa to contest
your father's will, and buy yourself a house, forget it,
mademoiselle.' His voice, with its soft warning and
accurate guess, startled her.

She stared up at him. 'If I had known——'

'You would not be here.'

'Yes. After all, Robert Harben is a stranger to me,'
she said defensively.

'Why should you help him? Is that what you are
trying to say, *mademoiselle*?' He was watching her with
narrowed eyes.

She lifted a defiant eyebrow and gazed directly at
him. 'I can't afford to be as generous as you, sir. You
are aware, Monsieur Fontaine, that I need to safeguard
my future.'

'Your future is already secured in Domaine du Fontaine.'

'Domaine du Fontaine?'

'The villa my father left you is there, *mademoiselle*.'

'Is—is it your estate?' So he was wealthier than she had imagined.

On a non-committal shrug he said, '*Oui*.'

'It is not where I choose to live. Now that I have a choice. . . Of course, I am willing to donate a piece of the jewellery for Robert Harben's release. But for the rest. . .'

He shook his head and looked at her mockingly. 'It will not be possible to give you the equivalent in money for these, *mademoiselle*.'

'Why not, *monsieur*?' She found it difficult to keep the alarm out of her voice. 'You have not long past said that the pieces are priceless.'

His black gaze studied her for so long that she felt uncomfortable. '*Oui*, and I stick by my word.'

She spread her hands. 'So why. . .?'

Gerard chucked her under the chin, and held out the purse. 'If you took this to a bazaar and tried to sell it to an Indian jewel merchant he would offer you a pittance.'

She swallowed. 'But I thought they knew the value of gems.'

'They do, but they deal mainly in Indian gold, which is of a high grade. They do not recognise Inca gold and may consider it worthless. The gems are dull and neglected. They might not be bought at all.'

'I do not understand, *monsieur*.'

'Then I'll explain. A French or European jeweller would know the value at once. If you took it to such a merchant he would still offer you a pittance. Why? you might ask. Because you are unaware of the true value.

But I happen to know their worth and who to sell them to. So, *mademoiselle*, I am your best buyer.'

'I see.'

'And I can't pay you till we reach Domaine du Fontaine. Meanwhile, can I keep this? I'll give you a receipt.'

Reluctantly she nodded, wishing she had not mentioned the jewels. But how could she have known the value? And where could she have sold them?

He slipped the pouch into a leather bag attached to his wide belt, then planted a quick kiss on her mouth, which startled her and made him laugh. 'Just a little thank-you, pretty lady.' His laughter gradually faded, and seriousness set in. 'But will Tipu take them? He has enough jewels of his own. He still might prefer to hold you hostage—so the masquerade stands. Oh, and I advise you not to mention this fortune. If word gets round, who knows? We may never survive to reach Seringapatam.'

She looked at him as understanding dawned. 'Perhaps those eyes I feel have something to do with the treasure!'

He frowned thoughtfully, digesting her words. 'No, I don't think so. By now all your possessions, including your saddle, would have been rifled. Since this is not the case, then I dare say you are suffering from an inner fear.'

Ramona bristled like an angry porcupine. 'Are you suggesting that I am mad, sir?'

He gave her a wry smile. 'Most certainly not, lady. You are a person who has the coolness of manner most superb. Alas, we all suffer from being over-imaginative at times. This may be your trouble.' He did not wait for her to speak, but called to the team to prepare their mounts for the southward trek.

As the party set off, Gerard told the team that the Tamil guide had pointed out that the main route to Seringapatam was dangerous. Many British and French troops with their Indian allies met on it, and frequent skirmishes took place over disputed boundaries. Therefore Rabin believed it would be safer to travel through the forest, which few humans inhabited. And, since the majority of the population down south were Hindus, and hence vegetarians, game abounded in the wilds.

Ramona spotted clumps of bamboo thickets and thorn bushes in the dusty and dry open forest. Gerard rode by her side most of the daylight hours, and they shared the natural beauty of the area. 'Look!' she cried, drawing his attention to a herd of deer. 'Aren't they beautiful? A lovely golden colour.'

'Yes, they're the largest breed of Indian deer, known as the sambar. And the spotted gazelle grazing near them are chital. We shall have to slay one for our meals occasionally.'

Her blue-green eyes widened in horror. 'No! Please don't kill those lovely creatures. I—— We can survive on lentils and bread.'

He tossed her a slightly irate look. 'We're in the forest now, far from villages or human habitation, so grain and flour are not readily available.'

'But alongside riverbanks and streams there are coconut palms. And I saw wild mango groves.'

'Yes, *chérie*,' this with studied patience, 'we could make do with coconuts, provided one of us can climb up to get them. I assure you, I have not tried anything like that,' he told her drily. 'It takes skill. But we'll try and oblige you for as long as possible.'

At night, as she and Nadine sheltered in their tent within the encampment surrounded by a protective ring of fires, Ramona listened a little fearfully to the natural sounds of the night: the call of prowling jackals, laughs of hyenas, grating snarls of leopards and the occasional roar of the tiger on its nocturnal hunt. She had never set eyes on these live animals, but knew they existed because of the skins she had seen on the whitewashed walls of villas of prosperous merchants in Goa. Obviously these beasts were attracted by the horses and mules tethered in the centre of the encampment.

One night Nadine became depressed, and tearfully confided in Ramona while they were preparing for bed in their tent. '*Mon amie*, I am of a mind that my Robert is dead.'

Ramona had not been herself of late because she had felt those unnerving invisible eyes on her more frequently, and Nadine's bald statement increased her nervousness. 'W-why do you harbour such morbid thoughts, my dear?'

Nadine began sobbing. 'My Robert, he—he was not an officer of the most important. Why would Tipu Sultan hold him prisoner and release others? I fear he might have been killed in battle and the British are unable to trace him.'

Ramona lowered herself to the French girl's mat, put her arms round her and rocked her a little. 'I do not think Gerard would have embarked on this journey if he believed your husband was dead. He probably has more information than you do that Robert lives. Why do you not ask him?'

'He does not wish to distress me, so he gives me false hopes. He is a man of much compassion. *You* ask him, Ramona.'

'But he will think I am interfering by probing into what is none of my business,' Ramona pointed out, disinclined to comply.

Nadine caught Ramona's hand and pleaded desperately, 'It is because you are not involved in my Robert's release that Gerard will tell you the truth. Perhaps he will pledge you to say nothing to me, but I beseech you to break that promise.'

Shifting uneasily away from her companion, Ramona bit on her lip. She sighed heavily and confessed, 'I dislike betraying confidences.'

'Oh, please, Ramona!'

Ramona perked up a little as an idea blossomed. 'Perhaps I can find a way round giving my word.'

Nadine's drawn face brightened in the semi-darkness of the lamp-lit tent. 'Oh, thank you, my dear. You will seek Gerard tonight? Now?'

Ramona blinked. 'What? He must be getting ready for bed.'

'No. It is his turn to keep the watch. You will find him outside. Perhaps on his rounds, inspecting that all the fires are lit and at a safe distance from the tents.'

'But how do you know, Nadine?'

'Jacques was on watch last night and he told me that Gerard would be on tonight.'

'They cannot get much sleep.'

'I dare say they doze in the saddle by day. Alas, Gerard does not know the muleteers enough to trust them to guard us at night.'

'He could trust my groom. He's been with me for six years.'

Nadine clicked her tongue impatiently. 'Then you can mention it to Gerard. Meanwhile, would you. . .?'

'Yes, very well,' Ramona agreed reluctantly, feeling certain that her mission would be futile. 'I'll change my shift and look for him.'

'No need to change, *mon amie*.' Nadine rummaged in one of her bags and pulled out a large silk shawl.

'There! It will reach your ankles and should preserve your modesty.'

Ramona settled the white fringed cloth over her bare arms and stepped out into a radiant moonlit night. She looked uneasily about her, but could see no one in the empty space between the tents and the group of animals tethered in the centre of the encampment. Moving behind the tents, she set out quietly to skirt the perimeter, around which the fires blazed. Then she felt the hairs on her nape rising; those invisible eyes were boring into her with evil menace. Breaking into a run, she looked back in terror and collided with a hard, muscular body.

With difficulty she stifled the scream rising in her throat. Two powerful hands caught her arms and steadied her. '*Diable*! What are you about, *mademoiselle*?'

Her breath came out in a sob of relief. 'Gerard! Thank God it's you.'

He frowned. 'What the devil are you doing out here on your own?' Then his brow cleared. 'If you are looking for your—your friend Jacques I left him snoring in our tent,' he commented drily. 'Unless of course he was putting on a show to deceive me, and now awaits your *liaison amoureuse*.'

'Stop! If I were having an affair with Jacques I would not hide it from you. What need would I have for doing so? But it is not so straightforward. As a matter of fact, I was looking for you, *monsieur*.'

He stepped back from her and folded his arms across his chest. They stood close enough to a fire for the light from flickering flames to play on him. She stared up into his stunning face, which was beginning to haunt her more than she desired.

Lines radiating from the corners of his eyes crinkled

as he smiled slowly. 'Ah, so it is with me you wish to have the dalliance? I do not object to the continuing of our all too brief meeting in the serai at Mangalore, *mademoiselle*—or to uphold the masquerade, should I say, *madame*?' He looked up at the sky. 'The pleasantly cool night, the brilliant moon are perfect for romance, and I am not immune. Life is all too short, so let us take what pleasure we can out of it, *ma chère* Ramona.'

The soft enticement of his voice silenced any protests her mind hoped to make and rendered it numb. His powerful arms, reaching out, enfolding her pliant body in his embrace, deepened the spell. She gazed in hypnotic wonder into the opal-black beauty of his eyes, framed with thick, meshed lashes. At first diffidently, then more confidently, her hands climbed up his arms, ever conscious of their muscular strength, and wound round his neck, caressing the thick darkness of his hair.

Ripples of elation raked through Gerard's body when he felt her soft fingers touch the bare flesh of his neck. Her shawl had fallen away from her bare shoulders, revealing thin straps that supported her muslin shift. His dark gaze fell to the high swells of her breasts, their nipples clearly visible through the transparent material. The black mole near her mouth added allure to the inviting lips now parted for his kiss. Her blue-green eyes engulfed him in their magic. Letting out a deep groan of surrender, he brought his mouth down hard on hers, opening it to taste and relish. *Dieu*, this was heaven!

Ramona responded with a fervour she would later come to rue. But now, with her mind dormant, her senses heightened and allowed her full pleasure. She inhaled deeply of his male scent, and felt him draw her away from the moonlight and into the shadow of a tent. His mouth left hers to plant tiny kisses down the long column of her slender neck. 'Oh, Gerard,' she breathed. 'I—I. . .'

'Do not speak, *chérie*. Not yet,' he murmured against her fragrant skin. And then his hand curved round the thin strap of her shift, lowering it from her shoulder. The shock of his warm palm cradling her naked breast made her jump, but he held her firmly. As she arched her back, Gerard brought his mouth down to kiss and gently suck her aroused nipple. A soft sigh of pure delight escaped her lips as her tingling body knew frustration, a yearning to experience full satisfaction from this man and this man alone.

Somewhere in her lethargic brain her conscience began a relentless probing. This pleasure she experienced was for the marriage bed and—Gerard was not for her. Besides, she remembered with a pang of guilt, she had come at Nadine's distraught behest, not to indulge in sensuous joys.

She pushed at him with dogged insistence. 'Monsieur Fontaine,' she panted, 'I think we have gone mad!'

Suddenly the laugh of a hyena shattered the silence, breaking the couple apart. Hastily she retrieved her shawl and wrapped it firmly round her shaking body.

His soft voice rippled with sarcasm. 'I might have known you would act the coward. Why did you come out here, Ramona? To tease and taunt me?'

She shuddered with self-contempt. 'No, certainly not. I—I came on behalf of Nadine, and. . .' She swallowed, ashamed to admit that she had been too weak-willed to resist his charm.

'And the moon affected you?'

'I-it was a folly which I hope not to repeat, sir.'

His mouth curved in derision. 'What ails Nadine? Or are you using her as some kind of excuse to cover your behaviour?'

She shook her head. 'Nadine is worried about her husband. She believes he is dead.'

He placed his hands on his hips. 'What?'

'I—I told her that you wouldn't waste time and money on this journey if you had the least doubt that her husband was alive.'

'Most certainly not! I have reason to believe that he is languishing in one of Tipu's vile dungeons, but living for all that. You may tell Nadine. Why she didn't ask me herself I find surprising.'

Ramona felt slight resentment towards her companion for causing her to bear the brunt of her troubles. 'Nadine feared that out of compassion you would lie to her about Robert's true state.'

'You can assure her, *mademoiselle*, that I would not lie about something so final as death. Nor would I waste my time seeking danger in Seringapatam for a dead man. Come, I'll take you back to your tent. I wouldn't have touched you had I known. . .' He gave a Gallic shrug. 'Never mind.'

The monsoons broke on the afternoon they sighted the city of Seringapatam. Its exquisite Indo-Saracen fort straddled an island in the centre of the Cauvery River.

The party took up residence in a large serai on the outskirts of the city. The downpour, which was not as violent as the torrential rains she had known in Goa, had ceased later on, and they were able to eat dinner outdoors that night. During the meal Gerard addressed the team. 'Tomorrow at dusk I must go into the city and visit a friend of mine, who also has influence with the Sultan. It is imprudent for everyone and the baggage train to arrive on his doorstep. Firstly, it will cause too much attraction, and secondly, my friend will

not welcome so many people and animals. I shall take
Ramona because she will be acting as my wife.'

'Did it not occur to you to ask me, *monsieur*?'
Ramona and Gerard now stood on a formal footing
with each other after that night of glorious insanity. It
was safer, but sadder this way, she had reasoned. Even
so, she fantasised secretly on the pleasures she had
experienced in Gerard's arms. No one could take that
from her.

'Would you accompany me, *mademoiselle*?' he asked
sardonically. Nadine and Jacques laughed.

She bowed to him and mocked sweetly, 'I may,
monsieur. Alas, I must think about it. If you will excuse
me.' She left for the seclusion of her drab chamber,
where she promptly undressed, sought her bed and fell
asleep almost at once.

The serai leased part of its yard to drivers with
vehicles, known as tongas, for hire. Late the following
afternoon Gerard took Ramona out in one of these
colourful contraptions harnessed to a sturdy pony gaily
decorated with beads and feathers.

Gerard gave the driver the name of the residence.
At the imposing wrought-iron gates, guards, who
apparently knew Gerard, saluted smartly and allowed
the vehicle in. A long winding drive led into a courtyard
neatly laid out with bright hibiscus in red, white, yellow
and pink, frangipani, casuarinas, watered by fountains,
and a tree with clusters of scarlet blooms which
Ramona knew as the Flame of the Forest, or known by
the locals as the Gold Mohur. The tonga came to a halt
at the bottom of double steps. Here Gerard dismissed
the vehicle and, taking Ramona's arm, led her up one
side to a teak door at the top. It stood open, and a
guard asked their names, explaining that he would
have to announce them to the sahib. Meanwhile they

could sit in the hall, where chairs of French design lined walls draped with pink watered silk.

The couple did not have long to wait. Ramona was surprised to see that the man who entered to welcome them was a European. He was of middling height and inclined to stoutness, but dressed in the latest mode of cream cutaway coat of shot silk and high cravat.

'Gerard, *mon ami*, welcome, welcome!'

'Armand!'

The two Frenchmen embraced and kissed each other on both cheeks.

'This is my wife, Ramona,' Gerard introduced, and to Ramona, 'This is my good friend Armand Dupres.'

Ramona smiled and held out her hand. 'How do you do, *monsieur*?'

'Ah! You impressed upon me that you would never marry, Gerard,' he accused merrily, wagging a thick finger. 'But, seeing how lovely the lady is, I can well understand.' Dupres gallantly bowed over Ramona's hand. '*Enchanté, madame*. If you please, would you both come in and meet *madame* my wife?'

'So, you too have broken your vow of bachelorhood,' Gerard teased.

Dupres moved his shoulders in an expressive Gallic shrug. 'It is the hand of fate, *mon ami*, is it not?' He escorted his visitors into a drawing-room.

This could be a villa in Goa or perhaps France with its European furnishings, Ramona thought.

She recognised immediately that the lady who set her embroidery aside and rose from the pale blue brocaded sofa to meet her guests was a Eurasian, and beautiful enough to take one's breath away. Indeed, she noticed with a twinge of jealousy that Gerard seemed quite overcome with admiration.

Dupres was clearly bewitched by his golden-skinned

wife; he caught her round her tiny waist and drew her forward for the introduction. 'Charmaine, *ma chérie*, meet Monsieur et Madame Fontaine.'

Charmaine Dupres's red lips parted in a happy smile that revealed startlingly white teeth. She held out her tiny hand to Ramona and appraised her with frank violet eyes. Her French was flawless, and Ramona guessed that one of her parents was probably French. '*Enchantée, madame*. It is most pleasing to meet Armand's friends from his own country.'

She turned to Gerard, who bowed over her hand, his lips brushing her fingers. '*Madame*, allow me to say that Armand is a lucky gentleman.'

'I am lucky too, *monsieur*.' Her violet eyes looked warmly at her husband. 'He is a husband most kind.'

The married couple might have been alone, for all the restraint Armand Dupres practised. He pulled his wife into his arms and was about to kiss her when she scolded him playfully. 'Armand, *chéri*, you are crushing my dress, and the dhobi complains that it is difficult to press.'

'It is a shade of blue that suits you, *madame*,' Ramona said sincerely.

'Thank you, *madame*. . .'

'Please call me Ramona.'

'And you must call me Charmaine. But pray be seated.' She gestured to the Louis XV suite. 'Would you care to have wine or coffee?'

'Coffee, please, Charmaine,' said Ramona, liking her petite hostess.

'And you, Monsieur Gerard?'

'Cognac is more to my liking, Madame Charmaine.'

'Armand, would you do the honours for Monsieur Gerard and yourself while I arrange for coffee to be brought in for Ramona and myself?'

Armand Dupres pecked his wife's cheek before she glided out of the room, and then sauntered across to a veneered wine cabinet on which were trays holding wine glasses and cut-glass decanters. He poured cognac into two brandy glasses and, holding them aloft, treaded carefully over the blue and gold carpet to where Gerard shared the sofa with Ramona.

He drew up a small fretted table, the only one of Indian workmanship in the chamber, and placed the glass on it. 'We will drink with the ladies when Charmaine brings in the coffee. She will no doubt order dinner for you as well, so please do not disappoint us by refusing.'

Gerard raised an enquiring eyebrow at Ramona. 'What say you, *chérie*?'

Ramona looked anxiously at Armand. 'But isn't it too late to give the cook the order? I do think it is unfair on him.'

'Karim always makes too much anyway, so it will be no extra work for him. So please say you will stay.'

Ramona smiled. This was the kind of hospitality she had experienced with the Portuguese community in Goa before her father had disgraced himself. 'How can I refuse?'

The evening turned out one of the best Ramona had enjoyed socially, till Gerard broached the subject of Tipu's prisoners.

They were all in a mellow mood while they sipped their after-dinner wine in the splendour of the drawing-room.

'I'm ashamed to tell you, Armand, that this is not an entirely social visit.'

Armand smiled genially. 'I know, *mon ami*. You want a favour, or perhaps need my help.'

'How perceptive of you, Armand; how did you guess?'

'From your expression, Gerard, I would have guessed nothing, for you were always good at keeping the face straight. Is it not? But now, your Ramona, she is different. Throughout the evening Charmaine and I have observed a restlessness in her manner and much trouble on her beautiful face. Is it not, Charmaine?'

Clearly ill at ease, Charmaine gave a hesitant smile and toyed awkwardly with a jet-black ringlet falling over one slim shoulder. 'Alas, it is true, Ramona. I hope you are not offended.'

'Oh, dear, am I so transparent?' Ramona asked ruefully. 'But no, I am not offended.'

'*Bien*! So tell us what is troubling you, Gerard,' Armand prompted.

Gerard placed his glass on the small table and rubbed the back of his neck absently. 'You are still in Tipu's favour?'

'*Mais oui*. Thanks to your showing me the art of making jewellery, I have made a small fortune, and receive orders not only from Tipu but also other clients. So, *mon ami*, I owe you much.'

'Tell me, what do you know of the British prisoners Tipu holds?'

Armand and Charmaine exchanged alarmed glances.

'This is dangerous ground, Gerard,' Armand warned. 'You are not spying for the British, are you? Because if you are, then be sure that I cannot help.'

Gerard laughed softly, leaned back on the sofa, stretched out his long legs and gazed up at the rococo ceiling. 'No, I am not a spy for the British, although my wife is part-English. I need information on behalf of a friend and compatriot. Nadine is married to a British officer who is reputed to be a prisoner of Tipu's.

When I last made enquiries Robert Harben was alive, but that was some months ago. I wondered if you could tell me whether he still lives and, if so, whether you would make an appointment with Tipu to see us.'

'Ah, Gerard, from what I hear, all the British prisoners died from an outbreak of a virulent disease.'

CHAPTER SIX

FEELING distressed, Ramona covered her eyes with her hand. 'Oh, poor Nadine. She did have an instinct that Robert was dead.'

Gerard sat upright and stared at Armand in shock. 'Are you sure?'

'No, he is not sure,' Charmaine intervened. 'Do you not remember, Armand, that we had it from reliable sources that a fever had raged through the fort and that *most* of the prisoners had died of it—not all? Monsieur Harben might well be alive. You must take Gerard to the Sultan, Armand.'

Dupres looked a trifle sheepish at his wife's chiding. 'But of course. You already know Tipu, Gerard. You do not need me with you. You were the one who designed his throne, and cut the jewels in the royal umbrella. How could he forget his former master jeweller?'

'But I have not been in these parts since then; he might have forgotten me.'

'I'll see the Sultan tomorrow and arrange for you to speak with him. Are you taking Ramona with you?'

'Yes, and Nadine and her brother. The more people we have to plead my friend's cause, the better.'

'If you are nervous of going, Ramona, you are welcome to stay with me,' Charmaine offered.

'That's very kind of you, *madame*, but I think I should be with Gerard. Besides, Nadine will need comforting—if her husband. . .'

Gerard stood up and glanced at Ramona. 'Time we left, Madame Fontaine.'

Though the address was a masquerade, it seemed a paradox to Ramona that she had to bear the name of the woman she resented and had caused so much unhappiness in her and Gerard's lives.

'Where are you staying?' Charmaine asked, shaking Ramona out of what threatened to become bitter thoughts. 'You can use our phaeton if you wish.'

Gerard bowed. '*Merci*, Charmaine, the phaeton will be much appreciated.'

'Where are you staying?' This time Armand enquired. 'I'll see you safely there.'

'It is not a very elegant place, I fear,' Gerard said. 'We are at the serai——'

'Serai!' the Dupres cried in unison.

Gerard sighed. 'There is a whole team of us, and the serai is appropriate for all our needs.'

Charmaine turned to her husband in dismay. 'Armand, you cannot let our friends stay in a serai when there is so much accommodation here. We have surely been imbeciles not to have offered them hospitality before now.'

Armand drew out a fine lawn handkerchief from his brocaded waistcoat and mopped his pale brow to cover his embarrassment. 'Forgive me, Gerard, it was most remiss of me not to invite you to remain here in the first instance. By all means, come for as long as you wish.'

Gerard caught Ramona's elbow and helped her to her feet. 'I will take advantage of your offer of transport, but it will not be possible for us and our group to stay here.'

'Why not?' Charmaine challenged. 'How can you

allow your wife to bear the primitive arrangements of the communal serai?'

'I assure you, *madame* hostess, that the serai might not be luxurious, but it is not primitive,' Gerard responded, trying to curb his impatience. 'But the reason we cannot come here is that there are muleteers and several mounts. We have all adapted ourselves to life in a serai, so it is no hardship. It caters to our basic needs and that is enough till we reach Pondicherry.'

Charmaine pooh-poohed that with an elegant flip of her hand, and Ramona realised that she was the dominant partner in her marriage. 'We have empty stables at the back and ample accommodation for grooms. We once had magnificent Arabs, but when Tipu Sultan heard about them he offered to buy the steeds off us for a fortune.'

Armand took up the tale. 'And, as neither of us is a very good rider, we let him have them. We used the money to purchase French furniture.'

'I find that singularly odd—about the Arabs, I mean,' Ramona mused. 'Could not the Sultan breed them for himself? Surely he has stables of his own?'

'Assuredly he has stables of his own,' Armand confirmed, and went on to explain, 'He also breeds ponies to sustain his cavalry. But for some unknown reason Arab horses cannot be bred in India. They have to be imported.'

Ramona shook her head in wonder. 'And the Arabs you had were imported?'

'Yes, they were given to Armand by a French officer who had to return to France. And he in turn bought them from the few surviving on an Arab ship. These horses are bad sailors and too expensive to lose, so not many are shipped. They are in great demand in

Europe, so few come this far east. As a result, they are priceless, and to own one is a mark of wealth.'

'I have an Arab. My mother gave him to me for my eighteenth birthday, but I do not know how she came by him. And I certainly do not consider myself wealthy.' Ramona forgot about the priceless Inca treasure.

'Then you must bring the Arab here, Ramona. It is a marvel that he has not been stolen,' Charmaine commented in awe. 'He is healthy?'

'Oh, yes; the trek from Goa was good for him, as he needs plenty of exercise. Alas, he will allow only my groom and me to ride him.'

'Then that's settled. Gerard, you and your team must move in with us.' Armand brought his podgy hands together in a loud clap of approval. 'I'll take you back to the serai and you can make arrangements to bring your team here.'

One disturbing thought intruded to remain uppermost in Ramona's mind: Gerard and she would have to share the same room.

The next morning the team arrived at Armand's villa. Nadine and Jacques were overjoyed at having to move into the equivalent of a French château, though its outer architecture conformed to the Indian design of domed kiosks on a flat roof.

Ramona was happy to see that Nadine and her brother struck up an immediate rapport with their hosts. She was also pleased that José and Midnight Grandeur were comfortable in the spacious stables and quarters for the grooms, along with the other muleteers and mounts. Except whenever she ventured near the stables she felt those unseen eyes bearing down on her back, with increasing malevolence. The tall north-

Indian muleteer hovered near by, but he seemed intent on attending to one of the mules.

Back at the mansion, Charmaine had already allotted Nadine and Jacques their rooms. 'I have selected the best guest suite for you two,' she announced to Gerard and Ramona, who followed her up the grand staircase in grim silence without exchanging looks. 'The servants have already taken up your baggage.'

They arrived at a plain teak door that hid the opulence beyond. 'There!' Charmaine said, a little out of breath. 'This suite contains three chambers and a bathroom.'

Ramona knew silent relief; she and Gerard need not share the same room, nor the vast double divan covered with pink brocade to match the curtains and heaped with silk-tasselled cushions.

'You like it?' Charmaine seemed disappointed that her guests had not remarked on the beauty of the rooms.

'Oh, yes, marvellous. I am quite dumbstruck at the splendour,' Ramona quickly assured her.

'We are indebted to you and Armand for favouring us with the best,' Gerard said, bowing to Charmaine.

'*Bien*! Then I will leave you to settle in.' She glanced at the teak clock on the marble mantelpiece above an ornate brass grate that had never seen a fire. 'We have luncheon at noon. So you have ample time to wash and dress before then.'

'Thank you, Charmaine. We'll see you at lunch.' Ramona smiled, and Gerard bowed again to their hostess. Politely enjoining them not to be late, she closed the door behind her.

After the sound of her swishing skirts had disappeared down the landing Gerard shrugged off his riding coat and flung it on an armchair near the bed. 'Don't stare at me like that, Ramona. I assure you, I have not planned this. I am as reluctant as you are to share this suite.'

Paradoxically she felt hurt. Did the night they had made love in the jungle mean nothing to him? She had to concede that even if it did he could not admit it any more than she could. That barrier of scandal was impossible to breach.

'I know.' Then, with typical feminine chagrin, she said, 'All my clothes are limp and worn from endless washing. I'll feel gauche and shabby next to the immaculately groomed Charmaine.'

He threw his head back and laughed. 'You look beautiful in anything and—nothing.'

Ramona felt discomforted, not knowing how to react to his words. They did not offend her; on the contrary, she found them stimulating, creating a tingling in her blood that spelled danger. She supposed a coquette would have slanted him an inviting glance, laughed and said coyly, 'Do you really think so, Gerard, my love?' She could feel heat in her neck and face. Heavens! It was she who wanted to say those words! Hastily she turned her back on him.

She heard him come up behind her, and closed her eyes, willing herself not to shiver at his touch. He placed his hands on her upper arms and gently rubbed them, setting off a pleasurable raising of goose-bumps.

'I did not mean to embarrass you, *chérie*. You do not know how hard this is for me.' How could he tell her that he had never had to strive against the charms of a woman or put up with resistance from one, without sounding arrogant? He knew an uncommon irritation with himself. Why the devil was he behaving like a lovesick fool? Lovesick! Where did that damn word come into all this? He had already convinced himself that she was the daughter of a sworn enemy and therefore out of his reach. Ah! That was the crux of the matter. She represented forbidden fruit and was consequently more desirable.

But he could not lay aside the past. He had to admit that the obsessive revenge he had felt twelve years ago had waned. Twelve years was a long time to bear a grudge. The target of his vengeance had died, and his mother was now middle-aged and forced to bring up young children when she could be enjoying a peaceful time.

Except occasionally he relived the bitterness and hurt of that fateful day in Goa when he had woken to a deathly silence. He had barged into his parents' bed-room. The bed had been unmade and no one was about. The dining-room and all the other rooms in the house had been empty. He had eventually collared the cook and the bearer in the kitchen. They had been talking in agitated whispers, their hands pumping about.

'What goes on?' he had demanded.

'Nothing, young sahib,' they told him, but he spotted the guilt in their faces. 'We are getting your breakfast.'

'Where are the sahib and memsahib?'

They looked at each other. 'We do not know. The—the sahib went out riding.'

'But he always wakes me first and then sees me off to school before he rides. I want to know what has happened!'

'Your mother has run away, my son,' his father said bitterly from behind him. Gerard spun round, horrified to see his father's drawn face.

'Why? Where?'

Silently Monsieur Fontaine led Gerard into the drawing-room and handed him a letter. Tears of rage, bitterness and heartbreak poured from the youth's eyes. 'She's gone with that bastard Dominic! I'll kill him! Does she know that the punishment for adultery is to be dragged naked on the main square and stoned? Does she?' His thin frame was shaking.

'It is no more the law, son. And, even if it were, she has yet to be found.'

'I'll find them! I'll find them and I'll kill them. I swear! I swear!' He collapsed in his father's arms and sobbed. Gerard did not go to school that day, nor the next, nor the next. He took a horse from the stables and rode through the countryside, totally disorganised and stricken. It was impossible to believe that the mother he had adored had done this to him. Hunger and lack of money forced him to return home. It was the doctor who met him on the veranda and told him that his father was ill with worry.

'You are wasting your time on worthless people. Your father is a good man and not very strong. It is your duty now to look after him. I have advised him to take you and go to Pondicherry. He has some property thereabouts.'

A few days later, after Monsieur Fontaine had recovered from his illness, he said to the distraught Gerard, 'I want you to promise me that you will not go in search of your mother and her lover, or try to kill them. You are to put your mind to your studies. As soon as we have packed we leave for Pondicherry.'

Alas, because of his parent's will he was now thrown into the path of the serpent's daughter, who might drag him into the same hell that his father and he had suffered at the hands of his mother.

'Why did you hoodwink Armand and Charmaine into believing that we are married, Gerard? They seem trustworthy enough to know the truth.' Ramona's voice

brought him back to the present. The thoughts reviving
his past put him on guard of who he was dealing with,
and the sooner the Robert Harben business was completed, the sooner he could install Ramona Dominic in
her villa and forget about her.

Abruptly he dropped his hands to his sides and
stepped back. 'It was necessary because Armand is a
friend of Tipu Sultan and he might well be prompted
to tell His Highness of our deception. As for
Charmaine, we have known her for only a day. It is
much too dangerous, taking them into our confidence.
Unless, of course, you are prepared to risk becoming a
concubine.' He wished he were not obliged to protect
her, as decreed in his father's will. How much easier to
let her vanish behind purdah and out of his life.

'Of course I don't wish to become a concubine. I
understand and agree that we must keep up the
masquerade.'

He spun away from her. 'Perhaps you would care to
use the bathroom first, Ramona. I'll wait in the other
room.'

She appreciated his consideration, but disliked his
remote tone. 'Thank you, Gerard.' She also experienced a blend of relief and frustration when he released
her. This intimate atmosphere with just the two of
them provoked temptation that would need herculean
strength of will to oppose. And Ramona could not
guarantee that she could withstand the attractions of
this man, whom she had seen and spoken to every day
for the past few months. He had improved on acquaintance, had seemingly grown closer—dearer. . .

Ramona shut her mind to further thoughts of Gerard
and persevered on what dress to select. She decided on
the lilac muslin gown she had worn in Mangalore when
Gerard had first kissed her.

Once she completed her toilet she knocked on the closed door of the adjoining chamber and called out that she had finished in the bathroom. Ramona then sauntered out on to the exquisitely worked projecting window with its fretted marble balcony. She looked down on a sunny garden displaying dazzling arrays of cannas and hibiscus. Beyond rose a hilly landscape. A gentle breeze stirred her washed and dried silver-gold hair, which she had formally brushed back into a loose chignon on her nape, with tendrils escaping to feather her temples.

It seemed a lifetime since she had left Goa, and more had happened on this journey than in her whole life before then. Now she realised that she had existed in a world of bitterness that could not be assuaged— till the advent of Gerard, like an archangel out of the night with a flaming sword to set fire to—to. . . No, I dare not say it, she thought, lest I plunge my brain into torment it could not cope with. She sighed.

'Why the sigh? Are you bored?'

She smelled his freshness as he came to lean beside her on the balcony. He had donned a cream shirt and burgundy waistcoat, with cream breeches and snowy cravat. His wavy dark hair had been neatly brushed back and secured in a ribbon to match his waistcoat.

'Not bored, sir. Just worried.'

'Why worried?'

She shrugged and shook her head. 'I don't know. I feel as if something is wrong.'

'Naturally there's something wrong. We have a dangerous errand to perform. That is, the release of a prisoner who may well be ill with a disease that we might all catch.'

She looked squarely at him, her hand on her breast. 'Do you think he has a disease?'

'I sense that he is suffering from something, something that could be contagious. Perhaps this is the reason he was not released with the others.'

At that moment a knock sounded on the door. Gerard answered it and Ramona heard the servant say that the sahib and memsahib would like a private talk with them in the small parlour before lunch.

When Gerard and Ramona emerged, the servant led them downstairs and showed them into an antechamber, where Charmaine rapidly fanned herself and Armand looked perturbed. He rose as the couple entered, and waved them to a couple of Louis XV chairs.

Gerard was the first to break the hostile silence. 'What's wrong?'

'Why did you not tell us?' Armand blurted out.

'About what?'

'That you are pretending to be husband and wife?'

Gerard and Ramona exchanged surprised looks. 'How did you know?'

'Madame Nadine's brother told us not long past.'

'But why would Jacques do that? We all agreed to say nothing. Why would he betray our secret now?' Ramona asked.

'I'll tell you why, *mademoiselle*,' Gerard said drily. 'He is besotted with you and is jealous that you should agree to masquerade as my wife when you could well be his in the true sense of the word.'

'B-but I am not attracted to him.'

'Ramona,' Charmaine said, 'it would be folly for you to go to the palace as a single woman. I fear that Jacques will make the mischief for you. If he cannot have you, *mon amie*, he will make sure that you suffer as the Sultan's concubine. And when Tipu sees you I fear this is what he will want.'

'Then it is best that I do not go to the palace.'

'Ah, but if Jacques spreads the word that a beautiful fair-haired unmarried European girl is here, Tipu will assuredly hear of it and want you in exchange for Nadine's husband.'

'That is precisely the reason why we arranged the masquerade,' Gerard explained drily.

Charmaine slapped the centre table with her fan in annoyance. 'But you reasoned without the vengeance of Monsieur Jacques, who is the lover scorned! Is it not? You are blind, I declare, Monsieur Gerard. What I am trying to say is that you and Ramona must have a proper marriage. If I am to spell it out—take the vows of matrimony. Else this girl will be sacrificed to a man whose ways are different from ours.'

Gerard rose slowly. 'What? A real marriage?'

Armand gave a weary cough. 'You heard Charmaine, Gerard. Why this reluctance?' He gesticulated wildly, swirling his hands around. '*Mon Dieu!* The girl is beautiful. Perhaps you would prefer her to marry that dolt Jacques?'

Affronted that Gerard should spurn her so adamantly, Ramona said angrily, 'I am not marrying anyone, *monsieur*. I will not go to the palace.'

'But you do not think of us. If Tipu finds out that we are harbouring someone he desires we shall all end up in the dungeons, and he will have you, for all that!' Charmaine said in high dudgeon.

'All right, if Gerard agrees, then——'

'Do you agree, Gerard?' Armand quickly interpolated.

Black opalescent eyes stared at Ramona, and in them she saw banked fury. 'Are you alive to what this means, Ramona?'

She spread her hands in appeal to her hosts. 'There,

you see? It is he who is not willing. He hates me and
would be happy to see me plunged into a living hell!'

Everyone started talking together.

'Hates you?'

'Living hell?'

'Pardon?'

'What madness is this?'

'*Mon Dieu*! Quiet!' Gerard bawled, and everyone
leaped out of their chairs. 'Quiet,' he repeated, but
softly, apologetically, and they all settled down again.
'Now listen to me, Ramona.'

'I'm listening, sir,' she said stiffly.

'Good. Will you marry me?'

Charmaine clapped gleefully and Armand beamed.

Ramona jerked backwards, almost toppling her chair
and herself. 'What?'

Gerard drew in a long tired breath. 'You heard,
mademoiselle. Isn't this proposal what everyone
wants?' He slapped his forehead in exasperation.

'B-but. . .' But what? She could think of not a thing
to say. And suddenly the humour of the situation
struck her and she began laughing, and so did Gerard
and their hosts.

Then, in the ensuing silence, Gerard said, 'We can
always annul the marriage later when we leave here if
you so wish.'

Charmaine made a move to speak, but her husband
touched her hand and pressed her to keep quiet.

Clearly taken aback, Ramona speechlessly let her
gaze wander from one face to another and finally settle
on Gerard. She expected to see derision in his
expression but it was solemn, not a gleam of mockery
in his iridescent eyes.

'I'm waiting for your answer, Ramona.'

She swallowed painfully. 'Can it be annulled?'

'If it isn't consummated,' he said casually, even managing an indulgent smile.

She heard the gasps from her hosts, and she herself felt a jolt of shock.

'But if it is consummated, *mademoiselle*, through an error of human weakness,' and now she detected faint irony in his voice, 'then we can always separate, but if we do the Church will not permit us to marry anybody else. It's as simple as that.'

She thought of her fate in Tipu's zenana on the one side, and being in bondage to Gerard Fontaine on the other. Though he was the son of her wretched father's mistress, she knew whom she must choose. 'I'll marry you, Monsieur Fontaine, for as long as it takes to get Nadine's husband out of prison. After that we separate.'

He stretched out his long legs, took his time examining his buckled shoes, and shrugged with a nonchalance that tended to vex her. 'As you wish. And now, Armand, where do we find a priest in this Hindu and Muslim populace?'

'Do not trouble yourself, *mon ami*; there are French barracks not far from the fort. Where there is a contingent of French soldiers there is always a priest. He has a small chapel, where he sometimes conducts Mass, but more often the service is held outdoors. We will go there tonight.'

'Not a word to Nadine and especially her brother,' Gerard cautioned them.

'Do not worry, Gerard,' Charmaine said. 'You two go with Armand and I will entertain Nadine and Monsieur Jacques.'

Just then a gong sounded. Charmaine rose. 'That will be the signal for lunch. Come. We will collect

Nadine and her brother, who are waiting in the drawing-room.'

When the meal ended Armand offered to show the men round the compound, and suggested that the ladies enjoy a siesta. Charmaine heartily agreed, and the three of them withdrew to their suites. Too jittery to take a nap, Ramona moved to the jutting window that overlooked a garden. She discovered steep steps leading down to it, and was about to take them when she spotted the three men entering the grounds, and quickly retreated to her bedroom. Here she paced to and fro, occasionally throwing herself into the deep armchair and sighing. She tried to find a way to avoid a marriage that neither she nor Gerard wanted. It was he who was making the supreme sacrifice to save her from the bondage of concubinage when he could be free. She would make it up to him, she vowed. Had she not always repaid her debts?

Soon after dinner Ramona, Gerard and Armand set off in the phaeton. The night was overcast, black, and a drizzle started as the carriage rolled out of the mansion but stopped when the vehicle approached the barracks. As the trio stepped out into the freshly washed air with just a hint of chilliness Ramona saw that they were in a flagstoned yard facing a small church. On the wall at the side of the arched door a lantern burned, and on the other side a bell dangled. Armand pulled on a rope that set up a clanging. Soon the door was opened by a young Indian, who enquired in Tamil what they wanted, and was told that they wished to see Père Philippe.

They were shown into a sparsely furnished parlour. A short while later Ramona heard the swish of a

cassock and faint rattle of rosary beads. A bearded
Franciscan priest made his appearance.

They all rose to meet him and introduced themselves. He asked, 'What can I do for you, my friends?'

Without preamble Gerard began, 'Father,
Mademoiselle Dominic and I wish to be married
tonight if possible, because we have to move out of this
town shortly.'

Ramona was not surprised to see that the priest
looked astonished. 'But *monsieur*, you have not given
enough notice. I fear I must publish banns for at least
three weeks before the wedding takes place.'

'There is no need for banns, Father. We are
acquainted with no one in Seringapatam except
Monsieur and Madame Dupres. I therefore entreat you
to conduct the marriage with the least fuss tonight. If
you refuse, then we'll hold you responsible for what
will be tragic results. It is a matter of life and death,
Père Philippe.'

After more persuasion from Armand and Gerard the
priest reluctantly gave in. First, however, he spoke to
Ramona. 'You did not say anything, *mademoiselle*.
Are you by any chance against Monsieur Fontaine's
decision? Do you agree that your marriage to him is a
matter of life and death?'

A tense silence followed.

Torrential rain had started—she could hear the
downpour hitting the flagstones. Though her heart
hammered from the enormous and irreversible step she
was about to take, Ramona answered calmly, 'Yes,
Father. If I remain single I might be forced to become
a concubine to a non-Christian. I fear I have pledged
to say nothing more. Monsieur Fontaine and I have
known each other since childhood and it is our intention to wed.'

'Well, in that case. . . I had better prepare myself.'

The ceremony was short, simple and impressive. The young Indian Christian who had ushered them into the church and Armand acted as witnesses. Ramona was filled with guilt to think that her mother's spirit must be crying out with rage at this union. Yet that seemed trivial compared to the fact that this was a loveless marriage. Even so, she knew growing dismay that once she left this church she would bear the hated name of Madame Fontaine. Most alarming of all: did Gerard hope to consummate the marriage? She knew he was too proud to force himself on her. Except she wondered whether she had sufficient strength of will to oppose him. Did she want to?

CHAPTER SEVEN

On the way back to the Dupres mansion a pulse hammered relentlessly in Gerard's right temple as he stared out of the carriage window and tried to distract his feverish brain by absently watching the activity in the bazaar. The downpour had stopped, bringing in its wake myriads of winged ants and moths, which swarmed round oil lamps illuminating the open-fronted shops. Outdoor vendors who had hurried in during the torrent were out again, building up dung fires and busily cooking crisp samosas, which they placed on banana leaves and sold to buyers. The appetising smell mingled with the acridity of smoke. As always, the locals, in their regulation clothes of long collarless shirts and calf-length dhotis for men and saris of various hues and textures for women, shouted across at each other, sometimes jovially, sometimes angrily, nearly everyone chewing betel-nuts packed into triangles of pan leaves. Sacred cows and bulls ambled along, helping themselves to vegetable and fruit, unhampered by stall-holders.

Gerard smiled faintly at the familiar yet never boring scene that prevailed through every bazaar in the sub-continent. Nevertheless, the view was marred by the serious step he had taken tonight. He breathed, deeply, silently. *Maudire*! It was obvious that Ramona was against this marriage, and it battered his pride to think that, of all the women he knew who had tried to lure him into wedlock, this one had succeeded, and, worse, with ego-destroying reluctance. How are the arrogant fallen, he misquoted in self-derision.

Shifting his gaze from the bazaar to the interior of the carriage, he saw that in the opposite corner Armand sat dozing, nodding with the swaying of the vehicle. Gerard envied his friend's ability to relax. But then, Armand had accomplished his good deed for the day and was troubled no more.

Gerard slanted a look at the girl seated on the same side as himself. She stared out of the opposite window, her face in profile, pale, traumatised and very beautiful. Madame Fontaine! Though for how long? He felt relieved that, if he succeeded in liberating Robert Harben and he stayed away from Ramona, he would be a bachelor again. Free! Alas, the thought brought no happiness and a mystifying gloom.

The fear on her face caused pity to touch him. He glanced down at her small hand, moving restlessly on the seat, and, leaning over, clasped it gently. But she jerked so violently that he hastily released her, angry that she should find him so repulsive. 'I'm sorry, *madame*,' he said coldly. 'It was not my intention to startle you.'

Confusion heated Ramona's face. 'I—I didn't expect. . . I fear my mind was far away.' Her thoughts, she reflected, were too frivolous for her to confide them to him even if she had meant to. Although marriage had not figured in her plans in Goa, she now felt miserable that the real thing should have been a secret affair totally lacking in romance. She would have liked all the trappings of a conventional wedding: the ivory satin gown with unlimited lengths of the heavy material, a long white lace mantilla, a bouquet of white flowers whose perfume would add to those decorating the interior of a church crowded with wellwishers, and wedding hymns played on the swelling notes of an organ, creating vibrations of awesome emotion. Beside her would be a tall, handsome man whom she loved and who loved her; as yet she could not give him a face. It was these fantasies that occupied her mind, and fantasies they had to remain. Gerard had brought her hurtling back to reality by the touch of his hand. She had not meant to offend him, felt compelled to apologise, except his face had grown hard and he turned to stare out of the window.

Not only Charmaine but also Nadine was in the drawing-room, excitedly awaiting the return of the trio. Both women rushed to congratulate the newlyweds.

'My friends, you have all my best wishes for your happiness,' Nadine gushed. 'How can I thank you for marrying for the sake of my Robert? But mark you this,' she said, wagging a finger portentously at them, 'you will not be disappointed in each other, I am of a certainty convinced!'

Armand stifled a yawn. 'Be that as it may, good ladies, I think we should retire and not keep the young couple waiting.'

They all mounted the stairs, stopping briefly on the landing to exchange a chorus of goodnights and knowing smiles, before retiring to their separate suites.

Once Gerard had secured the door an awkward silence clamoured in the high-ceilinged chamber. The couple stared at each other, Gerard's hands hanging helplessly by his sides and Ramona clasping and unclasping hers in a welter of anxiety.

'Gerard——'

'Ramona——'

They spoke together.

'What did you wish to say, Ramona?' Soft was his voice, evoking the magic she had known on that moonlit night in the jungle. Her fanciful recollection over a man who had married her against his will made her shudder in self-disgust.

Gerard stiffened and glared down at her. 'You don't have to tell me, *madame*. I can guess that you wished you had married Jacques instead of me.'

She was about to make a denial, but checked herself. Why not let him think that? It would keep him from attempting to make love to her, an attempt, she now admitted to herself, she would find it difficult to resist for whatever reason—a passing romantic notion perhaps, but more likely because he was stunning, alluring and also a gentleman. She must discourage him as much as possible—if this marriage was doomed to be annulled. A necessity because of the scandal dominating their lives. If they remained wed then, as the years rolled on, with every argument they would blame each other's failings on their parents' misbehaviour.

'Perhaps it would have been better if I had. But now it's too late, *monsieur*.'

A cruel curve twisted his mouth, and his eyes shot fires of rage that made her recoil inwardly, as if she had aroused the devil himself.

'Indeed it is not too late, *madame*,' he said with savage contempt. 'Fear not, as soon as Robert is rescued you shall be free and so shall I. I look forward to that day.'

She uttered a pain-filled exclamation and took a step towards him, but he favoured her with a stiff bow, and backed away. 'Goodnight, Madame Fontaine.'

She rose early from a fitful sleep, slipped into her well-washed riding clothes, showing signs of wear round the edges of sleeves and hem, and quietly descended the steps leading from the projecting window. The bloodshot sun peeped over the hills beyond the palace compound, where the sweet scent of jasmine and frangipani came wafting on the dawn breeze. Ramona wended her way to the row of neat stables at the back, but saw that no one was about. Remembering what Armand had said about Arab horses being exceptionally valuable, she ran round to Midnight Grandeur's stall and was relieved to see his elegant small head poking over the half-door. He whinnied softly when he saw her. 'I'll be with you in a moment, sweetheart,' she murmured, stroking his nose and long shining neck. 'I have to find your bridle and saddle.'

She moved away from him and began peering into empty stalls in the hopes that one would hold the tack. At last she found it at the very end of the row, but on her journey there she noticed that Sun King, Gerard's Persian stallion, was missing. Her thoughts were forestalled by the appearance of the tall northern Indian.

'*Salaam*, memsahib,' he greeted, bringing his palms together.

'*Salaam*—er—I do not know your name,' she addressed him in Urdu, which was the common language of the north.

He wore white garments and smelled faintly of woodsmoke. 'My name is Govind Lal,' he said quietly, clasping his brown hands behind his tall, thin frame. 'Do you want your black stallion saddled, memsahib?'

She felt distinctly uneasy in this man's presence, though he seemed harmless enough, not looking at her but keeping his eyes humbly cast down. And there was that uncanny resemblance she could not place. 'Do you know where José is?'

'He sleeps in the grooms' quarters near by, memsahib. It is not yet the hour for the servants to rise.'

He made her seem like an unfeeling tyrant. 'Then

please do not wake him. I can saddle Midnight Grandeur myself.'

'If you will allow me, memsahib, I will saddle him.' He reached for the tack and she returned to Midnight Grandeur.

While Govind Lal saw to the steed she said, 'I noticed Fontaine Sahib's stallion is missing.'

'*Ji*, memsahib, the sahib came before the dawn light and took his horse out.'

'He disturbed you?'

'*Nahin*, memsahib. I sleep little. I bathed in the river yonder and was saying my puja when the sahib came. I offered to saddle his horse, but he told me to go back to my prayers.'

'Do you know where he has gone?'

'Beyond the hills to the River Cauvery, memsahib.'

'Thank you, Govind Lal.'

He did not acknowledge her thanks, but stood aside as she swung into the saddle and rode away. If she had turned round she would have seen black malevolent eyes, and the enraged flaring nostrils of an aquiline nose.

She found a rocky path and followed it to the crest of a hill. From this vantage point she could see the wide river below. Palm, banana and papaya trees fringed its banks. Men and women were seated on rocks near the water, washing clothes. She was about to make a descent to the village to watch the people at work when she heard hoofs behind her.

Next moment Gerard had reined in alongside, and glared at her. 'What the hell do you think you're doing out here on your own?'

She glared back at him in angry indignation. 'I might ask you the same, sir! Midnight Grandeur needs exercise and I am giving it to him. It's as simple as that.

What I do and where I go is no concern of yours! I would not dream of questioning you on your whereabouts.'

He drew in his breath through clenched teeth. 'Have you not learned yet that it is the unwritten rule for European women not to go about by themselves in this country?'

'Oh, tosh! I've ridden up and down the banks of the Mandovi on my own in Goa and no one has tried to harm me or any other European girl. I don't see any danger here.'

'Goa is a safe haven, a peaceful Portuguese possession of no great value since the decline in Portuguese power. But Mysore is a rich estate in the hands of a ruthless tyrant. No one is safe, not even those villagers. Remember, they are mostly Hindu, and they resent him for a Muslim upstart; he overthrew their Hindu Raja. As a consequence, Tipu is at war with the former monarch and surrounding neighbours, who are intent on toppling him with the assistance of their British ally.'

'How singularly disloyal that you should speak ill of Tipu when he chooses your compatriots as his allies. You yourself have become prosperous through him.'

He eyed her coldly. 'Disloyalty does not signify. I am not a spy, I am a jewel merchant, lady. Being a jeweller is a highly skilled profession. I might be a Frenchman but I am not a soldier or at war with anyone, and hire my services to whomever requires them, regardless of who they are.'

She felt suitably mollified. 'Nadine mentioned that a truce has been called between the British and the Sultan.'

'An uneasy truce, *madame*. Any moment hostilities will erupt, and a European woman, more so one as beautiful as you are, can fare ill in the hands of the wrong person.'

'That means I can never come riding on my own, by your command?'

'Yes. For as long as I am your husband, I am responsible for you, *madame*.'

For a moment they glared at each other, then, lifting her chin, Ramona said mockingly, 'Oh, I could scarce trouble you. Tomorrow I'll ask José to accompany me.'

'Strange, I'd have thought you would grant Jacques that favour.'

'Perhaps I shall,' she said, slanting him a provocative look.

'Sorry, *madame*, but tomorrow we may be visiting Tipu. Today Armand has promised to see the monarch and arrange an appointment. That is—if Robert Harben is alive.'

Ramona's anger gave way to fear, her stunning blue-green eyes growing dark, troubled. 'Oh! And if he is dead?'

'Then Nadine will be distraught, but we'll be free to carry on to Domaine du Fontaine.'

She swallowed. 'And—and if he is alive I—I might be chosen as hostage if Tipu rejects my jewellery?'

'That's mere conjecture on my part. I cannot say what he'll do; he is an unpredictable man. Now, shall we return to Palais Dupres?'

She laughed softly. 'Is that what it's called?'

He smiled in faint amusement. 'Armand's grandiose name for it.'

They did not return immediately. Gerard led Ramona down to a secluded stretch of white sand on the riverbank and they gave rein to their horses. When they returned to Palais Dupres she felt exhilarated. Not even the thought of the appointment with Tipu in the near future or the threat that she might become a hostage dampened her spirits.

Ramona relished the leisurely breakfast of fresh fruit and croissants, which Charmaine explained she had taught her baker to make. They were light, and delicious eaten with fruit preserves. She remembered tasting them for the first time when her parents were together and her family and the Fontaines had enjoyed a picnic at one of the lakes in Goa. She wondered if Gerard remembered that day because a black-faced monkey had dashed down a neem tree and snatched the croissant from him just as he was about to take a bite. He had stared at the cheeky creature open-mouthed. He sat across from her and she glanced up to see him looking at her and chuckling quietly in memory, and Ramona laughed with him.

Abruptly he grew serious. 'Where is Armand?' Gerard wanted to know.

There was concern in Charmaine's Gallic shrug. 'He ate earlier on. He has gone to see Tipu, *mon ami*.'

Charmaine's words brought fear into Nadine's face; she made a pretence of eating and crumbled her croissant nervously, while her brother glowered at his and sat glumly without saying a word throughout the meal.

After drinking the last of the tea and coffee brought round by bearers in liveries, Charmaine rose. 'Come, my friends,' she said, smiling. 'We shall take a walk in the garden and then sit under my banyan tree. You have never seen one of a surety so vast. It is my practice to go there every day if it is not raining, and do my embroidery. But today I have guests and so we will the conversation make, *oui*?'

Ramona's heart went out to the lovely little woman who was doing her utmost to boost everyone's courage.

'I think I would prefer to retire to my suite, if you do not mind, Charmaine. I—I have the headache,' Nadine complained.

'Then the fresh air will do it good. See, it is a marvellous day! If you go upstairs you will only brood, and that will not do, *madame*. Besides, the servants must get their work done and you will be in their way.' She smiled sympathetically. 'There is no point in worrying, Nadine, *mon amie*. We must wait and see what Armand has to say on his return from the fort.'

A circular bench had been hewn round the enormous banyan tree. Its thick aerial roots sprouted from the branches and descended towards the earth but had to be pruned lest they grew into a forest. The tree was a natural aviary, and the exquisite bird-song compensated for the hours of idle chatter and the question shouting in everyone's mind: How was Armand faring with the Sultan?

It was nearing lunchtime when Armand made his appearance. He looked pale but relieved.

Before anyone could speak to him Charmaine said quickly, 'Ah, my love, you look strained. Would you care for a drink?'

He gave her a grateful peck on her cheek. 'No, *chérie*, I have just had one. I will not keep you all in suspense, especially Madame Harben.' He bowed to the white-faced Nadine. 'Your husband is alive, and some time ago recovered from a serious illness.'

'*Mon Dieu*! Serious illness!' Nadine cried out in horror. Ramona put a comforting arm round her, and the French girl started to weep. 'W-what did the Sultan say? Is he willing to release my husband?'

'He wants to see all of you this afternoon. He heard about your arrival at the serai and your transfer to my house. I fear nothing escapes Tipu Sahib. That's how you must all address him in his presence. Shall we go in to lunch?'

The servants would later enjoy a feast, Ramona reflected distractedly, as no one at the table did justice to the meal, and mountains of food were left over.

Up in their suite, Ramona checked through her dresses for something suitable to wear for the visit to the fort in an hour's time. She called out to Gerard, who was in the adjoining chamber. 'Shall I wear the evening gown?'

'No, wear something light and simple, and your hat. Its wide brim will partly hide your face, and Tipu will approve.'

She was faintly surprised that she should consult him about her clothes as if she were long married to him. After mulling over which dress to wear, she chose the yellow cotton now faded to pale lemon, the floral print long gone.

She took a quick tepid bath, and called out to Gerard when she had finished.

They both completed their toilet together and descended to the drawing-room, where the others soon followed.

But Ramona was alarmed at the sight of Nadine; she looked washed out, ill and thin. 'My dear, do you think it wise for you to go?' she asked in concern.

Nadine bravely straightened her shoulders, but stammered as she spoke. 'I—I must go, since this interview concerns me most. I—I will be all right.'

Tension filled the air. Indeed, Ramona found it difficult to stop herself from trembling.

'Charmaine will not be coming because there is not enough room for all of us in the carriage. I wish none of you ladies was going, but Tipu insisted on seeing Monsieur Harben's wife and Gerard's bride. Thankfully he was polite and genial, and I pray everything goes your way. There is one thing I must warn you about. I—I do not know how to say it,' Armand said, looking distressed.

'Just say it, *mon ami*,' Gerard prompted gently.

Armand cleared his throat and said, 'There are tigers in his courtyard.'

Nadine and Ramona gasped in horror, and the men's faces grew taut with shock.

'Tigers!' Charmaine squeaked. 'Then how did you get to see the Sultan, Armand? I do not see any scratch marks on you.'

Armand laughed nervously. '*Chérie*, tigers do not scratch, they wound deeply. These tigers have diamond collars and are on thick chains secured near trees at each corner of the main courtyard. They roar or snarl when anybody enters the precinct. The faint-hearted lose consciousness.'

'If they're on chains then we have nothing to worry about,' Gerard commented. 'Provided no one is tempted to stroke the beasts. They are a symbol of Tipu's status. He is known as the Tiger of Mysore and considers himself invincible. He will gain nothing by feeding us to his animals. So if you put on a brave face he'll admire that. I think it's time we were on our way.'

Ramona viewed the fort in awe. It was vast, imposing, built on a high eminence of rocks, and an architectural delight. The carriage crossed the drawbridge to the island on which the stronghold stood. Armand spoke to the guards, who all knew him and waved him through.

Outside the royal residence located inside the fort was a large tree-shaded yard, where animals and vehi-

cles were left with an attendant before visitors could
enter the palace grounds.

Soldiers stood guard in state uniforms of lilac sur-
coats, tied with pink sashes, that reached below the
knees. On their heads they wore flat turbans, which
looked like brimmed hats. The men marched back and
forth in front of the huge entrance door with iron studs.
Obviously the sentries were expecting the party, as
they pulled the structure ajar for each one to pass
through. Once all five Europeans had entered, the
door resounded as it rammed shut.

Nadine gave a weak shriek and leaned on her
brother. The other three stood as if chained to the spot
like those growling tigers beneath tall spreading neem
trees. The animals were enormous, obviously well fed,
and magnificent. It seemed apparent that they were
used to people coming and going, for they raised
themselves languidly on their forepaws, eyed the visitors with indifference and lay down again, to everyone's relief.

Gerard took charge then. 'Those animals are not on
very long chains, so they're too far away to harm us.
Also they're replete and annoyed that we have disturbed their siesta. Now, Armand, I assume Tipu will
see us in his audience chamber?'

'In the *diwan-i-khas*, his private audience chamber,
mon ami. Do you remember the way there?'

'Yes, I remember.' Gerard caught Ramona's elbow
and guided her through the centre of the courtyard,
while she glanced warily at the tigers, which had
resumed their nap. Arriving at one end of the square,
he led his group up a short wide flight of marble stairs
to an exquisite pavilion of scalloped arches supported
on pillars. A richly clad individual with a retinue of
servants welcomed them.

'I am Tipu Sahib's diwan. He has instructed me to take you to him.'

'The diwan is the chief minister,' Gerard explained to the others in French. 'Remember to bow to Tipu when we are ushered into his presence and address him as Tipu Sahib or Your Highness. Speak to him only if he questions you, but for God's sake don't question him. Understood?'

'But I will need to ask him about Robert,' Nadine said, her voice cracking. She was near to breaking down, Ramona could see with alarm.

'Gerard, Nadine is under tremendous strain. Is it necessary for her to see Tipu Sahib?'

Gerard slanted Ramona a withering glance. 'What do you think, *madame*? She is the main reason we are here at all and it is up to her to pull herself together if she wants to save her husband.'

Jacques, who was supporting his sister, turned on Gerard. 'You heartless swine! My sister——'

'Stop! Stop!' Nadine cried. 'Please do not quarrel. I—I dare say I am a coward. I swear to conduct myself with more dignity. It will not do to faint in front of Tipu Sahib.'

The diwan put an end to all talk. He led them into a large chamber with silk hangings and scalloped marble arches. At one end stood a circular throne on gold tiger legs and raised on a golden rod suspended above was a jewelled umbrella. On the plush cushions of the throne a man of proud bearing sat cross-legged. Ramona knew at once that he could be no other but Tipu Sultan. Around him hovered retainers in colourful raiments and European soldiers in tricorns, blue uniforms with gold frogging and smart calf-length boots. These must be the French mercenaries he employed, Ramona reflected.

As he approached the throne the diwan bowed three times and enjoined the others to do the same. Tipu seemed to grow impatient with his minister and waved him aside with a brown hand weighed down with enormous rings set with valuable stones of faceted brilliance. The sight of the magnificent gems, to say nothing of the ropes of pearls and necklaces of rubies and diamonds gracing the Sultan's strong neck, filled Ramona with qualms. She felt that her ancient jewellery, which Gerard intended to trade for Robert Harben's release, would tickle the monarch silly. He would probably have them all thrown into dungeons for daring to insult him with such a tawdry offer.

Tipu's black eyes lit up with pleasure as he saw the man who had been responsible for the making of his superb throne. 'Ah, Monsieur Gerard, it is a great pleasure to see you after so many months,' he said in flawless French.

Gerard bowed. 'It is an honour to be summoned to your presence, Your Highness, Tipu Sahib.'

'*Bien*! Pray introduce me to your companions.'

'This lady is my wife.'

Tipu twirled his stiffly waxed moustaches, which stood out horizontally like thick black needles on either side of his upper lip. His piercing black eyes scrutinised her from beneath straight black brows that were now raised almost to the flat brim of his turban. It was fashioned from yellow and black striped satin to match his surcoat, and decorated with ropes of pearls; a sapphire-encrusted holder supporting an aigrette of peacock feathers. His appraisal made Ramona conscious of her drab clothes.

Tipu favoured her with a charming smile. She noticed that he was handsome. '*Enchanté, madame*. Welcome to Seringapatam.'

'Thank you, Your Highness,' she acknowledged with a deep curtsy. A little flattery will help the cause, she thought.

Gerard smiled at her with approval and continued with the introductions. 'This is Jacques Janvier and his sister, Madame Harben.'

Tipu returned Jacques's bow with a brief nod, and stared at Nadine through narrowed eyes. 'You have come for your husband, *madame*?'

Gerard hastily said, 'May I speak on Madame Harben's behalf, Tipu Sahib? I fear she is suffering ill health.'

Tipu's cordiality changed to one of brusqueness. 'If it is the release of her husband Madame desires then I fear there will be a price. Every one of my British prisoners is to be exchanged for a price, and the prisoner Harben is no exception.'

'We have come prepared for that, Your Highness,' Jacques said quickly. And before Gerard could stop him he drew out a drawstring purse and handed it to Tipu. But the Sultan waved to one of his retainers to take it and ordered him harshly in Tamil to count the contents.

'One hundred gold pagodas, Your Highness,' the retainer said.

Tipu laughed scoffingly. 'Is that all?'

Gerard stepped forward. 'I have this.' And he handed over the purse of Inca jewellery.

Tipu shook his head in disappointment and handed back the gifts. 'Of gold and jewels I have plenty. What I need is an Arab horse. It is rumoured that one of you has one.'

Without hesitation Ramona said, 'It is I who own an Arab, Your Highness. You are welcome to him.' Her heart was breaking even as she spoke. 'But he will allow only my groom and myself to ride him.'

Tipu leaned forward, his dark countenance lighting up. 'No horse has ever rejected me, *madame*. And I have never ill-treated any. I will accept your Arab and his groom for the release of Lieutenant Harben. He has embraced Islam, Allah be praised. His name is now—Hamid.'

CHAPTER EIGHT

ON THE return journey from the fort Ramona strove valiantly to put on a brave face. Tipu had pledged to release Robert Harben the moment Midnight Grandeur was brought to him. She hoped and prayed that the stallion would allow the Sultan to ride him and thus save himself unhappiness. Nevertheless, Armand had assured her that the monarch, though renowned for his cruelty to humans, loved animals, as witness the condition of the tigers in the courtyard.

'But they are kept chained,' she pointed out.

'Not all the time. They are taken to a large railed-off field, where they are let loose. He has several tigers, out of which four are chosen daily to do "duty" in the main courtyard.'

Nadine could not stop apologising to Ramona for the loss of her steed, till after a time it began jarring on the girl's nerves. Even so, she said nothing to add to the distress of her overwrought companion.

Nobody spoke much on the drive back to Armand's palace. By rights, they should be rejoicing at Robert's release, and she was grateful to them for their sympathy in understanding the wrench it must be for her to part with Midnight Grandeur and José.

As soon as the carriage halted she could hardly wait for Gerard to hand her down. Once he did she lifted her skirts above her ankles and started racing round to the stables to bid farewell to José and her beloved horse. She had barely arrived at the back entrance when Gerard reached her. Swinging her up in his arms, he carried her into the house and climbed the grand staircase.

'Please let me go, Gerard,' she pleaded, stiffening her body and pushing at his chest. His strength was no match for hers and, his face wooden, no remorse in the hard pressure of his arms, he bounded up to their suite.

He kicked shut the door and stood her on her feet.

She began sobbing, trying to shove him out of the way. 'Let me go, Gerard! I will never see José and Midnight Grandeur again. They are the last link of my life with the part of the past that I loved. Could you not let me say goodbye to them?'

His face relentless, eyes opaque, he said, 'No.'

'Why?'

'Why? Because, *madame*, you will not only upset yourself more, you will also upset José and Midnight Grandeur. Oh, yes, animals know when something is amiss.'

'You're hard, cruel!' she accused, tears coursing down her cheeks.

'Call me what you like, *madame*, but you will not go down to those stables!'

'I want to tell José that I have not betrayed him. Or perhaps I have,' she contradicted in miserable confusion. 'At least I could have said goodbye to him and to my beloved Midnight Grandeur. What have I done? I have traded them for a man I have never met.'

'So you would rather offer yourself in Robert's stead?'

'It would be better than sacrificing José and Midnight Grandeur.'

'If I recall, it was you, *madame*, who willingly promised your stallion and your groom to the Sultan. Now you must abide by your word. They will be treated a lot better than if *you* were Tipu's prisoner.'

'Now that I think of it, didn't Armand give the Sultan his stable of Arabs? What does he want with my horse?'

'Yes, but some were too old and have lost their speed. He needs a spirited animal like yours, Ramona.'

She hugged herself and marched about in restless misery. 'Oh, why did I agree to come to Seringapatam with you?' She came to a sudden halt, her eyes flashing. 'Ah, but I didn't. You brought me here without consulting me. You thought more about your compatriots than of me. It is I,' she jabbed her finger at her chest, 'who has had to make a sacrifice; neither you nor they have had to give up a thing.' Her words were slurred with fury.

He regarded her coldly with eyes like black steel. 'I assure you, *madame*, that if Tipu coveted my steed I would have no compunction about surrendering him. It is unfortunate that I am not fussy about what breeds of horses I own, so long as they obey my commands and take me where I want to go.'

'Perhaps it gives you a sense of satisfaction to see the daughter of your mother's lover suffering.' She immediately regretted her words; rage shot from his opalescent eyes. He looked as if he was about to break her neck. He gripped her arms and shook her till her teeth rattled. But Ramona was also in a fury that overrode her fear. She broke free and lashed out at him, her mother's wedding-ring leaving a weal on his cheekbone.

'Damn you, woman,' he snarled, grabbing hold of her and crushing her against him. He locked his fingers in her hair and dragged back her head. But when he saw her tears he quickly let go of her. He felt disgusted with himself for losing control with someone weaker than he was.

Ramona stumbled to the bed and sat on it, crying quietly. She heard him move to the door and say drily, 'If you will excuse me, *madame*, I have a mission to perform before sundown.'

She knew what that mission was: the handing over of her horse and groom to that tyrant. Yet, despite her heartache, she had to admit that Gerard was right. It was through her own fault that José and her beloved Midnight Grandeur were leaving. She felt appalled at herself for losing control and hitting Gerard. Her ayah would have been shocked by her behaviour. As the picture of her wet-nurse rose before her she felt desolated.

Drying her eyes, Ramona left the bed and lowered herself into the wide comfortable depths of the arm-chair near by. She drew in a quivering breath and stared abstractedly at the brocaded silk coverlet. Darkness had fallen and still she remained stricken, her mind revolving without a solution to cure the pain, until loud knocking brought her back to the present. 'Yes, who is it?'

'Dupres Memsahib has sent me to tell you that dinner is ready, memsahib,' a servant relayed from beyond the closed door.

'Please tell Dupres Memsahib that I do not feel like eating. I am getting ready for bed.'

'*Ji*, I will tell,' the man promised and left.

Ramona quickly undressed and flopped on the wide, comfortable divan. She prayed Charmaine would not rush up to persuade her to go down, or send a tray of food. Thankfully no one came, and after a while she closed her eyes, but sleep evaded her. She turned on to her side and wept.

* * *

Several hours later Gerard quietly entered the suite and approached the bed. Radiance from the moon, pouring into the room through the projecting window, revealed his wife lying on her back atop the coverlet, her long silver-gold hair spread on the pillow, her face ravaged with tears. She had, no doubt, cried herself to sleep. His heart tightened as he gazed at her sad beauty. He was about to turn away and spend another night alone in the side-chamber, when she suddenly opened her eyes. They immediately filled with tears.

She raised herself and held out her arms, so slender, so silky. 'Gerard, I'm sorry I slapped you.'

He lowered his tall length to sit on the bed and gathered her soft body to him. Against her ear he said, 'Charmaine mentioned you refused dinner.'

'I—I did not mean to be discourteous, but how could I eat?'

'You must keep up your strength, *chérie*.' He felt the tears on her cheeks and heard the smothered sniff, an attempt to deceive him that she was not crying. 'Do not weep, my love.'

He held her slightly away so that he could see her face. Her stubborn chin quivered as she made a deter-mined effort to compose herself. Alas, she failed to stem the stream of tears.

'Forgive me, Gerard. I—I resent this weakness in myself.'

'I understand, *chérie*.' Lightly he brushed away her tears with his thumb. 'But weep no more. I have good news for you.' His hands began moving up and down the soft skin of her arms. 'José and Midnight Grandeur are back at the stables.'

Her face lit up with a radiance to match that of the moon. 'Oh, Gerard!' Then she sank back into gloom. 'But what about. . .?'

'Robert? He's here. First I'll tell you about Midnight Grandeur. The Sultan tried him out in the polo ground at the back of the palace known as the Field of Peacocks. Not surprisingly, your Arab would have none of him. He didn't actually throw Tipu, because José rushed forward to grab the reins and calm the horse.' He paused to smile at what he considered an amusing paradox: the powerful monarch who attempted to rival the one-time Great Mughal emperors and who had the whole of South India teetering on the edge of his sword could not maintain his seat on a spirited Arab.

Ramona gave his arm a shake. 'So, what happened?'

'Naturally he was disappointed, for he admired the steed. Said he'd not seen a horse so magnificent. But, being an ace horseman himself, he realised that the animal was beyond training and it would be cruel to break him forcibly. Moreover, he doubted whether that practice would succeed.'

'Oh, I am indeed grateful to the Sultan. What made him release Robert?'

'It was certainly not out of the goodness of his heart,' he said with faint scorn. 'I had an alternative plan, should Midnight Grandeur reject Tipu. I again offered the Sultan your Inca treasures. This time I impressed him with their enormous value, informed him that he could own as many Arabs as he pleased if he contacted a French dealer in Mahé—it's a French settlement on the west coast.' He took a breath and continued. 'This Frenchman is not only a trader in Arab horses, but also a jewel merchant and an expert in ancient jewellery.'

'And Tipu agreed to take them?'

'Yes, after some doubt. He sent for his top court jewellers, who are a Dutchman and Frenchman. It did not take them long to confirm that the jewellery was genuine. In fact, they were in raptures over it.' Gerard shook his head wearily. 'But still the Sultan was not satisfied. He sent for his Master of the Horse and enquired if he knew about Monsieur Lavelle's horse dealings and whether the Frenchman was honest. He was assured that the man in question did deal in Arabs—in fact, that his rare shipment of horses came on Arab vessels. And at last Tipu was convinced.'

Ramona smiled happily. 'Oh, Gerard, I'm so pleased. How can I thank you?'

'Ah, all in good time. But I haven't finished yet.' And her spirits sank. 'We must leave here at first light tomorrow. Rumours are rife that fighting might resume with the hostile states and their British ally, and we do not wish to be trapped. Tipu may intern Robert again, and this time you, because of your English blood, might have to go with him.'

'Then we had better get some sleep now,' she said anxiously.

His voice deepened. 'Not till you have thanked me, *madame*. You asked me how.'

'How, Gerard?'

'Kiss me, *chérie*.'

She gazed at him in the moon-drenched room, her heart beginning a rapid tempo. His clean-cut features, shimmering desire in his eyes and the persuasive caress of his hands on her arms dissolved what remnants of resistance she possessed; she doubted she had any left against his potent charms.

The small flame igniting her body burnt away the self-imposed ghosts of the past—his mother, her father.

She raised her arms, sliding them round his strong nape, urging his head down, her eyes half closed, drugged with passion, and pressed her parted lips to his. His mouth devoured hers, while his hands moved down her arms to encircle her back and waist, drawing her closer to him. Then, still holding her, he gently lowered her till her head rested on the high pillows.

Not lifting his moistly caressing mouth from hers, Gerard released her from his embrace and rapidly shed his clothes, tossing them anywhere. He dared not be fussy, else she might change her mind, and that would destroy the only chance he had of making love to her. I'm an opportunist, he scolded himself. But this woman had the power of a goddess over him and, like it or not, he was becoming a besotted dolt. His superb body, gleaming silver in the night's light, ached with a desire he had not known before. The one-time ogre of guilt—their parents' scandal—went soaring out of the projecting window.

The thin material of her nightgown felt like an armour plate, and, curbing his impatience, he untied the bow of the ribbon slotted through the neckline holding her garment modestly in place. Gently he eased her shift off.

Lifting his mouth from hers, he raised himself into a sitting position, keeping his hands on her slender waist, dewed with perspiration, and stared down at her body, the voluptuous curves of her breasts, full and upright, their nipples jutting taut, begging for his caress. He stroked the curves of her hips and slender thighs and admired her long, shapely legs. Whatever the sins of her father, the bastard and her mother had created the most perfect woman between them. Gazing deep into her bottomless eyes, he knew she was his to possess, for tonight at least. His eyes slid to the enticing silver-gold triangle and his hand lightly caressed it. He heard her audible pleasurable intake of breath, and laughed softly in triumph; he knew she was fully aroused. Even so, he vowed to give Ramona and himself maximum enjoyment before he took her. His hands moved smoothly up her body and cupped the fullness of her magnificent breasts, his thumbs stroking the nipples. The faint rose perfume wafting from her heated body created a headiness he had not known with any wine, woman or song. '*Chérie*,' he murmured as his mouth captured hers again.

His male scent acted like a love potion on Ramona. She felt him shudder as her mouth responded to his. His hands, caressing her breasts, generated a fever in her body and flames in her loins that only he could quench. She raised her arms and laced her fingers through his thick hair, then with more force, motivated by increasing passion, she caressed his broad back, revelling in the strength of his rippling muscles and his hard arousal throbbing against her. As he stroked the nub of her desire she moaned deep in her throat and opened to him like a bedewed bud in the sun.

Then he moved.

All the passion that had gone before was wiped out of Ramona from the searing pain of his action. She wrenched her mouth from his and cried out.

But Gerard waited. *Mon Dieu*! This was the first time he had taken a virgin. He stroked her hair, planted tiny kisses on her cheeks, eyelids. 'Sweetheart, it's always painful the first time for a woman.'

'I—I know, Gerard, but I did not think it would hurt as much as this.'

'*Chérie*, relax and I'll be as gentle as I can.' When next he moved, the pain vanished. Now, in his masterly way, he aroused her all over again. At last she responded, curling her limbs round him and digging her nails into his muscular back as their slick bodies joined in mating rhythm, carrying them on a cloud of ecstasy till their perfect climax.

In the aftermath they lay relaxed, in each other's arms, both conscious of the irreversible step they had taken in cementing this marriage; they were bound together as man and wife. The excitement of the day and the vigorous lovemaking, however, dispensed with thought and brought on a healthy tiredness that plunged them into deep sleep.

Sharp knocking at the door brought them wide awake. 'Gerard, get up, my friend. Did you not remember that you must leave shortly?' It was Armand.

Gerard's eyes snapped open. He felt a heaviness on his chest and saw that Ramona's head lay on it and that his arms still cradled her. She too stirred, and looked towards the shut door.

'Sorry, *mon ami*, is it very late?' Gerard asked.

'No, but I thought it better to rouse you early.'

'Thank you, Armand. We'll see you in a trice.'

While the talk was going on Ramona had slipped out of bed, retrieved her nightdress and lit a lamp; the moon's rays had shifted, but there were no signs of dawn. She unpacked her riding outfit and hastily made for the bathroom. In the meantime Gerard scrambled into the clothes he had strewn over the carpet last night.

He was ready to go in when she emerged fully dressed from the bathroom. While he washed she began stuffing her things into the makeshift petticoat bag. 'We should have done our packing last night,' she remarked.

He laughed as he came out, drying his ears with one of Charmaine's embroidered guest towels. 'Instead of making love?'

She slanted him a provocative look. 'Yes.'

He flung the towel on the bed and snatched her round the waist, but she swung away from him. 'Gerard, I do not think you are anxious to leave here.'

'No, my love, I'm not. I want to take you back to bed and make love to you there all day.'

'You know it can't be done. W-we foolishly lost our heads last night.'

'A glorious, exquisite foolishness, *chérie*.'

She evaded the subject. 'Gerard, help me to pack your bag.'

He sighed and began ramming in his expensive clothes with a carelessness that shocked her.

Before they descended to meet the others Gerard pulled her into his arms and kissed her long and hard. 'That's to remind you that we'll make love tonight.'

She looked at him in mock horror. 'What? In a tent?'

'*Mais certainement*, my charming wife. Out in the open, if needs be.'

They laughed as he swung the bags on his back and guided her down the grand staircase.

Armand and Charmaine were waiting for them in the vast marble stairwell. They looked agitated. 'My friends, we are sorry to hustle you away from here, but Madame Harben is anxious to be gone from Seringapatam and threatened to leave with her brother and her husband if you preferred to stay on,' Charmaine said.

Ramona frowned in surprise. 'But you are not hustling us. It was arranged this way. So why should Nadine feel anxious?'

'You have not seen Monsieur Harben yet, Ramona?'

'No.'

'You soon will. He has become a devout Muslim and is reluctant to leave Seringapatam. Also, he seems indifferent to his wife, and hints about returning to the fort.'

Ramona sent Gerard a worried look. 'Is this true?'

He nodded. 'We tarry, my love; let us be on our way.'

'The cook has replenished your stores and I have made up a hamper of food for all of you. It should do for the next twenty-four hours,' Charmaine told them. 'Come, Armand and I will say goodbye to you outside. Everyone is ready to start.'

They said their sad farewells and joined the party. Ramona cheered up when she saw José waiting with his own mount and Midnight Grandeur in the drive. 'Oh, José, I'm so happy to see you are still with us,' she said in Konkani.

José beamed. 'I am happy too, memsahib, and I think Midnight Grandeur is also happy.'

She nuzzled the stallion's satin neck. 'We must never be parted again.'

The rest of the party had already started out towards the front gate when Gerard, Ramona and their grooms caught up. The moon's rays were bright enough to see by as they made their way out of town. With Rabin and Gerard in the lead, the column returned to the serai and then branched off east, heading for the British-occupied territory known as the Carnatic.

Two hours later, as the sun spread its dawn light, Gerard called a halt at a quiet spot on the south bank of the River Cauvery.

The two ladies helped the cook sort out the contents of the wicker hamper that Charmaine had ordered packed for her erstwhile visitors. There was a choice of Indo-European food to suit everyone's taste. When the travellers had settled themselves on a grassy patch Ramona caught her first sight of Robert Harben.

She had expected to see an emaciated individual of
sickly pallor, dressed in ragged British uniform. Not
so! This man had the ruddy complexion of good health
that made it difficult to imagine that he had been
imprisoned in a dungeon. He was of medium height
and, though lean, certainly not half starved. If anything, Ramona would have wondered what troubled
Nadine were it not for Robert's apparel. He was garbed
in the white robes of a mullah, his head wrapped in a
white turban, and in his hand he held wooden beads.
He seemed to be in a world of his own as he stared
absently into the distance.

Nadine nervously offered him a croissant on a white
napkin. 'Darling, would you care to eat that?' she
asked him in English.

He stared at her with little recognition. 'Thank you.
Are we going back to the fort? Tipu wants me to see
the new mosque he is having built.'

'N-no.' Nadine bit her bottom lip, trying to hold
back her sobs.

'Where are we going? Why have you taken me away
from Seringapatam?' Then he seemed to become aware
of the others. Brusquely he demanded in his gruff
voice, 'Who are these people? Are they the British,
come to capture us?'

Gerald gently moved Nadine to one side and sat
down beside Robert. 'No, sir. You are a British officer,
and your wife and her brother asked me to help rescue
you from Tipu Sultan. You were his prisoner.'

Robert looked outraged and he glared at each of
them in turn. 'Prisoner? I have never been Tipu's
prisoner. I am his mullah and he is building a mosque,
where I will conduct prayers. I insist that you take me
back.'

Ramona could only gaze in amazement at this man,

who appeared to have astonished everyone. What had become of him? She glanced at Nadine and saw that her eyes were tightly shut in pain.

'I'm afraid that's not possible, *monsieur*,' Gerard said. 'Your wife and brother-in-law are escorting you to Fort Anglia, to your compatriots. You must report yourself to a British commanding officer.'

Enlightenment showed in his hazel eyes. 'Now I know—it's you who is taking me prisoner. That's what you've done. But Allah has ways of punishing the wicked.'

'Lieutenant Harben, your place is here with your wife. She has undertaken a hazardous and extremely uncomfortable journey to have you released from Tipu Sultan,' Gerard told him quietly but firmly.

Robert Harben stroked his brown beard, and he looked in surprise at Gerard. 'Wife? What wife? I have no wife, sir.'

'*Mais oui*, Robert Harben!' Nadine yelled in fury, and made everyone jump. She put her face close to her husband's and stabbed at her chest with her finger. 'I am your wife. We got married in Bombay, remember? Here!' She shoved her ring finger under his nose. 'See that? You put it there. And let me tell you. . .' Nadine jumped to her feet and walked towards a neem tree a short distance ahead and, leaning against it, began sobbing. Ramona was about to follow her but Jacques had already leaped up, and approached his sister. He put a comforting arm round her and she sobbed into his shoulder. 'Oh, Jacques, what shall I do?'

Jacques had been sulking for days, and now he erupted. 'It's your fault, Fontaine! You should have made enquiries about that. . .that imbecile.'

'I did make enquiries about Lieutenant Harben, Monsieur Janvier, as you are well aware. We knew he was alive. How the devil were we to assume that he would lose his mind?'

'We have wasted time and money to save this lunatic,' Jacques raved on. 'Leave him here and we'll continue to Pondicherry. That's where we intended to go in the first place.'

Nadine tore herself out of her brother's arms and stared at him in horror. 'Leave him here? My Robert? Never!'

'But Nadine, *chérie*, he's a madman. What use is he to you?'

'He is my husband. For better or worse, I will stay with him. I love him.'

'My good sister, he is a different man from the one you married. Oh, I agree he is physically fit, but his mind is sick, he is conditioned to another world, another culture. He is not for you.'

In the lull that followed Ramona yearned to help Nadine. She said quietly to Gerard, 'We must think of what to do.'

Gerard gave a short dry laugh. 'I have thought, *chérie*.'

'And?'

'And we start eating the delicious croissants Charmaine has packed for us. That's what we'll do now. I confess, I cannot solve problems when I am starving.' He lowered his voice to just above a whisper. 'Are you not hungry, *chérie*? After last night you should be.'

A faint pink stained her face, but she smiled. 'Yes, yes, I am indeed famished.'

'So, la! When we have satisfied our hunger we can think with calmness.' Without further ado Gerard tucked into the croissants and downed them with

freshly brewed lemon tea. He grimaced when he saw
Ramona adding milk to hers.

She persuaded Nadine and Jacques to eat, and
pointed out that the subject of their worry was enjoying
his food without a care in the world. After Robert had
finished he rose, walked to the edge of the river and
stood staring out over the muddy water.

Nadine regarded her husband with grief-stricken
eyes. 'He is a stranger,' she said to no one in particular.

'He has had a traumatic experience, Nadine,' Gerard
told her in sympathetic tones. 'He probably was in a
dungeon originally and promised that his treatment
would improve if he embraced Islam. He might return
to normal if you are patient. Shouting and screaming
will not improve matters. He might seek solace in his
new identity and you will have lost him forever.'
Nadine nodded but looked unconvinced.

Shortly after, the column resumed its trek, skirting
villages but keeping near the river whenever possible.
Towards sundown, while Ramona was admiring the
spectacular sunset that changed the sky to purple and
the river to scarlet and gold, a distant chanting reached
her ears.

'What's that?' she heard Gerard asking Rabin. 'It
sounds like a riot, or perhaps a skirmish.'

'You wait here, sahib, I'll take one of the muleteers
and see what is going on. We will go on foot,' the guide
said. The tall north Indian offered to accompany him
and the two set off towards the sound.

The sun had almost disappeared in the west when
the men returned.

'It is no fighting, sahib,' Rabin explained.

'Then what's going on?' Gerard asked.

Rabin looked at the ladies and hesitated. 'It is not
nice for the memsahibs to see. We Hindus believe the

rite is honourable, but sahibs and memsahibs do not like.'

Ramona had ridden up to Gerard and she saw that he had gone pale. He sucked in his breath sharply. 'Is it. . .?'

Rabin nodded sombrely.

'What is it?' Ramona chipped in a little restlessly. 'Why do you talk in half-sentences?'

Gerard stared at her. 'They are about to perform the rite of—widow burning.'

CHAPTER NINE

FOR a second or two Ramona felt suffocated. She put her hand to her bosom as if persuading her lungs to function.

'Have you heard of suttee before, Ramona?'

She stared at Gerard in open horror, choking a little as she tried to clear her throat. 'Y-yes. But it is outlawed in Goa. We gave it little thought, as if it was a thing of the past. It is terrible to know that the rite is practised elsewhere. Is there nothing we can do to save the poor woman?'

Gerard looked disturbed and asked the guide, 'Is the woman agreeable to offer herself?'

The north Indian answered instead, '*Ji*, sahib, the woman has agreed to become sati. It is a sacred rite for Hindus and must be honoured. Those who refuse to burn themselves on their husband's pyre are damned forever.' He had been speaking with his eyes cast down, but now he lifted them for a moment to look at Ramona, and she experienced a shaft of fear. Again that nagging familiarity about him touched her. How could she forget someone as sinister as this man?

A thought slipped briefly through her brain, like a plate dipped in and out of water, without time for it to take hold. Her dead ayah's image surfaced; she had run to Goa to escape the terrible rite. 'But if the woman is not willing she should not be forced to. . .to sacrifice herself,' Ramona said defensively.

'That is your view, memsahib.' The insolence in Govind Lal's voice was so slight that she could well

137

have missed it. 'But a true Hindu widow who refuses to fulfil her destiny is cast into hell.'

'Enough of this gloomy talk,' Gerard cut in irritably, 'Govind Lal, return to the mules.'

The muleteer touched his forehead in deference. 'As the sahib wishes.'

Gerard spoke to the guide. 'Rabin, we must avoid this crowd and make a detour.'

Ramona looked at him, aghast. 'Aren't you going to find out whether that woman is to be burnt against her will?'

Gerard sighed. 'My lady wife, there is nothing we can do. She might have been heavily drugged of her own free will or against it to escape the worst of the pain. In her trance-like state, it will not be possible for her to tell us whether she has consented or not.'

'The sahib is right, memsahib,' Rabin replied in Tamil; he obviously understood their French. 'This is a very sacred rite and it is best not to interfere, else you will bring many curses upon us and perhaps death; there are some in the funereal party who carry arms. Come, let us go another way.'

Ramona felt wretched, and angry with Gerard for making no move to try to prevent the cruel atrocity, as she considered it. She could not enlist the help of Nadine and Jacques because they already bore the tragedy of Robert Harben's mental instability. What could she, a single woman, do on her own? Gerard, on the other hand, with his potent personality, might be successful in persuading the chanting crowd that the woman was being murdered, and save her from so horrifying a death. She pleaded with Gerard again to try to help the hapless victim.

He refused. 'You are being unrealistic, Ramona. In

no way can we battle with a crowd of chanting people committed to the cause.'

'You don't even know how big the crowd is,' she argued. 'How would you like to be burnt alive?'

Gerard's face showed pale beneath his deep tan. 'Very well, we will watch the cortège from a distance. See for yourself how hopeless our meddling would be.'

Not far from the river was a field of towering sugar-cane. Gerard led the column into the midst of it, signalling for them to dismount and remain perfectly still.

Peering through thick purple stalks, Ramona watched the procession approach. It was a flamboyant affair of caparisoned elephants with gold and silver embroidered cloths spread on their backs, and on top of these were silver howdahs shaped like small pavilions, all except one crammed with people. Enormous throngs pressed round the animals and especially the elephant that carried a single occupant in its solitary howdah. She was a young woman—younger than I am, Ramona reflected, the hairs on her nape rising— dressed in a scarlet and gold sari, bedecked in jewellery of forehead pendants, nose-rings and thick gold neck-laces studded with rubies, diamonds and sapphires that flashed in the final throes of sunset. The woman gazed ahead, unseeing, heedless of the chanting crowd. Priests in white were in the lead, and just behind them six men carried a bier on which lay a body covered with garlands of marigolds. The crowd was now close enough for Ramona to hear the funereal chant: '*Ram, Ram. . . Ram nam sat hai. . . Ram, Ram.*' 'The name of God is great,' Ramona automatically interpreted, her body quivering with horror and compassion for the fate of that defenceless woman who was being given all the honours of a saint.

Once the procession had dwindled out of sight,
Gerard signalled for the column to mount their horses
and continue the trek while the light lasted.

He rode alongside Ramona. 'Now are you satisfied
that there is nothing we can do against that horde?'

She nodded, unable to speak from the horror still
curling in her stomach while she visualised the beautiful
young woman. There had been men on the outskirts of
the crowd armed with long-barrelled muskets, and a
number of people carrying spears and swords. She was
forced to admit that it was impossible for their party to
outwit that mass. The woman had probably consented
to undergo the burning, she tried to console herself,
but it proved useless.

That night they camped near the Cauvery Falls.
After supper Ramona took a stroll to watch the silver
cascade and its boiling spume as it joined the river
below. She stood on a rock and inhaled the freshness
of the water and the misty spray in the hopes that it
would cure the sick feeling she experienced from
wondering whether the young woman had perished in
suttee.

'It's beautiful, romantic in the moonlight. Would you
not say, Madame Fontaine?'

Ramona recognised Jacques's voice. She glanced
over her shoulder and smiled at him. 'Yes, indeed it
is.'

'You are not helping your husband to make up the
bed tonight?' he asked derisively.

'No.' She felt slightly annoyed that he should still
feel piqued over her marriage, and sought to divert his
mind. 'How is Robert?'

Jacques gave a Gallic shrug. 'He enjoys the
Mohammedan cook's company. They say their prayers

together. He is quiet and watchful and disinclined to talk. Sometimes I catch him staring at Nadine.'

'Give him time. He'll probably recognise her in a couple of days.'

She stiffened as she felt his hands on her waist, moving her round to face him. 'I do not want to talk about Robert or Nadine or anyone else. I want to talk about you and me. Why have you been avoiding me, Ramona, *chérie*?'

'I haven't.'

He wrapped his arms around her and began crushing her to him.

'Jacques, you are hurting me!'

'Give me a small kiss, Ramona, *amour*. I know you do not love Gerard. It is me you care for, *oui*? It is out of fear that you married him, is it not?'

Ramona frowned in bewilderment. 'I don't understand.'

He dug his fingers into her waist. 'You understand well, *madame*. Do you not know that Gerard is an expert in unarmed combat? Surely he has mentioned it to you?'

'No, he has not. Where did he learn it?'

'From an itinerant Japanese who heard about his skill in cutting precious stones. Gerard watched the man doing his routine one day and wanted to know about it. He became so interested that, instead of charging the Japanese for the work, Gerard asked that he teach him the exercises.'

Ramona felt afraid, not of Gerard's accomplishment but of Jacques, for he was strong and appeared intent on crushing her to death. 'Please, let me go!'

'No, you'll like this.' And he brought his mouth down brutally on hers. She tried to struggle, push him off, but he hurt her all the more so that she decided to remain still in the hopes that he would relax his hold, enabling her to break free.

He released her quicker than expected.

'Ah, how touching!' Gerard's mocking words had Jacques pushing away from Ramona so fast that she almost lost her balance and splashed into the river. Quickly she steadied herself and stared at Gerard.

'It was her fault, Gerard. I didn't want to, but she insisted.'

My God, Jacques was terrified of Gerard—she shifted her gaze to stare at him, appalled by his cowardice—and his lies. 'It's not true!'

Gerard ignored her. 'Go to bed, Jacques,' he said with quiet menace. 'We make an early start tomorrow.'

Jacques stumbled away. '*Oui, oui, Gerard, mon ami.*'

'Why do you not go after him, *madame*?' Gerard asked, giving her a mocking bow.

'I do not wish to. H-he forced himself on me. He hurt me.'

'Really? I saw no sign of a struggle, *madame*.' His voice chilled her as if she had been sprayed with ice.

'That's because I couldn't. He was squeezing the life out of me. H-he bruised my lips. If you hadn't come. . .'

'What, *madame*? I have spoilt your fun. Is it not? Have you forgotten that you once said you should have married Jacques? Are you trying to cuckold me, *madame* wife?'

'Do not be absurd, Gerard. The man was trying t-to violate me. I assure you that I am not in the least attracted to him.'

'I do not believe you, *madame*. Now that you have had a taste of passion you want to experiment with other men.'

She looked at him through narrowed questioning eyes. 'Gerard, are you by any chance jealous?'

His chilling and bitter laughter caused her to cringe inside. 'Jealous? No, *madame*, do not flatter yourself. I am not surprised that you have the makings of a coquette.'

She raised her well-shaped eyebrows in cynicism. 'Of course not, *monsieur*. Why should you be surprised? Am I not my father's daughter? But never forget that you are your mother's son!'

He gripped her elbow and began pushing her along. 'Come, *madame*, it is late and we have to make an early start on the morrow.'

'I will not bed with you, sir!'

'But I will bed with you, Ramona, my beautiful wife.'

In spite of herself, she felt sensual excitement. His voice alone, though laced with contempt, had the unholy power to rouse her desire. 'You would force yourself on me, sir?'

'There'll be no need, *chérie*; you'll give yourself to me with all the wantonness of a whore.'

Ramona gasped in outrage. 'How dare you, sir? You know full well that I am no. . . You were the first man I—I've known.' She despised herself for stammering like a seventeen-year-old.

They had entered their lamp-lit tent by now. 'True, and whether you like it or not I shall be the *only* man you'll know. You used your woman's wiles, tears, to tempt me into consummating the marriage.'

She glared at him, aghast. 'What? It was you who came to me, sir!'

'Did I?'

Her eyes wavered. She felt hot blood pulsing in her cheeks as she recalled that it was she who had raised

her arms in invitation on the night he had returned
from Tipu's palace.

'Enough of talk, *madame*. Now strip.'

Ramona bit her lip to stop herself from crying. A
deep hurt and indignation spread through her being.
Despite his hatred of her father, Gerard had never
before shown this extent of disrespect to her. He now
put her on a level with his virtueless women. Or
perhaps he fussed over them more than he ever did
with her. She watched him undoing his shirt, then
turned and made for the entrance. 'I will not share this
tent with you, *monsieur*!'

In a couple of strides he reached her and spun her
round to face him. 'Oh, yes, you will, *madame*.'

And that was his undoing, Gerard thought in self-
contempt. He had but to touch her and his blood sang.
What the devil was he doing with his life? Before he
had married Ramona he had known exactly where he
was going, but now his future lay shattered, unpredictable. He had broken every pledge he had made himself, and for all the wrong reasons. First, he had sworn
to remain single, no matter what. Second, he had
promised to escort Ramona to her villa and then
continue as before. But everything had gone awry. He
could no longer deny that he had become more deeply
involved with Ramona than he had done with any other
woman. Moreover, he had betrayed his father and
himself by marrying her, the daughter of the man they
both hated. Why had fate allowed this to happen? And
why had his father insisted that he escort Ramona?

Then there was the Satan of jealousy plaguing him.
He should have been relieved to see that fool Jacques
embracing Ramona and her passive, encouraging
response to him. It would hasten the separation they
had agreed upon. At least she had been honest in

stating that she should have married Jacques instead of him. Then why the hell had she not done so? But all this did not explain his overpowering jealousy. And he was damned if he would allow Ramona to cuckold him right here under his nose! Come what may, the woman was his wife and he would see to it that she fulfilled her conjugal rights, and he his!

'Where will you go, *madame*? You cannot go to Nadine's tent. She now shares it with her husband and is doing her level best to save her marriage.' Damn the woman—she had the most alluring eyes.

'I do not know where I shall go, sir, but I refuse to stay here with you. You have made it clear that you intend to behave worse than an animal. Give them their due, they do not rape!'

She almost smiled with satisfaction when she saw him taken by surprise. 'Rape! A strong word, coming from you, *madame*.'

'In truth it is, but then, if you consider me lower than—than a common slut, why should it matter what word I use? It certainly makes my meaning clear.'

She refused to cry, yet those betraying tears glimmered on her lower lids.

Maudire! He cursed himself for succumbing to her wiles. Gerard gathered her to him, his eyes closing with the ecstatic feel of her soft body.

Ramona recalled how he had accused her of using her feminine ways to seduce him, and anger at herself for repeating her mistake caused her to attempt to struggle out of his arms.

A mistake.

He tightened his hold till she was crushed against him. Try as she might to evoke the revulsion she had experienced in Jacques's embrace, she failed hopelessly.

This was Gerard.

This was rapture.

This was a kind of magic she could not name, dared not.

Even so, she tested her dwindling will, refused to give in, pushing at his bare chest where he had undone his shirt. The touch of his flesh seemed to burn her palms.

Her struggles enraged and aroused Gerard. His mind went blank except for the fury. He kept her crushed to him with one arm and the other hand grabbed the silver-gold coil of her hair and dragged her head back. She opened her mouth to cry out. Without mercy, his came down in savage possession.

The moment she felt his probing tongue her whole body grew pliant, unresisting; her own tongue curled against his in response. They were discarding each other's clothes, anxious to reach the enticing flesh beneath. This was pure desire, she thought. Shame and guilt would come in the aftermath, but for now. . .

Lust, that was all it was, he thought as he divested the last of her clothing and his. It could not last, any more than it had lasted with his women of the *demi-monde*, shipped out from France to satisfy the sexual needs of Frenchmen in India. He would bear the blame after he and Ramona had made love for forcing himself on her, except that her reaction had not led to rape.

Their lovemaking was quick, fierce and marvellous. Afterwards she snuggled up to him, sighing with satisfaction, feeling safe and protected in his strong embrace.

The party resumed the trek before dawn, and except for brief stops for meals they pushed on. Occasional rain fell, but as they approached the east coast there were frequent downpours, accompanied by flashes of lightning and roars of thunder.

Ramona and Gerard had little time together because she had to share with Nadine again. The tent Gerard and she used had to be cut up for covers on the mules to safeguard the baggage from becoming soaked in the rain, and preserve the supply of food which now had to be rationed. Villages were few and far between. Gerard, Robert and Jacques now occupied one tent. As the column headed east the stark rocky landscape turned to lush greenery, and as the party neared the plains leading to the coast it changed to jungle.

The weather grew hot, humid, like that of the west coast. One steamy morning when the rain had kept off Ramona offered to help the cook clear up the remains of the breakfast, when to her surprise someone spoke to her in English. 'Madame Fontaine, may I speak to you?'

She did not even recognise the voice. Looking up from her kneeling position while she gathered up the plates, she stifled her surprise. Robert Harben stood near by. He no longer wore the Muslim garb he had donned at breakfast. Now he appeared in simple European clothes of a clean shirt, brown waistcoat, breeches and boots. His head of light brown hair was bare, but he still kept his beard.

'Please call me Ramona. I am an acquaintance of your wife.'

He smiled, and his hazel eyes lit up. 'Yes, I know, ma'am. I'd be offended if you called me Mr Harben.'

'Naturally, Robert.'

'No, not Robert—Hamid.'

She laughed sheepishly. 'Oh.'

'Allow me.' He helped her to her feet and, offering

her his arm, guided her some distance out of earshot
of the cook and muleteers.

'You're English, aren't you, Ramona?'

His speech was clear and his eyes had lost that glaze
they had shown soon after his release. She prayed that
he had returned to normal.

'I am partly English. Why?'

'Nothing. I feel more at ease in the company of my
compatriots.'

'I understand. But you did marry a French girl.'

'Nadine is very beautiful. Unfortunately I can't
remember much since—since I was imprisoned. I begin
to recall snatches of the past occasionally, though not
my brother-in-law or my marriage. But I have not
forgotten Gerard.'

Who could? she asked silently and drily. 'And do
you still hanker for Tipu Sultan and life in his fort at
Seringapatam?'

'I did at first. But something always stopped me from
taking a pony and returning.'

'Yes, now that I think of it, it does seem odd. I vow,
sir, it was your love for Nadine, locked somewhere in
you, that prevented you from going back. And I am
sure that is what Tipu expected.'

He frowned. 'Do you think so?'

'Most certainly, Rob—er—Hamid!'

They walked on in silence for a while till he brought
her to a stop under a silk-cotton tree. 'I'm worried
about Nadine.' And Ramona could have skipped for
joy. He would not worry about his wife if he did not
care for her.

'Perhaps I can help,' she offered quietly.

'It's that brother of hers. He does not talk directly to
me. I find it humiliating when he speaks to his sister as

if I am not there and refers to me as an imbecile. I have been plotting to kill him.'

Ramona started and took a step back. He spoke the last sentence in a determined manner, and she knew that he was capable of carrying out the cold-blooded act without any qualms.

'Oh—er—Hamid, you must not do that. It's wilful murder.'

'To slay an infidel is no murder.'

She felt shocked to hear this man speak so calmly. 'But you must be patient with Jacques. He is not used to—to the situation.'

He laughed. 'You mean, he has to learn to accept me for what I am?'

'Yes, something like that. But you seem to have adapted to your surroundings, and eventually you will go back to what you were before your capture.'

He looked up into the branches of the tree. 'We are never the same after an experience, ma'am, and I fear I will not surrender my Islamic beliefs.'

She said nothing; who was she to advise about religion?

'You disapprove of my conversion, Ramona?'

'No. Not at all. I think people should be free to practise whatever faith they believe in. However, I am curious to know why you became a Muslim.'

'At first it was because I wanted to be free of the stinking dungeons where we were thrown after our capture. We were promised that we could enjoy a better life if we embraced Islam. Most of us did. The others used their new religion for convenience, but as I studied the Koran I became impressed.'

She raised her well-formed eyebrows. 'The Koran is written in Arabic. You know that language?'

'I know only the Arabic in the Koran. Mullahs taught us.'

'I see. You said you were worried about Nadine. I cannot remember whether you told me what the matter is.'

'She has become very thin; she dislikes me being a Muslim. She says I should revert to Christianity, but I have never had a rigid belief in any other faith, hence it was easy to convert. I'm afraid I shall not throw off Islam,' he vowed with a determined lift of his head.

Ramona spread her hands in an expression of bafflement. 'Why have you brought me out here, Hamid?'

'I want you to convince my wife that it is futile for her to try and change me. I think this is what she wants to do. The alternative is a divorce.'

She felt distressed for her Nadine. 'Oh, no, I think she is very much in love with you, and for you two to part will break her heart.'

His eyes lit up with pleasure. 'She loves me?'

'Oh, yes, why else would she have persuaded Gerard to bring her to Seringapatam? However, I dislike meddling in other people's affairs. Nadine herself might resent me for this. But if you care enough about her then I will tell her that she must take you as you are. But you too must accept her for what she is. And this might mean that there could be arguments over religion.'

'But you will talk to her, Ramona?'

'Yes, I will. Tell me, though, do you love Nadine?'

'Yes, very much. It's a strain not being able to share her bed.'

Ramona yearned to help but could see no way of doing so. She thought for a while till an idea took hold. 'If it isn't raining tonight I'll sleep outside, and then you and Nadine can share the tent.'

His eyes shone with happiness. 'I knew I could rely on your aid. Nadine and I will always be grateful to you.'

She smiled, happy to be of use to the two people she had grown to like. 'Good. I think we'd better go back to the others. The column must be ready to move off.'

She and Robert had to brave the jealous glares of the other three as they appeared together and found the whole party waiting for them.

Gerard glowered at the pair. 'What have you two been doing? Practising your English?'

She gave him a sideways glance. 'However did you guess, *monsieur*?'

He played along with her. 'I dare say it was difficult, *madame*. Shall we go?' He gave the order and the cavalcade advanced. Rabin advised Gerard to branch off and follow the River Ponnaiyar, which would take them almost directly to Pondicherry. It rained off and on in the lush river basin and the air became steamier. All the European travellers suffered from prickly heat and harassment from flies and mosquitoes.

That night, when the tents were pitched, the rain teemed down and Ramona was forced to sleep inside, thus depriving Robert of visiting his wife. But she had a chance to talk to Nadine.

At first the French girl rebuffed her, but Ramona persisted. 'I know you were suspicious when you saw Robert and me together, but I assure you it was perfectly innocent. He confided in me because I can speak English and I'm his compatriot.'

Nadine unrolled her mat and spread her bedding. 'What did he say?'

Ramona felt relieved that she had unbent a little. 'He's worried about you. He says you have become very thin.'

Nadine straightened from her task and faced Ramona, her face glowing with happiness. 'So he does remember who I am!'

'Yes. But he is now a devoted Muslim and has stressed that he does not want anyone, not even you, to interfere or criticise his new faith, and insists on being called Hamid. Also, he finds Jacques's behaviour towards him humiliating. Your brother's life will be in danger if he isn't warned. It would be best if you could talk to Jacques, tell him to keep away from Robert.'

'Why should my husband confide in you and not me?' Nadine asked petulantly.

'It might be because he isn't fluent enough in French to explain what he means. It was easier for him to use me, since I am well versed in most languages. I do not intend to boast. The study of different tongues is my profession.'

Nadine nodded. 'Hmm. I understand.'

'He also wanted to sleep with you tonight. I offered to move my bedding outside, but it's raining. Sorry.' Even so, Ramona felt heartened to see Nadine so happy.

But the next night, when they encamped again, it was dry and Ramona slept outside, as promised. She saw Robert creep in, and relaxed.

She woke in blind terror when a hard hand clamped over her mouth.

CHAPTER TEN

THE hand clutching Ramona also squeezed her nostrils. She lashed out with arms and legs, catching the assaulter in a vulnerable spot. He grunted and relaxed his suffocating fingers. Ramona screamed. She heard the man flee, and almost immediately after came Gerard's ringing voice.

'What goes on?' The next instant as he bent, peering down, he recognised her. '*Sacre*! Ramona! What are you doing, sleeping outside the tent?'

By now everyone had gathered round her, including Nadine and Robert. A distressing suspicion troubled Ramona. Gerard had appeared so swiftly after her shriek that she wondered whether it was he who had frightened her. She had to find out. 'I—I'd like to speak to you alone, Gerard.'

Ramona sat up, grasping the sheet, holding it up to her neck to hide her figure, visible in the near-transparent shift. But now reaction of her terrifying experience made her body tremble.

The waning moon cast enough light for Gerard to notice Ramona's state. He ordered those crowding round her to go back to bed. He spotted Robert going into Ramona's tent with his wife, and his trim eyebrows rose in astonishment.

'I—I. . . Robert wanted to be with Nadine, s-so I let him use the tent while I slept out here,' Ramona explained, stiffening her body to stop it from quivering.

'So that's what the secret conference was about yesterday morning.'

There was no mistaking the easing in Gerard's voice. She nodded but could not bring herself to say more.

He dropped on the mat beside her. 'Why did you scream, *chérie*?'

'Someone tried to harm me. He grabbed my mouth and nostrils. I—I couldn't breathe. So I thrashed out at him and. . .'

'And you caught him where he least expected.' He grinned. 'Resourceful of you, my love.'

Her suspicions grew as she saw that he was fully dressed. 'But what are you doing close by, Gerard? Should you not be in bed?'

He narrowed his brilliant eyes on her. '*Madame*, I was looking for Robert Harben. I thought perhaps he had absconded; he is not quite himself yet. What are you implying? That I was the one to harm you, or paid someone to do so?'

She had the grace to flush, thankful for the colourless light of the moon, which seemed to weave its way through the dark patches of cloud. 'I'm sorry if I slighted you. But I—I find the attack baffling. I mean, I do not own valuables any more. Tipu possesses them now.' Suddenly she said, 'Gerard! I-is Midnight Grandeur safe?'

Gerard shook his head. 'If the attacker wanted to take your horse he would have done so without disturbing the camp. All right, come with me.' She was about to push her feet into her shabby shoes when he yelled, 'Stop! What do you think you're doing?'

She hastily drew her feet back and looked at him in surprise. 'I'm about to put my shoes on, what else, sir?'

His mouth a grim line, he bent and turned each shoe over and rapped it on the sole. 'You have not yet learnt that you should make sure there are no scorpions lurking inside, especially during the rainy season.'

She pushed her hand through her tumbled hair. 'I am in no state to remember such details, sir!'

'I'm sorry, Ramona, but those details will keep you alive. There could even have been a krait coiled in there.'

She shuddered at the thought of the tiny brown snake. Despite the size of the krait, its bite was even more deadly than a cobra's. She swallowed nervously as she slipped into her shoes and threw the sheet round her shoulders.

Gerard led her to the makeshift corral, where the horses were gathered. Ramona gave a happy, 'Oh,' when she saw Midnight Grandeur, and called to him softly. He whickered and trotted up, tossing his head. She and Gerard stroked him and ran their hands over him to see if he fared well.

'I was right, it's not your horse the attacker is after, Ramona; it's you. Now think back. Have you made enemies? What about those clients you did translations for? Did you by any chance displease any of them?'

She squeezed her eyes tight and pondered. As far as she could recall, she had offended nobody. She shook her head and grimaced. 'I can think of no one. The only enemies I had were your mother and my father.'

'Yes, *chérie*, but they were our enemies; we were not theirs.'

She looked at him in a daze. 'I'm not sure what you mean.'

He smiled patiently. 'What I'm trying to say is that they are our enemies because they harmed us. We are not theirs, because we did not harm them. What need is there for their vengeance? Besides, your father is dead and my mother is sailing to the opposite side of the world.' He leaned against the branches of the

hastily erected corral and immersed himself in thought.
'You got on well with your servants?'

'Yes. They worked for Mother and me for years.'

'You do not suppose they resented your leaving
them to fend for themselves?'

'No. I offered to bring them with me, but they chose
to remain in Goa. Besides, I believe you gave them
money.'

'*Oui*, as you say.' He sighed. 'We cannot hang about
all night, wasting time guessing, when it could be spent
on sleep, which we will need if we are to be refreshed
for our journey tomorrow.' He placed his hand on her
back and escorted her along. 'You will share Nadine's
tent, and Robert and I shall sleep just outside, in front
of the entrance.'

'I don't think Robert will like that very much,' she
said with a smile in her voice.

'Robert will need to practise patience the way I have
to till we reach our destination,' he said, feeling sharp
disappointment that he was so close to her, yet they
could not bed together. And now, with this latest
attack on Ramona, he had more to worry about.

The following day it rained off and on, and Rabin led
them via a village bazaar selling large straw umbrellas
which could be fixed to saddles and keep the rain off a
wide area. Since the trees the column travelled beneath
were tall, there was no danger of the umbrellas being
caught in low-lying branches.

In the afternoon the rain held off and the sun
pounded down, but the umbrellas had another advantage in serving as sunshades.

So it went on day after day. The column skirted
flooded fields where peasants laboured with their oxen
yoked to ploughs. Women with their saris hitched up
planted paddy, and Ramona would have enjoyed the

scene if she did not feel again those unseen eyes boring into her. It will drive me insane, she thought.

Then another dangerous incident occurred which convinced her that someone meant to do more than just frighten her.

One morning, when she took the precaution of tipping her shoes, a krait fell out of one of them. She was so petrified as she watched it glide away that she could not scream. Nadine saw the snake, and her screech of terror had everyone dashing in.

Ramona calculated that whoever had placed the reptile in her shoe had heard Gerard's warning to her and hoped she had not heeded it. But who would kill her this way, and why?

She looked up at Gerard, who had put an arm round her shoulder, her eyes huge and terror-stricken. Meanwhile Nadine had become incoherent and threw herself into her husband's arms as soon as he entered the tent. Everyone was talking together in a variety of tongues. And Ramona understood them all.

'What happened?'

'Did a leopard come in? What? In broad daylight?'

'Impossible!'

Gerard held up his hands. 'Quiet, if you please!'

Silence fell. 'Tell us what happened, Ramona.'

She took a few shuddering breaths and pointed to her shoes. 'A krait was in one of them.'

Gasps of horror.

Gerard stared at Ramona. 'Where did it go?'

She caught her temples and shook her head.

'It's—it's outside somewhere.'

'I'll come back when you and Nadine are dressed,' he said, hustling everyone out of the tent.

'*Notre Dame!*' Nadine exclaimed when they had gone. 'I'll be relieved when we reach Fort Anglia.

Perhaps the army will release my Robert and I can persuade him to return to France with me. No more snakes and scorpions with the bite most deadly!'

Ramona scarcely heard her companion babbling on. She was staring at the shoes, thinking that if she had not heeded Gerard's warning she could by now be in her death throes. She could not bear to wear the shoes again. So, stowing them away, she pulled out a pair of sandals. 'Now I can see what is lurking in them,' she muttered to herself.

'*Oui*, that is an idea, very good,' Nadine remarked in admiration, and took out a pair of sandals for her own use.

A while later Robert came to collect his wife, and Gerard arrived shortly after.

Ramona held out her hands to him and he strode forward, kissing each one in turn. 'Gerard, I'm afraid.'

'So am I. So am I, *chérie*. I am now convinced that someone wants you dead.'

'Yes, someone in this group, Gerard.'

He looked down at her hands and rubbed his thumbs along the soft skin on the backs of them. 'Let's start with each person. I doubt whether it is any of the muleteers, since none of them met you before this trip.' She nodded agreement and he went on. 'There's Nadine——'

'Oh, not Nadine, surely? You saw her terror. I could not imagine her handling a snake.'

'I have my doubts that it is her, though she may be a brilliant actress. But we have to consider that she and you were the only ones in this tent and therefore Nadine is a prime suspect. All right, let's proceed with the others. Jacques?'

'It could be,' she said, feeling miserable. 'What proof is there that he is the culprit?'

'None, I fear. Besides, he does have one important factor in his favour, and that is I am a light sleeper—I would have wakened at once if he had tried to leave the tent.'

'Last night could have been the exception, Gerard. He could have slipped something into your drink.'

Gerard laughed incredulously. 'No, I doubt it. The cook served the drinks. Well, I suppose Jacques could have bribed the cook. But I would have felt the effects on waking.'

'"Hell hath no fury like a woman scorned",' she misquoted, and, seeing his quizzical look, she explained. 'Or so said an English author, William Congreve. He wrote it with a jealous woman in mind, but it could easily apply to a man.'

'Ah! I see. Janvier could be seeking jealous revenge? But why would he want you out of the way? It is me he would wish to do away with to leave you free for him to woo.' Even so, there lurked scepticism in Gerard's eyes. 'I doubt whether Janvier would go to such lengths.'

She raised an eyebrow. 'Really? Do you think I am not worth it?'

Gerard laughed easily and dropped her hands— much to her disappointment. 'Oh, you are, *madame*, but not for someone as shallow as Jacques. He does not have deep emotions like his sister. Perhaps women are different.'

Pain touched her heart; he obviously felt the same slight emotion for her as he accused Jacques of. She did not wish to prolong her thoughts, so said, 'Do you suppose Robert has anything to do with the snake incident? He might wish to be rid of me to share his wife's bed. Remember, he is not quite—er—quite normal.'

'No, Ramona, I am certain Robert would not go to such extremes. His mental health improves daily, and to me he is a lot saner than the sane. Who else is there?'

'Rabin?'

'I think we can rule him out. What would he gain by your death? Then there is José, a long-standing servant of yours. You know him best, Ramona. What do you think?'

'With me gone, he would lose his job. And if he wanted Midnight Grandeur he would just take him, sell him and return with a long story that the horse had run away. Why should he want to kill me? It would be out of malice, and José hasn't a malicious bone in his body. Moreover, he is a devout Christian; he once mentioned he would like to join the priesthood.'

Gerard smiled sceptically. 'The best of Christians have been the worst of murderers. Never mind. After José there is one more suspect left.'

She frowned. 'Who?'

'Me, *chérie*, your husband. I have the prime motive of doing away with you. Would you not think so?' He advanced and slipped his arms loosely round her waist.

Her throat felt suddenly dry; simultaneously his arms around her evoked a familiar thrill. 'You're going to bring the scandal up?'

'Mm. I fear so. Firstly, I would want you dead because of your father, *chérie*. Alas, he sensibly died before I could wreak vengeance. Nevertheless, he generously left a beautiful daughter and, since my revenge is so profound that it demands satisfaction, I need a victim. And who better suited than you?' He had drawn her so close that she could feel the strong thump of his heart.

Her own heartbeats thundered in her ears and the

sensuous play of his hands made her blood flow with warm ecstasy. 'And secondly?'

'Secondly, I would want my freedom, unfettered by marriage to a hated enemy's daughter, easily resolved by your death.'

Their mouths were so close that she could smell his fresh breath. 'Y-you would scarce put a snake in my shoe after giving me due warning. If you wanted to kill me, sir, you would. . .'

His mouth played lightly with hers and distracted her from what she was saying. 'I would do what, *ma chérie*?' He kissed the mole near her upper lip. At the same time he parted her blouse from her skirt and caressed the bare skin of her back in light circles.

She was not sure what they were talking about. His hand had moved round to the front and was inching up her rib-cage towards her breast. 'What?'

'How would I kill you?'

What was this outlandish talk of killing? They were making love! 'You—you would perhaps stab me.'

'Where, *chérie*—here?' His hand moved up to caress her breast and the taut nipple.

'Gerard. . .'

He repeated the love-play with her other breast. 'Or here?' He bent his head and sucked the throbbing pulse in her throat. 'Or here?'

She drew in her breath sharply and stared into his opalescent eyes as he straightened his head. Her whole body ached for him. Then, to her utter frustration, he was pulling away from her, dropping his hands. 'Think about it, *chérie*. But I promised my father I would see you safely to your villa, so it's not I. Come, *chérie*, I hear the cook calling us for breakfast.'

Ramona gazed at him, appalled, her body afire, clamouring for his possession. Could he not tell? And all he could think of was breakfast! She hauled herself together, tucked in her blouse, patted her coiled hair and, lifting her chin proudly, said, 'Yes, I could do with breakfast. I'm starving.'

He smiled slowly and her heart jolted. 'Are you, Ramona, *chérie*? So am I, so am I.' And she knew he did not mean food, like the hints he had spilled out not long before. So why had he not. . .? But of course he could not, with the risk of someone walking into the tent.

Gerard bowed courteously and offered her his arm. 'Allow me.'

Faith and charity! He must be the most charming man in the world.

At breakfast everyone commiserated with Ramona. The muleteers, José and Rabin, later told her how distressed they were about the terrible incident.

Gerard came to a decision. He called the group together and told them his plans. 'I have decided that the safest and fastest way we can move on this journey is to travel at night.'

'Then when will we sleep?' Nadine queried.

'*Madame*, I haven't finished yet. Later you can ask questions.' He let his eyes scan the expectant faces. 'We will stop for no more than four hours. No need to pitch tents except if it's raining. Then we push on. This way we'll arrive at Fort Anglia in the least possible time. All right, Nadine, what more have you to say?'

'It takes at least an hour to cook food. We'll therefore have only about two hours' sleep.'

'Then we'll have to be quicker. And you ladies can help the cook. No elaborate meals. If possible we'll camp near a village and buy fresh fruit there.'

'So we go back to bed again now?' Jacques asked with a trace of mockery.

Gerard refused to be ruffled. Jacques's question was sensible. 'No, we'll camp at noon and rest for four hours.'

He had been talking in rapid French, then he translated in Urdu and Konkani for the muleteers and José. Rabin understood French, so there was no need for a repeat in Tamil.

It did not rain, hence there was no need to erect tents. Everyone by and large remained in full view of each other, so it felt safe. One problem: the ladies could not bathe in privacy and it was much too dangerous to allow them to seek a quiet spot along the riverbank on their own. So Ramona suggested that she and Nadine put on their thick drawstring petticoats, fasten them round their necks like tents and wade into the water, and, once submerged to their chins, they could bathe with due modesty. Thus it was agreed.

Late that evening the column came upon a festival in full swing. Rabin explained that it was called *Nag Panchami* in honour of the cobra deity. The occasion occurred outside an exquisitely decorated temple, its façade abounding with brightly painted statues of the innumerable gods and goddesses that comprised the Hindu Pantheon. Small earthenware lamps with naked flames called *chirags* outlined the building, and lamps in food stalls shed enough light for all at the fair to see.

Gerard handed the cook a gold pagoda and told him to stock up what food he could from the vendors. He then bought everyone the equivalent of a dinner each and, after eating, urged them to push on. But a gathering in front of the temple aroused Ramona's curiosity. 'Gerard, can we not leave our mounts here and take a look at what's happening? I see a lot of women. We've been in the saddle for weeks now. Let us enjoy a little entertainment.'

He did not feel too happy about the group mingling
with the crowd, especially Ramona; it was easy to
commit murder in that jostling, merry, brightly clad
throng, accompanied by the 'zing-a-ka-zing' of hand
drums and vibrating twang of sitars, capable of drowning out screams for help. 'They are probably perform-
ing a fertility rite, to ensure they have many sons.
There is a shortage of males in this country due to the
number of battles fought.' He hoped the explanation
would satisfy Ramona. It did not.

Her peacock-blue eyes looked beseechingly at him,
and he damned himself for an idiot. 'Oh, Gerard, let's
enjoy ourselves for a little while.'

He agreed with a resigned shrug. He told the muleteers and Rabin to remain with the animals while his
European travellers took a look round, then they in
turn would stay on guard while the Indians wandered
about. They agreed.

Gerard held on to Ramona as he led the others to
the gathering of local women. As the Europeans were
all taller than the tiny Tamils, they could look over
their heads with ease. And immediately Ramona
recoiled.

The crowd had left a wide circle in the centre, and in
the midst of it was coiled an enormous black cobra,
hood spread. Beside it sat a man whom Ramona
recognised as a Brahmin priest, his oiled hair scooped
back in a tight knot above his nape, the white horizontal lines on his forehead proclaiming him a devotee of
the God Shiva. He did not seem in the least afraid of
the snake and it appeared quite docile till one of the
women advanced to throw a garland round it, then it
rose higher and hissed, its forked tongue shooting in
and out. The woman darted back and tossed a coin to

the priest. He started chanting in a language Ramona had never heard.

'What's he saying?' she asked in an awed voice.

'My guess was right. It's a fertility rite and the priest is chanting in Sanskrit.'

She looked at Gerard in admiration. 'You know Sanskrit?'

'A little.'

'I'm surprised, because it is an ancient Aryan tongue, passed down mainly by Brahmin priests and only to their successors.'

He did not enlarge, but pressed a coin into her hand. 'Toss it to him.'

'But I'm a Christian!'

'What does it matter? You've enjoyed the show, now reward the priest.'

'I suppose that's one way of seeing it.'

She was about to toss the coin over the heads of the gathering in the direction of the Brahmin when suddenly Nadine pushed past and entered the deadly circle. The priest motioned her to remain at the edge of the crowd and slowly move in a circle towards him. Ramona watched in horror. Whatever had taken possession of Nadine? 'Gerard, aren't you going to call her back?'

'No, she'll be all right if she listens to the priest.'

By now Nadine had reached the Brahmin and handed him a pagoda. He steepled his hands, thanking her for the coin. Then he handed her a garland and urged her to place it over the cobra, but Nadine shook her head and gestured for him to do so. He not only popped the garland over the snake, but he also sprinkled its hood with coloured powder. Then he began chanting. When he had finished he motioned to Nadine to return to the crowd the way she had come. She looked pale and shaken when she joined her husband.

'Why did you do that, Nadine?' Ramona asked. 'That cobra could have bitten you.'

'I heard Gerard say that this ceremony was a fertility rite. I thought I would try it. Now, please, no more of your questions.'

Out of curiosity to see how Nadine's husband reacted to her behaviour, Ramona took a peep at him and saw him looking in amazement at his wife. But he said nothing.

'If you all have seen enough, let's get back to the muleteers and give them a chance to enjoy the entertainment. I see the locals are about to give a performance on that platform. We'll be able to watch it from our horses,' Gerard said.

Ramona recognised the act as an extract from the great Indian epic known as the Rāmāyana. Her ayah had told her bedtime stories from the classic, but this was the first time she had seen it enacted and found it fascinating.

Gerard allowed everyone to stay till the fireworks display started, which made the animals restless. So he ordered the column to advance.

The exhausting trek and little sleep made everyone fretful over when they would arrive at their destination. Rabin offered consolation, stating that, now that the river was broadening and the land levelling out into lush green plains, it would be a matter of days before they reached Fort Anglia. Their hopes were dashed when Nadine became ill.

One day she retched up her meagre supply of food. 'I cannot move another step,' she told her fellow diners after Robert brought her back from the bushes where she had been sick. '*Sancta Maria*! I shall surely die if I mount a horse!'

Gerard rose and called to the muleteers, along with Jacques and Robert, to pitch a tent. 'Ramona, stay with Nadine till Robert has made up her bed. I fear we cannot move till she is better. Perhaps the water is contaminated.' He turned to the cook. 'Ahmed, you will need to boil the water for us to drink in future.'

'*Atcha, sahib,*' the cook consented.

Rabin suggested they sleep beneath trees at the edge of a fallow field, which Gerard agreed to, and the party remained for three days, mainly drowsing in the steamy heat. At the end of that period Nadine had not improved, so Gerard ordered a couple of the muleteers to take their mounts and some money and find a village where they could buy a cart. Rabin said he knew the countryside, and offered to go along with them. Gerard agreed, provided that the guide left instructions and a map of the route to Fort Anglia, a precaution should none of the muleteers return.

To everyone's relief, they arrived back within four hours with their mules hitched to a covered cart bought from a village a few miles ahead.

Gerard inspected the vehicle and said to the others crowding round, 'It's been well used, but it seems sturdy enough. It should cover the distance to Fort Anglia. I think everyone is well rested, so let's resume the trek. Ramona, I think you should stay in the cart and keep an eye on Nadine.'

'No, I shall,' Robert spoke up. 'She is my wife and I have a right to be with her.'

'So you have, but Ramona can attend to her. You can ride alongside the cart. You forget that Ramona is a woman and needs rest from riding more than we do.'

'Oh, do not worry about me, Gerard, I enjoy riding

Midnight Grandeur.' She turned to Robert and said kindly, 'You go in and care for Nadine. She'll feel better for it, I'm sure.'

'Thank you, ma'am,' he said with a grateful smile.

Ramona rode beside Gerard in companionable silence. Suddenly he commented, 'There's nothing wrong with Nadine.'

'I do not think that is a particularly good joke,' she said with distaste. 'It's somewhat sick, I would say.'

'It's no joke. I thought you, with your sharp eyes, would have realised by now.'

'Really, Gerard, you are speaking in riddles. I should have seen what?'

He laughed comfortably, and she was about to remonstrate with him for enjoying himself at a sick woman's expense when he said, '*Chérie*, she is expecting a baby.'

Her eyes opened wide and her face broke into a smile. 'Oh, Gerard, how wonderful! I must go back to the cart and congratulate them!'

Just then Rabin, who was a few paces in front, held up his hand to call a halt. He pointed ahead.

Ramona shaded her eyes and followed the guide's extended arm. In the distance she caught sight of uniformed men on horseback. Through the cloud of dust their animals kicked up she observed that they wore shakos and bright red coats, gold frogging and buttons glittering in the late-afternoon sun.

It was Gerard who put her thoughts into words. 'If I'm not mistaken, those are your compatriots, Ramona—the King's Dragoons.'

CHAPTER ELEVEN

GERARD pulled down the brim of his hat to shade his eyes and peered intently at the advancing cavalry of ten men.

Foreboding touched Ramona. This group looked like a reconnaissance or search party. Either way, it meant trouble. Vaguely she sensed it had something to do with Robert Harben. Saying nothing to Gerard, she wheeled Midnight Grandeur and cantered up to the cart. Lifting the back flap, she warned the couple inside, 'The British Dragoons are approaching. For your own sake, Robert, do not mention that you have embraced Islam. Leave it to me to explain.' She heard Nadine's gasp but had no time to say more, and trotted back to Gerard's side just as the soldiers reached him.

The Captain saluted, and Gerard nodded affably. 'What can I do for you, *Monsieur le Capitaine*?'

'Good afternoon, sir. You are French, I presume?' the Englishman said with an almost indefinable sneer.

Gerard inclined his head and smiled easily. 'Is it not plain, *monsieur*?'

The Captain chose to ignore what he considered impertinence. 'We have information that deserters are on the run and we are here to make certain you are not harbouring any.'

Ramona had to clamp her teeth together to stop herself from gasping, and admired Gerard's calm and daring front.

'I fear I do not understand what you are talking about, *Monsieur le Capitaine*. Perhaps you could start by informing us what your name is and where you come from.'

The Captain looked astounded. Obviously he was not accustomed to such insolence, least of all from this arrogant Frenchman! Ramona could almost feel what the officer was thinking. His face, already pink from heat, turned scarlet with indignation; in contrast, his eyes, like blue steel, stared coldly at Gerard in the hopes of intimidating him. 'I would have thought by now that word would have reached you, sir.'

'I regret to say, *Monsieur le Capitaine*, that it has not.'

'I am Captain Palmer,' he said with brusque importance and a trace of hauteur. 'Do you also want to know the names of my men?' he added cynically.

'Your name will suffice, Capitaine Palmer. May I know who sent you and who are the deserters you want, British or sepoys?'

Gerard's humorous condescension did nothing to improve Palmer's temperament. 'I come from the commanding officer at Fort Anglia, a British stronghold, in case you don't know,' he said with cutting disdain.

'I know very well, *monsieur*. It was built to replace Fort St David demolished by the French.'

'And we in turn razed Pondicherry Fort.' The Captain smiled complacently.

'So, *touché*,' Gerard said. 'And you are looking for deserters? Pray, what are their names?'

Clearly Captain Palmer objected to this interrogation. 'It is I who should be asking you the questions, sir. May I know *your* name?'

Gerard lifted his shoulders in a Gallic shrug and said mildly, '*Mais certainement, Monsieur le Capitaine*. My name is Gerard Fontaine and this is my wife. You surely do not suspect a Frenchman of being a deserter from the British Army?'

It was as well the Captain could not see his men grinning broadly behind his back, Ramona mused, else they and Gerard's party would be in for a rough time. Even so, she had to give Captain Palmer credit for observing etiquette. He nodded courteously to Ramona in acknowledgement of Gerard's introduction. 'My pleasure, madam.'

'Captain Palmer.' She bowed her head. It would not do to antagonise him, she reflected, eyeing the long curved sabres dangling from his riders' belts. She felt a little pity for the poor men, whose faces, unlike their Captain's, were of an unhealthy pallor and streaming with perspiration. The cause, she assumed, could be blamed on the thick woollen material of their jackets. Faith and charity! Could not some merciful outfitter have designed a uniform suitable for this climate?

He turned to address Jacques none too politely, 'And you, sir, who may you be?'

Jacques looked at the Englishman blankly, for he spoke only French. 'What's this imbecile saying, Gerard?'

'He wants to know your name.'

'Tell him to go to hell!'

But Gerard knew better. 'I fear my compatriot neither understands nor speaks English. His name is Jacques Janvier. And I assure you, *monsieur*, that neither of us is involved with deserters. But I am keen to know whether the men in question are British or sepoys.'

'British,' came the sour reply.

Captain Palmer's gaze swept over the gathering and came to rest on the cart. 'Who's in there, Monsieur Fontaine?' And Ramona felt her heart leap.

Gerard remained unruffled. 'Madame Nadine and her husband.'

'Is there something wrong that they are travelling by cart?' A glint of curiosity appeared in the cold eyes.

'Yes, *monsieur*. Madame Nadine is with child and feeling unwell. Her husband insists on staying by her side.'

Ramona's apprehension grew as she noticed that Captain Palmer appeared unconvinced. He had not travelled the distance from Fort Anglia to be fobbed off with what might well be lies. 'I would like to see Madame Nadine's husband. Perhaps the lady would not mind if your wife stayed with her for a while, Monsieur Fontaine, till I have had a word with her spouse.'

Gerard spoke in rapid French to his countryman. 'Jacques, tell Nadine that a British reconnaissance party is here, searching for deserters. Robert might be down as one. Get her to tell him to say he was Tipu's prisoner and that we rescued him. Nothing more.'

Jacques nodded and rode back to the cart.

'What did you say to him, sir?' Captain Palmer demanded, his eyes narrowing with suspicion. 'Were you sending some sort of warning?'

Gerard chuckled quietly. 'No, *monsieur*. Jacques is Madame Nadine's brother and I asked him to tell her gently that we are surrounded by British soldiers. Is there anything wrong with that?'

'No,' Captain Palmer growled grudgingly, but he bristled with disbelief.

A few moments later Robert climbed from the cart and advanced to meet the Captain, and Ramona saw with relief that he was wearing European clothes, but his words alarmed her.

'You are Madame Nadine's husband?' Captain Palmer enquired.

'Yes, Captain. I am Lieutenant Robert Harben.'

Captain Palmer looked round smugly at his men. 'And could you explain what you are doing here, Lieutenant?'

'I am travelling with my wife. She and my friends are French. I was Tipu Sultan's prisoner and Monsieur Fontaine had me released.'

Captain Palmer twirled his upswept flame-red moustaches, his eyes sparkling with triumphant glee. 'Monsieur Fontaine had you released?'

'Yes, sir.'

His steel-blue eyes lanced at Gerard, but Gerard returned his stare without flinching. 'You sound as if you are a—er—friend of Tipu Sultan, sir.'

'I am. All Frenchmen are.'

The Captain was so taken aback that he rocked in his saddle, which made his horse sidle.

'You have the effrontery to admit that on British territory, sir?'

'I do. We are escorting an Englishman and his wife, and as soon as we have taken them to their destination I shall proceed to my own domain, *Monsieur le Capitaine*.'

'Now that is a singularly tall story, sir. I must ask you all to accompany me and my men to Fort Anglia.'

'With pleasure, *Capitaine*; that is our destination. We wish to convey Monsieur Harben and his wife—at their own request, mind—to the commanding officer at the fort.'

Ramona decided it was time she spoke up. They could not give in that easily. 'If you think Lieutenant Harben is a deserter, Captain, I assure you he is not. He has had a trying time in Tipu's dungeon, and to

save himself from the harshness he and his fellow
prisoners suffered he consented to convert to Islam.'
She swallowed and dashed on. 'That's why he is alive.
You should know that Tipu did not honour the Treaty
of Mangalore. He agreed to exchange prisoners, but
kept a few back. Among those was Lieutenant Harben.
He was of unsound mind when Tipu Sultan agreed to
release him.'

Captain Palmer gaped in astonishment at Ramona.
'Madam, you are British?'

'Does it not sound like it, Captain?' she asked drily.
Strange, she thought, how few people detected the
Portuguese half of her. Perhaps living most of her life
with her mother and physically resembling her had
conditioned Ramona into believing that she was indeed
wholly British.

'I'm sorry if I have given offence to you and your
party, madam. You will appreciate that it is my duty to
round up any British soldiers. Many have deserted
from the Dragoons and the East India Company Army.
Worse, a number have absconded to Tipu's camp! Can
you credit that?'

Ramona's red lips curved faintly in irony. 'I'm hardly
surprised, since the British Army insists that their men
wear thick uniforms fit for the European climate.
Perhaps if they wore the cotton and muslin garments
of Tipu's men they might not only stop deserting but
also live longer. Moreover, the Sultan does not shoot
deserters—he no doubt believes cowards are unworthy
of a precious bullet.'

Ramona glanced at her husband, expecting to see
condemnation in his eyes, because with her forthright
outburst she could well be endangering them all. And,
heavens, she had spoken like a traitor! It was as well
that Tipu, the British and French had signed a truce.

But she was delighted to see that Gerard's opalescent black eyes were radiant with humorous approval.

She could not say the same for Captain Palmer; he looked disagreeably at her. 'Madam, it might be a good idea for you to write the Governor General and present your views to him,' he remarked with scathing sarcasm. 'Perhaps he may even consent to employ you as Commander of the British Army in India, despite your admiration of Tipu Sahib like the French.'

His men laughed and he joined them.

'*Mon Dieu*, that's a notion most excellent, *Monsieur le Capitaine*,' Gerard said amiably. 'I feel sure my wife would make a commander of the first class. Not for her the ordinary rank of—er—Capt—er—junior officer.'

The laughter disappeared from Captain Palmer and his men. He glowered at Gerard. 'We tarry, sir, with idle talk. Be so good as to come willingly with us.'

'*Mais oui*, since we are travelling to the same destination, why not, *mon capitaine*?'

However, during the next twenty hours before they reached the fort, a cool rapport sprang up between Captain Palmer and Gerard. Ramona assumed they both recognised the leadership quality in each other. The Captain unbent a bit more when Ramona offered him and his men some of their supper, of a quality far superior to frugal army rations. If the journey had been longer she felt convinced that they would have all become friends.

The monsoons were at their height and the River Ponnaiyar had burst its bank in places. Rather than delay and skirt the miles of flooded areas, Captain Palmer ordered everybody to wade through a shallow part. He led the way and the others followed without demur, since it was apparent that the officer knew the

area well in the wide green belt of the Coromandel
Coast.

At dawn they spotted the Union Jack fluttering atop
Fort Anglia, veiled in sea mist rising from the Bay of
Bengal just beyond. Unlike Fort Aguada in Goa,
Ramona saw, this one was small, white and more like
a villa than a fort.

'It's eight miles from the borders of Pondicherry,'
Captain Palmer informed Gerard. 'As soon as you
have seen the commanding officer and are refreshed
from your travels you will probably be allowed to cross
the border. Only, of course, if he clears Robert of
being a deserter. But the CO is a rascal if ever there
was one!'

Ah! Conflict brewed here, Ramona thought. Since
Captain Palmer was known at the gatehouse, the
guards saluted him and allowed the party to pass
through to the vast flagstone forecourt. Here he urged
the Europeans to dismount and gave his troops orders
to take the muleteers to the barracks of the *suwars*,
the Indian cavalry, and make them comfortable till he sent
for them.

Ramona felt anxious about Nadine and helped her
down from the cart. 'Would you like to rest somewhere, Nadine?' she asked, and looked with entreaty
at Captain Palmer.

But Nadine was adamant. 'No, *mon amie*, I think we
should stay together. I do not feel too ill, but I shall do
so if you all leave me, no?'

'I certainly won't, darling,' Robert vowed. 'Come,
hold on to my arm.'

Captain Palmer waited for them at the bottom of a
series of shallow wide steps that led up from the
courtyard. 'You are taking us to the commander of the
fort, *Capitaine*?' Gerard asked.

Palmer sighed. 'We have to report to Colonel Farnell—he's the commanding officer and an East India Company man. His office is at the end of this corridor.' As Gerard strode alongside him the Captain confided, 'The EIC think they are the lords of India. But now their wings have been neatly clipped. Good old Pitt brought out the India Act, which prevents Company servants from taking more money than they earn out of the country. That's put an end to the millionaire nabobs. Thieving lot, I dare say.' He looked round at the group. 'Well, here we are. Good luck to you.' And Ramona suffered a bout of fear as she saw two orderlies with fixed bayonets standing at ease on either side of a stout door. The soldiers snapped to attention and saluted the Captain. He returned it and said, 'I wish to see Colonel Farnell on behalf of these people. Will you give him the message?'

'Sir!' the orderly shouted, and rapped on the solid wood, reinforced with bands of iron. A gruff voice bade him enter. He disappeared for a minute and came out again. 'Colonel Farnell will see you, sir!' He stood to one side and Palmer led the four people in.

They stepped into a sparsely furnished large high room, its whitewashed walls lightly strewn with gekkos. From the ceiling a bamboo screen fan swung listlessly, pulled by ropes attached to it by someone seated out of sight on the other side of the window.

Colonel Farnell rose, tall and sinewy, from behind a heavy desk. He slid brown fingers through his thick white hair and raised bristling black brows. His pale grey eyes, the whites bloodshot, looked suspiciously at the party. His skin shone like polished leather, deeply tanned, betraying that he had spent many years in the country and seen a number of campaigns.

Captain Palmer saluted, and the Colonel returned it

with a light touch of his forefinger to his temple. 'Sir, I
met these people while out reconnoitring. They said
they wished to see you.'

'Then perhaps, Captain, you would be good enough
to introduce them.' Farnell's voice was quiet and as dry
as burnt wood.

'Er—yes, sir.' Palmer cleared his throat. 'This
is——'

'The ladies first, Palmer.'

By now the Captain's face had gone a deep shade of
red. 'Naturally, sir. Behold Madame Fontaine and
Madame Harben.'

The girls gave quick curtsies, and Farnell bowed
politely to each in turn. 'Ladies, delighted.'

'These are Monsieur Fontaine, Monsieur Janvier and
Lieutenant Harben.'

Farnell nodded stiffly. 'Gentlemen. So I would have
thought it was a French matter that brought you here,
but I see we have one Englishman among you.' He
dismissed Captain Palmer. 'That'll be all, Captain.'

'There are two English people among us, *Monsieur
le Colonel*. My wife is one,' Gerard said almost non-
chalantly, and that brought the commander's attention
to him.

His pale eyes glanced from Gerard to Ramona, and
a faint smile touched his thin lips. 'I see we have an
Anglo-French alliance here. But my prior concern is
with Lieutenant Harben. Pray state your business,
Lieutenant.'

Robert came forward. 'May the ladies sit down, sir?
My wife is—is indisposed.'

'But of course, I was about to suggest it.' He gestured
to upright chairs against the wall. 'Perhaps you gentlemen would draw them forward?'

There was hostility in his voice, and Ramona

believed that Colonel Farnell would be a hard man to deal with. And, since he had invited Robert to speak first, she felt sure that he suspected the officer of deserting.

Once he had seen his wife settled comfortably, Robert winked at her, no doubt to cheer her up, and said in a relaxed voice, 'I fought with Brigadier Matthew's force against Tipu Sultan, but, alas, we were all taken captive. However, after signing the Treaty of Mangalore, Tipu released most of the prisoners, not all. I was among those forced to remain. My wife is French and, as you may be aware, Tipu favours the French.'

The Colonel fixed Robert with a daunting stare. 'Go on.'

'My wife persuaded her brother and Monsieur Fontaine to come to my rescue.'

'I see they were successful. So what do you want from me, Lieutenant?'

'I would like to be disbanded with honour, sir. If needs be, I'll buy myself out.'

'And you are able to prove who you are?'

Gerard stretched his lips and cursed himself for failing to remind Tipu to surrender Robert's identification papers, assuming that the Sultan had kept them.

Robert looked round in dismay at his companions, then helplessly at the Colonel. Unlike the rest of his troops, the commanding officer wore a cool shirt and cotton breeches. Impatiently he thrummed his fingers on the glossy black desk with its small piles of papers, anchored with paperweights to prevent the breeze from the punkah wafting them away.

'I regret, sir, that I have no identification on me, but I'm sure Brigadier Matthew must have sent word here and to Madras, informing of my colleagues' and my deferred imprisonment.'

'Then I'm afraid that I must prevent you and your party from leaving this fort till I can verify who you are. If we have no information to support your statement then I fear we shall have to send to Madras for further enquiries. If they cannot provide anything then, Lieutenant, you will have to remain here till we contact Bombay and Calcutta.'

'Do you suspect Lieutenant Harben of being a deserter, *Monsieur le Colonel*?' Gerard asked quietly, so as not to give offence. They all needed the colonel's good will.

'I'm sorry, Monsieur Fontaine, I am in no position to voice a personal opinion. We have as yet to interrogate Lieutenant Harben. But for the time being you will be shown to your—er—quarters. I trust they will be comfortable.' He summoned an orderly and told him to see that these ladies and gentlemen were placed in the guest rooms. 'There will be a few minutes' delay till the orderly returns with some of my men.'

His smile sent a chill down Ramona's spine. She knew that this man did not trust any of them.

Her fears were realised when the tramp of boots heralded the arrival of the Colonel's men. On hearing the sharp knock on the door, the Colonel called, 'Enter!' And, to her astonishment and dread, ten men armed with bayonets marched in.

Gerard's face turned ashen with shock. 'What's this, Colonel?' he asked. 'Are you. . .?'

Colonel Farnell looked with mock sadness at Gerard. 'I fear, *monsieur*, that I am forced to imprison you till we know more about you all. But I assure you that you will not be subjected to any harsh treatment, and you will be sustained with reasonably good food.'

'But this is outrageous, *Monsieur le Colonel*! None of us is armed, so our intent is not to cause any trouble. We come peaceably. Therefore, would you be good enough to let us be on our way? Pondicherry is but a short distant off.'

The Colonel shook his head. 'I'm sorry, but you are here in suspicious circumstances, which might prove detrimental if we allow you to go free.' He nodded to the uniformed Sergeant. 'You know where to take them, Sergeant Grimmond.'

The Sergeant saluted. 'Aye, sir!'

The Colonel waved his new prisoners to the open door. 'If you please?'

Gerard headed the party out and immediately they were flanked by the soldiers, the Sergeant in the lead.

Ramona thanked God that her fears of their being thrown into dungeons did not materialise. The men were separated from the women. Ramona felt relieved to see that their so-called cells were passably comfortable. And, though the windows had bars, the doors were wood, and Ramona heard the bolts being shot from the outside. A wave of panic assailed her, but in order not to daunt Nadine she showed a calm exterior.

It was a different matter with Nadine; the moment the bolt shot home she collapsed on one of the two narrow bunks pushed against the whitewashed walls and burst into a storm of sobbing.

This disturbed and frightened Ramona. She took a deep breath and prayed that she would not lose control. Lowering herself, she sat beside her distraught companion, whom she had come to regard as a friend. They had been through much together and grown close. 'Nadine, my dear, please do not be so upset. You will not only harm yourself but your baby. For the little one's sake, you must calm down. Robert would be greatly worried if he knew.'

'It is for my Robert I cry, *mon amie*. They will surely shoot him as a deserter. Perhaps even now they—they are blindfolding him and thrusting him against a wall and—and. . .' She broke into fresh sobs.

'That's absurd!' Ramona said forcefully to lend truth to her words. 'They cannot shoot him without a trial. It is not the British way, I assure you. Besides, if Colonel Farnell is of such a mind, which I doubt, there is Captain Palmer of the Dragoons, who is not his best friend. And the Captain was amiably disposed to us. He would see the end of Farnell if Robert was—was. . . He wouldn't dare!' Ramona became aware that she was thinking aloud rather than trying to comfort Nadine.

Even so, the outburst seemed to have a rallying effect on the French girl. She sat up slowly and fumbled for a handkerchief. Ramona offered her a ragged one which she had washed and used time and again to save unpacking a fresh pile. Nadine accepted it and dried her eyes. 'You think so, Ramona?'

'I do not *think* so. I know so! Be of good cheer, and pray.'

'*Mon Dieu*! I would feel better for a bath!'

Ramona felt the same. She swept her gaze round the room and spotted a bamboo screen near one corner. Glancing behind it, she saw a metal tub filled with cold water, a basin and ewer and a section for their basic needs. A drain sloped to a hole in the corner. 'You can have your bath, my dear,' she called to Nadine. 'There's plenty of water. I can wait.'

They took it in turns to bathe, and Nadine spoke for both of them. 'It is wonderfully refreshing, *mon amie*, but what we need is clean clothing, no?'

'Yes, I'd have appreciated that,' Ramona said on a wistful sigh.

And then the air was shattered by gunshots and cannonade.

Nadine began screaming. 'They have shot my Robert!'

Ramona felt stunned but soon recovered to put her arm around her friend and say soothingly, 'No, it isn't that, I'm sure.'

'Then what is it?'

'I don't know, Nadine. Sit down and try to be quiet. You must think of your baby.'

All grew silent again. Ramona moved to the door and pressed her ear to the wood in a vain attempt to eavesdrop.

A sharp rap had her reeling backwards, her senses dazed. Then, shaking her head, she pulled herself together and asked, 'Yes?'

'I've brought yer breakfast, ma'am. Colonel's orders. 'Ave I yer permission ter enter?'

'Come in,' she summoned with a touch of haughtiness. She promised herself she would not be a cowed prisoner.

'Yes, ma'am.' The bolt scraped and the door pushed open. In marched a trooper, carrying a tray laden with plates and pastries and a pot of tea with cups and saucers. He looked around to put it down but could see no table. He shouted to someone in atrocious Tamil, and within a short while a sepoy entered, carrying a round table. He salaamed and departed.

Just as the young trooper placed the salver down, Nadine began sobbing again. He looked uncertainly at the two women and prepared to withdraw. To Ramona's dismay, she saw another soldier standing in the doorway, a bayonet at the ready.

'Pray, what goes on?' she asked, willing herself not to tremble.

The trooper shrugged. 'Don't know what yer mean, ma'am.'

'We heard cannonade.'

'Oh, that! It's to let 'em all know a prisoner has escaped, ma'am.'

Nadine and Ramona exchanged anxious looks. 'What prisoner?' Ramona asked.

'Top brass Frenchman. Been 'ere not above an hour, I says. Some fool's in for a flogging.'

'What is the name of the escaped prisoner, Private?'

He shrugged, then called to his friend. 'Oi, Mike, what's the name of the Frenchie that's done the bunk?'

'Name of Gerard Fontaine.'

CHAPTER TWELVE

By the time the orderly brought Ramona and Nadine their breakfast, Gerard was well out of the fort and nearing the French settlement of Pondicherry.

In his mind he thanked his Japanese friend who had taught him a system of self-defence and unarmed combat that had earlier stood him in good stead. It was also a stroke of luck, he reflected, that Colonel Farnell had ordered his three male prisoners to be housed in separate cells, ironically for the reason that they might contrive to escape. He had unknowingly made it easier for Gerard in that he would not be encumbered with the other two men. Alone, he could move quicker and think freely, unhampered by suggestions from others. Gerard felt a mite sorry for the hapless guard who had had to bear the brunt of his violence.

He recalled that soon after he had been locked in he had stretched his weary body on the narrow bed in the sparse cell. After a while his mouth had become parched in the stifling heat and he had risen to help himself to water, which he'd assumed lay in a tub in the partitioned area of the makeshift bathroom; but he had found only a little liquid at the bottom of a pitcher. He had swallowed the last drop, and this had given him a brainwave. He'd called to the guard, who had answered from beyond the door.

'What d'yer want?' the man asked.

'There's no water here, *monsieur*, and I'm thirsty. Would you be so good as to fill the pitcher?'

The guard grunted. 'Aye. Stay away from the door. Sit on your bed. Call out when you've done that.'

This man had his wits about him, Gerard thought in admiration; he intended making sure from the distance of his prisoner's voice that he was well out of the way. 'All right, *monsieur*, enter, if you please.'

The bolt slid back cautiously and the door creaked open a slit. As it widened, first the bayonet appeared, held in its combat position, and then the guard materialised. A tall, well-built man, he sported a slight squint. 'You stay right where yer are, mister. No hanky-panky, yer hears?' he told the leg of the charpoy. 'Now pass me the pitcher. Go on!'

Gerard fetched the jug and held it out languidly to the guard. But as he made to take it Gerard grabbed the hand clutching the bayonet and at the same time brought his foot up. Crack! The heel of his boot caught the guard squarely on the chin. He crumpled without so much as a sigh. It had all happened with a swiftness that made a mockery of lightning. Immediately the guard dropped, Gerard dragged off his scarlet uniform jacket, disconnected the bayonet from the gun and, throwing off the hard mattress, cut large strips off the webbing from the bed, which he used to gag and truss his opponent. He then slotted the bayonet back, shrugged into the red coat, slammed on the shako and peered out into the narrow corridor to see if anyone was about. There were two other guards some distance off. They had left their posts to chat to each other. Hoisting the bayonet to his shoulder, he marched down the passage and out in the yard. Continuing to a row of stables near the guard-house, he propped the gun in a corner, grabbed the first saddled pony, mounted it, and with impunity cantered out of the fort, mingling with uniformed riders heading that way. On the slushy, rutted road, he lagged behind, veered away from the others and broke into a gallop.

Now shrugging out of his jacket, he hid it and the shako in a tight clump of bamboos and, remounting, rode alongside the River Ariancopang till he spotted the French-held Ariancopang Fort, its fleur-de-lis flag stirring lazily atop a tall mast on the highest turret.

The day was clear and steamy, and from his stunted shadow Gerard knew it was nearing noon when he arrived at the gatehouse. He enquired whether he could see Capitaine Dumouriez, a long-standing friend of Gerard and his father. But he was having difficulties because the guards needed written identification of who he was. He explained that he had mistakenly been taken prisoner at the British Fort Anglia and had made his escape. His wife and friends were still imprisoned there and he needed Capitaine Dumouriez's help to get them out.

His tale, instead of gaining the sympathy of the French guards, deepened their suspicions. 'Why would you, a civilian, be imprisoned in an *Anglais* garrison, *monsieur*? Those limeys would not imprison even a French soldier now that we have a peace treaty with them.'

Gerard boiled with impatience. Nevertheless, he showed an impassive exterior. 'Then tell me, *monsieur*, how am I to approach Capitaine Dumouriez?'

The answer was a Gallic shrug and a pursing of lips in concentration. At last he beamed at Gerard. 'Why do you not write a note to *Monsieur le Capitaine* and I will have it delivered, no?'

This was what he'd been trying to convey to this fool in the first place, Gerard thought in exasperation. He smiled amiably. '*Merci, Monsieur le Caporal*, I will do just that. Have you any paper?'

Within a short time Capitaine Dumouriez himself appeared at the guardhouse. The slim officer greeted his friend with gusto. 'Gerard, *mon ami*! What brings you here, in this heat? Why are you not enjoying the pleasant climate of your plateau?' The two men embraced and patted each other heartily on the back. Gerard glanced at the Corporal in amused triumph, and that worthy gave him a shamefaced grin and a helpless shrug.

Gerard returned his attention to Captain Dumouriez. 'I fear, Pierre, I am in trouble.'

'That is sad news, Gerard. But come, let us go to my quarters. We can discuss your problems more favourably after lunch and a cool glass of wine, no?'

'Excellent, *mon ami*, but first may I trouble you for a bath?'

'Of course, you would be welcome to a change of clothes also, but. . .' Pierre Dumouriez's dark eyes in a deeply tanned face glanced at his compatriot's superb physique and sighed with yearning '. . . I fear, Gerard, that my clothes will not fit you. Do not worry, the dhobi can wash yours while you bathe, and in the scorching sun they will dry and be ready for wear within the hour.'

'That is most kind, Pierre.'

The Captain took his friend's elbow and guided him to the officers' quarters, where he possessed a comfortable suite of rooms. He called to his servant and told him in a medley of French and appalling Tamil to arrange a bath for Gerard Sahib and to send in the punkah wallah to operate the overhead screen fan. To Gerard's surprise, the man grinned and nodded. 'You mean, he understood you, Pierre?'

Captain Dumouriez gave a deep-throated chuckle and waved politely for Gerard to be seated on one of the chintz-upholstered chairs in his lounge, and chose the matching sofa opposite.

The punkah wallah arrived, salaamed, and sat against the wall, where he began his boring task of pulling at the rope attached to the screen fan.

'*Mais oui*,' Pierre began, 'my servant, Manian—that is not his full name, which is unpronounceable, as it is with Tamil ones, you comprehend?—would make a linguist most proficient if he were in France, and would earn a fortune there.'

The word 'linguist' caused Gerard's heart to twist in anguish and longing for Ramona, still a captive, his wife and the woman he loved——

Love! He felt stunned. It had finally come to the fore of his consciousness. He should be relieved but was not, simply because he had reneged on his own vow never to fall in love, and least of all with Ramona, the daughter of the man he hated.

Love for a woman had destroyed his father.

It would not destroy him!

Never!

He must exert all his moral strength to fight against it.

Pierre, who had been lolling indolently on the sofa, sat up and stared at his friend. 'What is it, Gerard? *Mon Dieu!* You have gone so pale that I would say you are about to be sick.'

Gerard recovered instantly and flashed his friend a quick smile. 'I'm very well, *monsieur*. The long journey from Goa has possibly caught up on me.'

'Ah, then perhaps a drink will help, no?'

Pierre strode to an exquisitely carved teak cocktail cabinet and, waving to a tray containing cut-glass carafes, asked, 'What is your preference, *mon ami*?'

'A brandy, Pierre, if you please.' He accepted the balloon glass and swallowed the contents in one gulp.

Manian appeared then, immaculate in white livery with a band across his turban embroidered with a row of gold fleur-de-lis. He spoke passable French but with an accent that made Gerard wince. The servant informed Pierre that the sahib's bath was ready.

'*Merci*, Manian. Now, if you please, collect the sahib's clothes and have them washed by the dhobi.' Pierre forsook Tamil and spoke in French; obviously he found the local tongue painstaking. 'Tell the washerman to return them as soon as possible, for the sahib has nothing else to wear.

'Go with Manian, Gerard, and pass him your garments. There is a large robe in the bathroom; you will have to wear that for lunch, I regret, but there will be only you and me and the bearer who serves the meal.'

Gerard returned to the lounge in a calf-length cotton robe, which he had found hooked up behind the bathroom door. He felt refreshed from his bath, reluctantly elated from his acknowledgement of his love for Ramona and worried about her being in captivity, although he felt certain that neither she nor his friends would be ill-treated. For the time being they were safe. Even so, if Colonel Farnell decided that Robert Harben was a deserter and liable to be shot, the others would be condemned as collaborators in assisting his desertion.

Pierre rose, glass in hand. He too looked as if he had taken a bath, and had changed into buff breeches, black buckled shoes and a full-sleeved white shirt. 'Ah, Gerard, you look much better. How was the bath?'

'Wonderfully cold. I have not known the water to be so chilled in these parts.'

'Ah, because it is well water. The river water, *mon*

ami, is exceedingly murky. *Eh, bien*, shall we go in to luncheon, or would you prefer a drink first?'

'I'm ready to eat.'

Pierre led them to an adjoining room with a small lace-covered round table laid out with silver cutlery, wine glasses and two decanters of red and white wine. 'This is the breakfast-room, which I use for one or two guests. The dining-room is for formal occasions when I invite the other officers. Usually we contrive plans on how to oust *les Anglais*! Alas, they are gaining ground in colonising this vast country. We are now making headway in our campaigns farther east beyond Siam.'

The meal consisted of three courses of French cuisine. 'It is a long time since I tasted home food, Pierre. Excellently prepared. I'm afraid none of the local cooks I've employed has been able to master the art. Remark you, I like local dishes too, so I have not lost out.'

'The French cuisine is easily explained. I have a French cook! He is expensive, our Jean-Marie, and all the officers share his services. Alas, I cannot stomach the Indian food.' He rubbed his abdomen and grimaced. 'It gives me the gripes most terrible, and brings on purges most painful!'

Gerard felt grateful to Pierre for keeping the conversation on food to indulge his appetite, and temporarily divert his mind from his troubles. They carried on in this vein, enjoying the meal and sipping excellent burgundy. After the dessert they retired to the lounge, where Pierre poured out more wine.

'Now, *mon ami*, let us discuss what is worrying you.'

Gerard felt mellow and able to tackle his problem with a relaxed mind. He told his friend everything of importance since his meeting with Ramona in Goa up to his escape from Fort Anglia. To avoid mentioning his mother's scandalous behaviour he said she was dead. And this was how he saw her.

Pierre listened intently, on occasions interrupting to clarify a point, but mostly absorbing Gerard's narrative with a nod of understanding and occasional sips of wine.

When Gerard finished, Pierre rose and began pacing the room, a frown of concentration creasing his smooth, tanned brow. 'Hmm. But where do I come in, *mon ami*? How can I be of help? Will the British listen to me, one of the "Frenchies", as they call us?' He laughed good-naturedly. 'We are at peace now, but how long will that last? It is but natural for the French and British to be at war. For this reason Tipu Sultan chose us French as his allies, perversely because he knows we are ever the enemy of the British!'

'That's true, Pierre. However, I remember that you had a very good British friend: Brigadier Bingley of Fort St George, Madras. Perhaps if you had a word— unless. . .' his heart sank '. . .unless he has left.'

Pierre beamed. 'No, my friend, Bingley is still in Madras. He was my prisoner when we captured Madras, and I his when the British captured Pondicherry! We struck up a rapport and treated each other well. He often invites me to Madras, and I ask him here. So what favour do you want from him?'

'Could he confirm that Lieutenant Harben is not a deserter but taken prisoner by Tipu, which is the truth? Otherwise Colonel Farnell might take his time verifying the information, and meanwhile my wife and friends will languish in the heat. There are no fans in those rooms of confinemnt. But how long will it take for you to contact the Brigadier?'

Captain Dumouriez pursed his lips and thought, but Gerard detected a sparkle of mischief in his eyes. 'Let us see. Madras is more than a hundred miles from here, is it not?'

'I believe so. You should know, Pierre.'

'*Oui, oui*, it is so. *Très bien*. We have special carriers.'

'You mean, swift riders? I can go there myself if you give me the necessary written introduction.'

Pierre shook his head and wagged a forefinger. 'No, no, *mon ami*, in order to relay quick messages we use carrier pigeons. It was our mutual interest in homing and racing pigeons that sealed a friendship between Bingley and myself. We both have private dovecotes to indulge our hobby. Now, let me see.' He fingered his lower lip. 'If I send a message to my *Anglais* friend, say, within the hour, I should receive a reply some time tonight or early tomorrow, depending on how much he knows about your Lieutenant Harben. I should imagine the Bombay authorities would inform Madras of Harben's imprisonment with Tipu, rather than its less important Fort Anglia. *Alors*! When your clothes are washed we will depart for the dovecote.'

At first Ramona had been overjoyed to know of Gerard's escape, but as the morning wore on and the oppressive heat increased in the fanless room, causing perspiration to trickle down her body and face, she suffered depression as negative thoughts filled her mind. Had Gerard escaped to save his own skin? Had he left her and his friends to fend for themselves? She was forced to recall that his mother had forsaken him and his father in the selfsame way. Disappeared when they had needed her. It was with much anguish that she felt ever alive to the fact that he had his mother's blood and could well have inherited her disloyal, craven trait.

With a trace of shame Ramona noticed that Nadine had no such traitorous compunctions about Gerard. She positively glowed. 'I knew it!' she enthused. 'Our Gerard will get us out from here. He knows many influential people; therefore he will seek them out and *voilà*!' She snapped her fingers in delight.

Ramona had to admire Nadine's faith. 'Do you really think Gerard will rescue us?'

Nadine glared at her friend. '*Mais certainement*! How can you, his wife, doubt that he will do so? You do not take the care of your words, *mon amie*. La! To have so much mistrust of the man you love!' She shook her head in disapproving amazement.

'But I do not. . .' Ramona bit her lip to stop herself from stating that she did not love Gerard. Faith and charity, it was not true! She *did* love him. I love Gerard, she repeated silently to herself in wonder. For the second time that day she felt stunned.

Nadine put her to more shame. 'You should be worrying whether he is safe and has not been overtaken by miscreants. No, all you are troubling over is: will he rescue us? I do not comprehend you, Ramona.'

Perhaps Nadine would understand better if I told her of the scandal that clouded the lives of both Gerard and me. Ramona felt tempted to confide in her, but thought better of it. The shameful secret was not only hers but Gerard's and it was not her place to repeat it without his consent.

'. . .by tonight at the latest, just you see,' Nadine was saying, and Ramona had no notion what she was talking about.

'I'm sorry, I didn't catch what you said.'

Nadine rolled her eyes and snapped irately, 'Stop pacing about like a caged imbecile and attend to what I am saying!' She smiled ruefully when Ramona came to a sudden halt and gave her a hurt look. 'I'm sorry, *mon amie*, I was convincing myself that I felt sure Gerard will be here tonight to deliver us from this stifling den. Though I am thankful that we have a spacious chamber for you to pace! And that we are not chained to a grimy wall!'

Ramona laughed and Nadine said, 'There, how much more beautiful you look, *chérie*, when you laugh. Your peacock-blue eyes shine like rare jewels and your skin it glows like the colours of a ripe apricot.'

Ramona moved to sit beside her friend and hugged her. 'Oh, Nadine, you are so good for my morale. Let's hope Gerard does help us; it would not be healthy for you and the baby to be locked in here.'

Nadine patted Ramona. 'I think that you should stop this hectic pacing, for it will make you feel hotter. So lie quietly on your bed—you will feel a lot cooler.'

'And through my fault, Nådine, you are unable to rest. How thoughtless of me.' She plumped up the pillow for her friend and retired to her own bed, where she stretched out but could not unwind. She heard Nadine sigh and, glancing across, saw that the French girl had closed her eyes. Ramona envied her ability to shut her mind off from troubles.

Ramona willed her tense body to relax. Her ayah had taught her how to relieve tension by the ancient Indian practice of yoga. 'In your mind tell each part of your body to "float", Ramona *baba*. Start with your toes and finish at the crown of your head.' The good ayah's voice spoke in her head. Gradually she found herself drifting, floating. . . At least here there were no unseen eyes boring into her back. . .

A faint brushing against her cheek accompanied by a vague smell of freshly washed clothes startled Ramona awake. She widened her blue-green eyes and stared into the iridescent depths of her husband's.

'Gerard!' Spontaneously she flung her arms round his neck. 'Oh, Gerard, you came,' she half sobbed, half laughed. His cream full-sleeved shirt and cotton fawn breeches were spotless. In addition she saw that his hair had been cut to his nape and curled attractively. He's more irresistible than ever, she thought, seeing him with the eyes of a woman who acknowledged she was in love.

Ramona felt surprised that she had slept through all the noise going on around her. The door to the room stood wide open. Not a guard in sight. Robert Harben and Nadine were hugging and kissing each other, and Jacques was there too, laughing with joy. Nadine said in a high-pitched excited voice, '*Alors*! What did I tell you, Ramona? Did I not say Gerard would rescue us? And for shame, *mon amie*, you thought he had absconded to save his own skin!'

The blood went out of Ramona's face. She felt chilled with fear of Gerard. He had been sitting beside her on the bed, his eyes and face suffused with happiness and—dare she assume?—love. Now his expression grew harsh, the eyes like black stones. He stiffened away from Ramona, pulled her arms from his neck and abruptly rose. His nostrils flared, his jaws clamped rigid, muscles pulsing in rage, and his hands clenched. He had his back turned to the others and none saw his wrath. His voice was wholly nonchalant as he said on a short laugh, 'Ah, I do have a trusting wife. Do I not?' To Ramona's ears the words were loaded with contempt.

She felt she could cheerfully strangle Nadine for her thoughtless outburst. But she soon turned the blame on herself. Why did I not keep my thoughts to myself? This way all would have been happy. Now she sought for appropriate words with which to soothe him. Unable to find any, she decided to change the subject altogether. 'Then—then we are free?' She avoided his eyes and looked across at the others.

It was the taciturn Robert who spoke. 'Yes, my dear, at last, thanks to your heroic husband.'

'*Le bon* Gerard will tell us all when we are safely away from here in a carriage provided by his friend,' Nadine finished.

'A carriage?'

'Yes, *madame*,' Gerard said, making no attempt to disguise the dryness in his voice. 'But only for part of the way. Robert, Nadine and Jacques are bound for Madras. You and I, my lady, are bound for Domaine du Fontaine. That is, after we stop the night at a French fort to accept the hospitality of Capitaine Dumouriez, who made your freedom fact.'

'I see,' she said with a calmness she did not feel. 'Then perhaps we should leave now?'

He bowed stiffly. 'Of course.'

There were guards in the corridor, but none stopped them. As soon as the party reached their carriage in the courtyard, awash with the scarlet-gold rays of sunset, they encountered Captain Palmer. 'Ah, Monsieur Gerard, I see Farnell released you all. So he found out the Lieutenant wasn't a deserter?'

'*Bonsoir, Capitaine*, I am happy to see you.' Gerard nodded to the officer. 'As it happened, I escaped and found help in Pondicherry. Your good officer Brigadier Bingley of Madras provided proof that Lieutenant Harben was no deserter and that we were not guilty of harbouring him.'

Harben spoke up then. He saluted smartly, though he wore civilian clothes, and Captain Palmer graciously acknowledged it. 'Sir, I shall ask to be disbanded from the army. Nadine and I hope to settle in her villa at Mauritius.'

'Good, good, Lieutenant. I thought you would be going home.'

'No, sir. The voyage will be too trying for Nadine. Perhaps after the baby is born. . .'

'Yes, yes, of course. Well, let me wish you all safe travelling. Glad to have known you.' He shook the men's hands and bowed gallantly over the ladies', then stayed till the carriage with its train of mules and muleteers rumbled out of the fort.

At dusk the travellers arrived at Ariancopang Fort. Gerard had ridden alongside the carriage and related the outcome of his escape from Fort Anglia.

The party enjoyed an excellent dinner with Captain Dumouriez. Ramona found him entertaining and charming, traits inherent in all the Frenchmen she had met. Certainly she had fallen under the spell of one in particular, she reflected, and it was proving painful, considering that he did not return her feelings. More-over, she knew uneasiness that she had yet to confront Gerard alone, because of Nadine's innocent outburst.

As was his custom, Gerard treated her with meticu-lous courtesy streaked with a trace of coolness, which warned Ramona that he still regarded her with dis-pleasure.

'Ah, such beautiful ladies!' Captain Dumouriez gushed, and finished with a nostalgic sigh. His guests were seated in a large dining-room with an elaborate gilt-framed portrait of the stout King Louis XVI staring down haughtily from the wall.

'Are you not married, Captain?' Ramona asked after swallowing a dainty mouthful of delicious teal cooked in a wine sauce.

'Not yet, *madame*. But I hope to be.'

'And, if I am not being meddlesome, may I enquire where your lady-friend is? Why did you not invite her to dinner?'

'Alas, I did not know whether you would be here tonight, else you could have had the pleasure of meeting Colette. Perhaps you think that at the age of forty-five I am too old to take a wife?'

Ramona laughed. 'Of course not.'

'But if you stay another night you will meet Colette. I might add that she is a widow, but handsome for all that.'

Gerard quickly said, 'I'm afraid we must make an early start tomorrow, Pierre. I am—and I'm sure the rest of the party is—anxious to reach the end of this trying journey. Besides, it would be taking advantage of your hospitality by depriving you of your quarters.'

Captain Dumouriez did not protest too vigorously, and Ramona guessed that he was not overly keen on upsetting his arrangements for another night, which meant that again he would be compelled to occupy the sofa in the lounge while his male guests took possession of his bedroom and the ladies his opulent guest room. From the subtle perfume clinging to the vast four-poster, Ramona suspected that the good Captain was no celibate. She wondered with a stab of jealousy whether Gerard's bed in Domaine du Fontaine also betrayed traces of scent.

Nadine noticed nothing. She felt thankful to bathe and change into a clean nightshift.

Ramona had feared that the looming confrontation with Gerard and the excitement of seeing her new home on the morrow would prevent her from sleeping. But no sooner had her body sunk into the bed than she dropped off. Just before sleep claimed her she reflected with yearning, I wish Gerard were here beside me.

CHAPTER THIRTEEN

IN THE golden light of early morn the party said their goodbyes on Captain Dumouriez's veranda, thanking him for giving them shelter and hospitality.

There were tears in Nadine's and Ramona's eyes as they kissed sad *adieu*.

'I doubt that we shall ever see each other again, *chérie*,' Nadine said, sniffing. 'But we can write, no?'

'Of course, my dear. As soon as we are settled in I shall write to you at the Madras Fort, and if you have already left for Mauritius then I'm sure the letter will be sent on.'

With Nadine gone, Ramona reflected with a heavy heart that she would have no lady-friend to turn to for comfort or diversion.

Jacques came forward and kissed Ramona's hands, then her cheeks. He whispered into her ear, 'You should have chosen me for your husband, *chérie*. I would have made you happy.'

She was half inclined to think so too. Returning his kisses on either side of the face in the French mode, she smiled sadly. 'Goodbye, Jacques.'

'*Au revoir, Ramona, chérie.*' Jacques stood aside to allow Robert Harben to say farewell to her.

He kissed her formally on the hand. 'It was good knowing you, Ramona, and I am ever obliged to you and Gerard for your help in bringing Nadine and myself together again.'

'I'm glad I was able to give you both some aid. And now I'm sure you will enjoy a happy future together with the new baby.' She lowered her voice and added, 'Are you still a devotee of—er——?'

'Yes, ma'am, nothing will turn me away from Islam,' he said resolutely. Then with a twinkle in his eyes he added, 'Rest assured, however, that I shall not take another wife!'

She laughed. 'I wish you both luck.' Ramona's spirits lifted to see that Robert had mentally recovered and that he worshipped Nadine.

Meanwhile, Gerard had moved away and was talking to Rabin and the muleteers. He handed each a purse of money, all except José and Govind Lal. Then, turning to the rest of the party, he said his goodbyes.

He started with Jacques, and as Ramona watched she likened them to a couple of enemies declaring a reluctant truce, both faces wooden and a mere touching of the hands, no observing French custom.

A smile of liking appeared on Gerard's face as he came to Robert. 'You will no longer need the services of the guide and the muleteers and their animals. Your baggage has been tied on top of the carriage, and there's enough food for the journey to Madras. If not, I have instructed the driver and his assistant to buy some at the bazaars and hamlets you pass.' He smiled encouragement. 'It's a journey of over a hundred miles to Fort St George, I fear, but the coast road is flat and good.'

'Our thanks, Gerard,' Robert said quietly, but the look in his eyes displayed that he was deeply moved. He swallowed and said, 'You and Ramona are going to your place on horseback?'

Gerard nodded. The two men shook hands. To everyone's surprise, Robert used the Muslim words of farewell, '*Khuda Hafiz*.'

Gerard took Nadine in his arms and kissed her

fondly. 'Take care of yourself and the little one, *chérie*. Who knows? We might all meet again. I think you have forgotten that my father left me a villa in Mauritius.'

'Marvellous, *mon cher*! You and Ramona must come!'

Although Ramona had grown fond of Nadine, and knew that Gerard regarded her as an old friend, she could not prevent a faint streak of jealousy, and chided herself for being small-minded. Perhaps if she and Gerard were not at present in conflict, Ramona pondered wretchedly, she would have viewed his leave-taking of Nadine in a different light.

Amid calls of '*au revoir*' and 'goodbye' and clicking of the tongue from the driver to urge his animals forward, the vehicle rumbled towards the northern gate of the fort, which gave way to a bridge leading to Pondicherry and thence to join the coast road.

Gerard led Ramona, José, Govind Lal and the two pack mules out through the north-eastern gate, and also crossed a bridge over the Ariancopong into the enclave of Pondicherry. The riders stirred up dust that hung in the still air. The road stretched for one and a half miles to a thorny thicket pierced with a small, sturdy mud fort that had sentries. The travellers were allowed to pass when Gerard showed the guard a permit. It was a long, hot and tiring trek through Tamarind copses, mango and coconut groves and village bazaars till they began climbing the slopes of the hills comprising the Eastern Ghats. Gerard called a halt for lunch during the most exhausting part of the day, when the sun hammered down from a white-hot sky and the glare hurt the eyes. The foursome ate in the deep shade of a spreading neem tree.

Late afternoon the group reached the heights of the

Ghats, where the weather became pleasantly balmy. They passed a magnificent stronghold.

Unable to contain her curiosity, Ramona asked Gerard, 'What's that?'

'That's Gingee Fort,' he pointed out in a neutral voice as if he were explaining to students. And she knew he still held her in contempt. 'It is the site of many a bitter battle between first the Mughal Emperor Aurangzeb and a Deccan Sultan, and lately between two Deccan Nawabs, one with French allies. It is now British.'

'And we are on British territory?' She felt a little happier that he was actually speaking to her. Faith! I'm like a beggar thankful for crumbs, she thought in self-derision.

'Officially, yes. Now they own vast areas of the Carnatic, but few Englishmen to oversee it.' He looked searchingly at her. 'You seem tired and anxious. I can understand the tiredness, but why the anxiety?'

They were riding along a smooth stretch of ground with little but shrubs visible in the distance.

'I fear I'm going insane again, Gerard.'

He glanced at her sharply. 'What is it?'

'I—I can feel those menacing eyes on me once more. I did not experience the malice during our imprisonment, nor when we were at Captain Dumouriez's quarters. But—but. . .' She lifted her hand from the reins, brushed back a wayward tress and inhaled a shuddering breath.

He stretched out a hand, copper-gold in the sunset, and touched hers. 'We are in sight of Domaine du Fontaine, Ramona. Look, there are the walls. After a few days' rest you will be back to normal.'

'Yes, yes, I suppose so,' she said, and smiled at him

uncertainly. 'And is Domaine du Fontaine on British territory?'

'No, it used to be the palace of a small independent Raja and he sold it to me.'

'Are you not afraid you'll be caught in the crossfire if hostilities break out?'

'It is not of much strategic value to the British or French, who are the main contenders for this country, because it is way out in the wilderness, with no roads within moderate distance. Besides, it does not have enough water or fuel to house an army.'

'Then how do you manage?'

'A well in the garden provides enough for about two dozen people. Colveram is a township fifteen miles away where meat and fish is available, but it is reached with difficulty through a narrow defile.'

She thought it odd that he had not attempted to improve life here. 'Is there no way to increase the water supply?'

He smiled as he looked ahead. 'There is, but I prefer to keep it this way.'

'Why?'

'Because, lady, if we have plenty of water, food and fuel we'll have armies and wars on my doorstep.'

'And where is the villa your dear father left me? Is it within those walls?'

'Yes, a few hundred yards from the palace. It used to house one of the Raja's favourite concubines. He looked after her well, and the villa is stolidly built. Do not concern yourself about it; you will not be needing it. You'll share the palace with me.' And with slight contempt he added, 'Even though you believe I am craven enought to abandon wife and friends.'

Gerard was still coming to terms with his feelings for Ramona. He marvelled at the extent of her power to hurt him. The last woman who had done that was his mother, but with his father's love and encouragement to involve his mind in work and ambition he had developed self-confidence and toughness of spirit, which had led to success. Other women had mistrusted him, but he had laughed and shrugged them aside. Ramona was different. Although he had admitted to himself that he loved her, he was not quite sure whether he was truly in love. He hardened his jaw. Fontaine, you thought you knew it all. You know nothing, he told himself.

They had reached the huge wrought-iron gates with guards installed just inside.

The men cheered in delight as they recognised Gerard, and, dragging back the gates, said in Tamil, 'Welcome home, sahib.'

He addressed each one by their long, difficult-to-pronounce names. 'I am happy to be home. This is the memsahib.'

They grinned in delight, placed their palms together. 'Welcome, memsahib. May you have many sons.'

She was not sure about the many sons, but she immediately liked these men, and smiled at them. 'I am happy to be among you.'

And then her eyes were drawn to the building looming ahead. She had expected something on the lines of a converted French château, similar to Armand's and Charmaine's mansion in Seringapatam. Gerard had made no changes to his palace, had sensibly not interfered with its exquisite Indo-Saracen architecture. It seemed to be built on a high plinth, the whole structure white, but now washed in gold with the last rays of the sun. It was enormous, its roof a series of gilt-covered domes, and to her seemed large enough to

house an army. But, of course, without enough
reserves of water it would be useless.

The long path from gate to palace entrance was wide
enough to take carriages and perhaps, in the Raja's
time, a column of elephants. On either side of the path
and against the palace walls were tall sandalwood trees.
In small beds bloomed cannas in pink, red, white and
yellow, hibiscus also in a variety of colours, jasmine
and frangipani. Even this early in the evening, per-
fumes filled the air.

'Is that scent also from the sandalwood trees?' she
asked, inhaling deeply.

'No, *chérie*, sandalwood gives off no perfume in its
living state. Only when the wood is cut does it become
aromatic.'

His '*chérie*' cheered her up, encouraged her to talk.
'And where does the water come from for these plants,
Gerard?'

'I've had pools sunk to collect monsoon rain. When
they dry up, then the beds are empty except for the
deep-rooted plants and trees, which look after
themselves.'

She had expected to see a number of servants
awaiting them in the large marble forecourt, but spotted only four men, in cotton liveries of blue and white;
she remembered that it was not possible to feed a lot
of people, so the size of staff had to be kept low, since
access to and from the little township of Colveram was
arduous.

Gerard greeted each delighted servant by name and
introduced them to their new memsahib. He helped
her dismount, gave orders for José and Govind Lal to
be housed and the animals stabled.

One of the servants was Raschid the Muslim cook,
and the others general factotums. They walked dis-

creetly behind their master and mistress as Gerard led them through arcades enclosing courtyards. Over his shoulder he asked the cook to scramble up some supper, as he and Ramona were famished, and to bring it up to the zenana. The other servants he dismissed.

The word 'zenana' almost brought Ramona to a halt. She was tempted to ask Gerard what he was doing with harem quarters and whether he kept it filled with concubines. But she decided against disgracing herself and him, with the servants making a slow departure and in danger of overhearing her.

When they proceeded alone together Gerard took Ramona's hand. She snatched it back. 'Do you maintain a zenana, Gerard?' she questioned, unable to keep the wrath out of her voice. 'Did the Raja leave you his concubines as well?'

Gerard grabbed her hand again and tugged her along. 'He offered them to me.'

'You—you mean, you are taking me to meet your— your women of pleasure?'

He stopped and swung her round to face him. She was almost persuaded that there was laughter radiating from his iridescent eyes. 'Would you object?' he questioned seriously.

She looked at him, aghast. 'What?' Faith and charity, this man was ten times as abominable as his mother and her father!

His smile, though still having its devastating effect on her, she thought, incensed, showed patient mockery. 'I said, Ramona, darling, would you object if I supported a zenana? Might I add that you are the chief wife?'

She tried to believe that he was talking to her tongue-in-cheek. Except she knew the reputation of European men in India, especially those of position. They had quarters in their back gardens that housed women for their pleasure. Some wealthy Portuguese who came piously to church in Goa, to Confession and Mass, Sunday after Sunday, and gave huge donations—no doubt to salve their depraved consciences—did the same.

'Of course I object! How dare you treat women as if they were playthings? We are as human as you are. You take advantage of these local girls because their fathers sell them to you. Oh, yes, I'm no naïve idiot; I know what goes on with you Europeans!'

It was his turn to be taken aback. He blinked. He had thought to arouse her jealousy, some recognisable proof that she cared a little for him. *Maudire*! He was besotted with this girl and he felt as if she had slapped his face by accusing him of ill-treating people of her sex. He wanted her to writhe with jealousy, as he had done when she had only smiled at Jacques and even the charming Dumouriez. *Dieu*! She was driving him to Bedlam.

He hauled her along, his lips thin with exasperation. 'See for yourself, *madame*!'

She put up a struggle. 'No, I'm not going to the zenana to be humiliated by you! Let go of me this instant!'

He let go of her hand but gripped her round the waist and tossed her over his shoulder. 'You're coming with me, *chérie*, like it or not. You promised to love and obey me.'

'And you promised to endow me with all your worldly goods, cherish, worship me and forsake all others! And, talking about worldly goods,' she shouted, her head banging against his back, 'I want the money for my jewels you so generously gave to Tipu Sultan!'

This was a farce, she thought vaguely, an[d] been an onlooker would have thought it hila[r] at the moment she felt pure jealousy, green [a]s sour as a lime. 'And you have the gall to take me by force to your den of sin!'

Gerard's sense of humour overrode his pique, and he roared with laughter. 'If nothing else, my love, you will keep me amused, and I'm happy to see that you remember our marriage vows.'

'I find nothing amusing in your throwing me over your shoulder like a meaningless sack of rice!' It was all she could do to hold back her laughter.

'A sack of rice is far from meaningless, *madame*. It is very important, the staple diet of this country. Without it, people would die.'

She dared to smile, despite being incensed. 'Are you saying that without me you would die, Gerard?'

Ramona almost sensed his smile. 'You would love that, would you not, *chérie*, having me fawning at your feet?'

'Yes.'

She felt him stagger in surprise and took her turn at laughing, until he reminded her where they were going.

'Keep still, or you'll knock your head against the walls at the sides of the narrow steps.'

Gerard climbed the winding steps till they reached a door. He opened it with the key stuck in the lock, then eased himself and his burden through. Setting Ramona down, he took the key out and used it to lock the door from the inside so that no one could enter.

Ramona looked round. They were on a flat roof with five evenly spaced large pavilions, each domed and arched, the arches draped with curtains. Lamps hung above the supporting pillars, and when Gerard lit the wicks they illuminated the whole area.

Nothing stirred.

No signs of occupation.

No voices.

'This is your zenana?' she asked, greatly puzzled.

He moved with an animal grace to the nearest pavilion and lifted the green satin drape. 'Yes. *Madame*, if you please?' He bowed and ushered her to enter.

Hesitantly she made her way towards it. 'Then— then where are your. . .?'

'Nowhere. There never were any concubines here.' Stifling a chuckle, he said with mock seriousness, 'I couldn't afford to keep them. There's not enough food or water. Remember?'

Ramona's humour asserted itself and she started laughing, and he joined her. Then she said with feigned wonder, her eyes huge and to him irresistible, 'Really?'

'Really! Those ladies did, however, leave some pleasant things behind.'

'What?' she asked warily, peering round the drapes.

'Beautiful clothes, some of them not worn.' He put his arm round her waist and gently steered her inside the building. She gasped as she spotted a large satin-covered divan with matching gold-fringed bolsters. At the foot of the bed was a large ottoman. Gerard drew her to it and, flipping open the cover, tossed out clothes of every hue and texture of material. There were richly embroidered kaftans, saris, short bodices, full muslin skirts braided in gold and silver, wide gold and silver-spangled shawls, long narrow pyjamas and also baggy ones. 'Oh, Gerard! They're beautiful. I think I'll wear this.' She picked up a pink embroidered kaftan.

'No,' he said, his voice husky. 'Wear this.' He chose a peacock-blue fitted short bodice and a pale green muslin skirt with a peacock-blue underskirt.

Her eyes widened as she stared at the exquisite garments. 'They are a little daring.'

'There's only you and I, *chérie*. And I want to see you looking like a goddess when I make love to you—soon.'

She looked down in dismay at her shabby travel-worn clothes. 'I cannot wear those lovely clothes without having a bath.'

He smiled into her eyes and chucked her under the chin. 'Nothing to worry about. Come.' He caught her hand and took her to another pavilion. 'In here.' He lifted aside a curtain.

'But there's no water in there,' she said in awe. The round marble sunken bath with jewelled flowers and plants set in the base was empty.

'Yes. Our Raja had it perpetually filled so he could cavort with his girls, till two of the wells ran dry. Now there's a copper tub on that pedestal and a small ewer to toss water over yourself. No lounging around in that jewelled marble. I'll wait for you to finish, then take my bath.'

He left her. She spotted a robe hanging up, and expensive soap. Ramona gasped as she tossed the cold water over her, but it was gloriously refreshing, prompting her almost to sing. She heard a knock on the door and exchange of voices and supposed their dinner had arrived.

As soon as she came out of the bath pavilion, Gerard went in, already dressed in a deep blue robe and clothes tossed over his arm. 'Won't be long, *chérie*. Then we'll eat.'

She arrayed herself in the garments he had chosen, swirling about to let the lamplight dance on the spangles and gold-braided hem of the skirt. The bodice fitted snugly over her full breasts and fastened with three emerald-studded clasps. She eyed herself with approval in the gilt-edged mirror of the elaborately hewn dressing-table of eastern design, and brushed out her silver-gold hair with the European-style brush, and on impulse decided to leave her tresses flowing. Then, picking up a muslin shawl to match the skirt, she draped it over her head. A trembling excitement rolled in her abdomen. To calm herself she stepped out of the pavilion, sauntered to the parapet of the zenana quarters and peered down through the stone fretwork overlooking the empty forecourt below. Lifting her gaze, she sighed at the beauty of the star-spangled indigo heavens.

She knew he was behind her before she turned. A faint smell of sandalwood and clean clothes greeted her nostrils.

Slowly he manoeuvred her round to face him. Her heart came to a sudden stop then raced on as she observed him in wonder. In plain clothes he had looked superb; in rich raiment he looked like an exotic god, she thought with romantic fantasy. He wore a muslin shirt tucked into full eastern pyjamas and a velvet embroidered waistcoat.

'Come, Ramona,' he said, taking her arm and drawing her to a table with two covered dishes, carafes of wine, and laid with crockery and cutlery. 'Let us eat. I'll wager you are as hungry as I am.'

She had not thought of food, but the mention of it stimulated her appetite. Indeed, the fish was delicious. 'I thought you had to send for meat and fish. I received the impression that no one was expecting us.'

'True. However, there is an artificial pond built at the back. It collects the monsoon rains and we breed some fish in there for emergencies, should the food run out. But during the dry season the water is low, so we do not have a lot of fish. What we're eating is carp, freshly caught.'

'That's why it's so delicious. You and your father thought of everything, Gerard,' she said in admiration. 'Forgive me if I'm personal, but how can you afford to maintain a palace like this, and where did the Raja go?'

'I'll answer the last question first. The Raja was forced to leave for greener climes to enable him to feed his court and huge menagerie of elephants, horses, bullocks and goats. He now owns a realm near Travancore, which has two monsoons a year and is therefore evergreen. To answer the second question: how do I maintain this palace? Gems, darling, gems.' His eyes lit up with pride. They were like gems themselves: rare black opals, Ramona mused. 'Fontaines have been a family of jewellers for generations. Once a year I travel to Golconda and buy rough diamonds. Then I cut, polish and set them in gold. As the French are expanding farther east, this jewellery is in demand. It is also needed for the internal trade; every Indian bride, rich or poor, must have jewellery, gold or silver for her dowry. More and more of the wealthy fathers choose the new faceted gems for their brilliance.'

'Then do you have a shop?'

He laughed, 'No, I'm happy to say gem merchants come from far and wide to buy from me or give orders. I do not have to roam the bazaars to hawk my wares.'

'Where do you keep all this dangerous wealth? Are you not afraid of being robbed?'

'I wouldn't make the fatal mistake most of the nobility in this country do. I keep very few gems here, because much of my work is commissioned and I have to complete it for the buyers who stay here till the job is done. Why do you ask where I keep the jewels? Do you intend to rob me?'

She pushed her plate away, and used the damp cloth dipped in rosewater to wipe her mouth and hands. Then, placing her elbows on the table, she looked at him squarely. 'Of course, why do you think I asked?'

He laughed softly and she smiled. 'You would not be able to get anywhere near them if I did tell you.'

'Why? I can always pick the lock or pay someone to do so.'

He raised an eyebrow. 'Not if you knew there were cobras down in the vault.'

She started. 'What?'

'Yes, darling. And only I know how to handle them.'

'Faith! I—I had no idea.'

'Oh, the vault used to be a temple. Still regarded as one. In them Priests keep cobras—which, as you know, are sacred—to safeguard the immense riches in the shape of gold and jewelled images of the Hindu gods.'

'But what if someone tried to steal the gems and they did not know cobras were there?'

'Oh, there's fair warning in Tamil, Urdu, French and English outside the vault. If it's ignored, then. . .' He shrugged.

'And has anybody. . .?'

He shook his head. 'They wouldn't dare.'

'How do you feed the snakes? And who fed them while you were away?'

'The sides of the vault are too steep for the snakes to climb. A Brahmin priest lowers eggs in a basket tied to ropes. The basket is hauled up once every two days and refilled. It is all done with great ceremony and chanting.'

'What if the cobras climb into the basket when it is

being pulled up?' she asked, unable to disguise her horror.

Gerard smiled widely, amused at her macabre questions. 'He manipulates the ropes so that the basket comes up upside-down.'

Ramona grimaced and shuddered. 'And you—how do you go in for the gems?'

'Through the door. It has an intricate lock on it which I designed, so only I know how to open it without a key. I wear snake boots, and the vibration of them on the floor frightens the cobras. They slither out of the way. If some decide to become defiant I wave my flaming torch at them.' Gerard put his glass down after draining the wine and looked across at Ramona. 'Have you finished?'

'Yes,' she said huskily as he took her hand and raised her to her feet. How brave he was. Indeed, his courage and strength were as sturdy as a pillar in a storm.

'Let's go to bed, *chérie*.'

The moment they entered the pavilion Gerard folded her soft body in his arms. 'I've waited too long for this,' he murmured, lowering his mouth on hers to tantalise and titillate. Then his kiss grew harder and more erotic as he widened her mouth to taste and enjoy.

Her shawl fell off and his hands moved with urgent pressure on the bare skin of her waist and midriff. His mouth left hers to push back her head and trail along her chin, her throat, her shoulders. She arched back, giving full vent to the unquenchable passion he aroused in her, setting her blood pounding in fevered ecstasy. He undid the clasps that held the bodice in place and swept the garment off her. Lifting her in his arms, he placed her on the bed and rapidly stripped. Tall, copper-gold in the lamplight, he represented the per-

fection of male beauty in her eyes. He removed the
last vestige of clothing from her and buried his head
between the valley of her high breasts while he caressed
and kissed the jutting peaks. Then his hand moved
down her flat abdomen, caressed the soft swells of her
hips and with his other hand sought and rhythmically
stroked the hub of her desire. 'Do I please you, *chérie*?'
he murmured, even as she moved urgently to his
titillation. His breath intoxicated her with its aroma of
wine.

'Gerard,' she breathed into his mouth.

'And you want more? Much more?'

'Mmm,' she whimpered in frustration.

'Why, *chérie*?'

'I love you, Gerard, darling.'

His eyes blazed down at her. He lifted her hips and
melted into her with a groan of deep pleasure, crushing
her to him, filling her with an ecstatic pain as they
moved in unison to another plane of bliss. I did not
know it could be as sublime as this, she thought.

As they drowsed, wrapped in each other's arms in
the replete aftermath, loud knocking and arguments
could be heard from beyond the zenana door.

Ramona pulled the satin coverlet over herself while
Gerard dragged on his pyjamas. 'Who the devil is
that?' he yelled.

'It is I, Yvette, your lover, *mon cher*! You could not
forget me!'

CHAPTER FOURTEEN

'YVETTE? *Mon Dieu*! What are you doing here?'

'What do you think?' asked the provocative voice. 'Monique heard it from Dumouriez's lady-love that you had returned. So I came as soon as I could. I knew after the long journey you would need me, Gerard, *amour*! And are you going to leave me to talk behind a closed door?'

'Go down and wait for me in the lounge!'

'Ah! You have a doxy up there, is it not?' The alluring tone had changed to one of anger.

'I said, go down and wait in the lounge, Yvette,' he repeated firmly.

'And what will you do, *mon chéri*, if I do not? I doubt that you will have the servants throw me out.'

'Do not tempt me, Yvette.'

In her shocked state Ramona heard an inelegant snort, a swish of skirts and receding footfalls.

Since the time the stranger had spoken Ramona felt as if a knife had been plunged into an already gaping wound in her heart. It did not take her agonised brain long to absorb that this. . .this Yvette was Gerard Fontaine's mistress—or perhaps one of his mistresses. She lay there, numbly gaping at him as he vented his anger on the sultry-voiced Yvette. Ramona felt defiled, sensually exploited by this man who treated women as if they were devoid of emotion—like game pieces to be picked up, put down, thrown out whenever the mood took him. Yet she chided herself for allowing him to hoodwink her with shameless ease; she should have known better. All the signs, the warnings were there, but she had let this handsome Lucifer delude her. She had deliberately ignored the portents and had foolishly fallen in love with him. In consequence she must suffer the humiliation of being his wife, forced to endure that which she could scarcely endure: another woman, or women, to share him.

As the sounds of Yvette faded down the steps Gerard turned his eyes on Ramona. For seconds they stared at each other. She said in a choked voice, 'Get out!'

'Ramona, listen. . .!'

Feeling sick, she shut her eyes. 'There's nothing to listen to. Leave me to dress. Go to the lover you cannot forget!'

His face turned white with fury, the eyes black steel, lips thin and colourless. 'I'll be back,' he promised through clenched teeth. Snatching up his shirt, shrugging into it, he left. She heard the key turn in the lock. So I'm his prisoner, his cheap plaything. Ramona bitterly blamed herself not only for falling in love with Gerard but also, to add to her shame, for admitting it to him not long past. How he must be rejoicing over his victory! How complete his revenge on her father through his mortification of her. She dragged herself out of bed, pulled out a modest kaftan from the ottoman, flung it on and waited for his return, her mind seething with jealousy.

Gerard hated locking Ramona in, but he did not want her following him and making matters worse. In high fu ʼ he bounded down the steps and headed for the opulence of his oriental lounge. What had got into Yvette? This was the first time she had left her comfortable apartments in Pondicherry to come to Domaine du Fontaine. In fact, he had rented her the chambers, but when he had lost interest in her had compensated by giving her sufficient money to live on—though he knew she had a string of French lovers and perhaps even a Nawab or two who showered her with riches.

And now he had fallen deeply in love and believed that he had won Ramona's heart. She had delighted Gerard by declaring her love for him. Now this! What jinx pestered him?

At one time he would have found Yvette ravishing in her scarlet taffeta dress with black lace ruching, the neckline cut so low that it barely covered the nipples of her magnolia breasts. Her thick black hair was piled high in ringlets, gleaming blue-black in the lamplight, and her heavily lashed blue eyes slanted upwards at the outer corners. He would have had to be blind not to acknowledge that she was a beautiful woman, but now he had no urge to sweep her up in his arms and make passionate love to her as he had done in the past. It was no fault of hers; it was his. As he viewed her eagerness to be with him by holding out her slim hands he felt pity for the girl.

He caught her fingers and bowed over them. 'I'm sorry, Yvette, but I must ask you to leave. You should not have come to the palace. I have forbidden you to do so before.'

'But *mon chéri*, it has been a long time for you, has it not? I thought to give you the pleasure most wonderful, no?'

He released her fingers. 'I'm afraid you are too late.'

Yvette's eyes flashed blue flames. 'Then I am right—you have a doxy up there!'

He shook his head. 'No.'

'Ah, is it some *pauvre innocente* you have seduced and are now keeping locked in your zenana?'

Gerard raised one eyebrow. 'No.'

Yvette's patience ran out. She stamped her foot and raised her voice. 'You are playing games with me, *monsieur*. Can you not tell me who your new paramour is?'

'It is none of your business, *mademoiselle*,' he said smoothly, 'but, if only to keep you off these premises in future, I'll tell you. The girl in the zenana is my wife. I married her in Seringapatam. That is all I am prepared to say.'

For a moment Gerard thought Yvette would have a fit of the vapours, and silently groaned, preparing himself for her tantrums. She turned white, backed to the brocaded divan heaped with fringed bolsters and, with a low moan, sank into its depths. She lay very still, only her magnificent breasts moving.

He strode forward to stare down at her. 'Yvette!'

The sharpness of his voice must have convinced her that he was not deceived by her false show of heartbreak. She sat up abruptly, touched her ringlets into place and looked at him wistfully. 'I have been a fool, *monsieur*. I had thought perhaps I could win you for my husband. Alas!' She sighed with longing. 'I should have known it is of a rarity that men marry courtesans. I ask that you answer one question: your wife is beautiful, *monsieur*?'

'Ramona is very lovely.'

She nodded and lifted her slim shoulders with an air of resignation. 'It is as I thought. You always chose the beauties for your bed.' She gave a self-derisive laugh. '*Oui*, I suppose I should feel honoured.'

Gerard knew acute guilt and embarrassment; Yvette had never spoken with deep feelings before, and he felt helpless to console her.

She rose slowly and patted his arm. 'Do not upset yourself, *chéri*, I will not make the trouble for you and

Madame Fontaine. I have never yet destroyed a marriage.' She perked up. 'And there are many handsome Frenchmen who are willing to pay court to me. But I—I liked you best.'

'I warned you, Yvette.'

She nodded dolefully. '*Oui*, as you say, *monsieur*.' Then, stretching up, she kissed him on both cheeks. 'Congratulations, Gerard, *chéri*. Your wife is lucky. *Au revoir*.'

He saw her to her carriage, cursing himself for causing her hurt. Yvette had an easygoing temperament that contained no malice, and he and she had enjoyed carnal pleasure. 'Will you be all right, *mademoiselle*, travelling at this time of night? Perhaps you would like to leave in the morning.'

She glanced at the vehicle driver and his assistant, and said in a nervous voice, '*Oui*, I would prefer to leave in the day, because I shall be journeying all night. But I think it would be wiser for me to go now. I am sure Madame Fontaine would object to your former paramour sharing her roof. No, *mon ami*, I will return to my apartment tonight. Perhaps you can spare a couple of armed guards?'

'Certainly, *mademoiselle*. I shall also arrange for refreshment for you to take.' He entered the carriage with her and at the gatehouse gave the necessary orders. He watched the vehicle roll out till it was no longer in sight, then retraced his steps with a feeling of dread; he feared he had already lost Ramona.

From the parapet Ramona looked down on the lamplit courtyard and watched in relief the glamorous Yvette—it had to be her—climbing into the coach. Then when she saw Gerard follow the French girl in her jealousy intensified. Though she was aware that a man as virile as he had not lived the life of a celibate, she had not expected his lover to arrive in person to shatter her dreams.

Ramona had no idea how to cope with a predicament she had not experienced before. Instinct prompted her to vent her wrath on Gerard, and she might have done so had he not left her alone to calm down. She feared an ugly scene would end in self-imposed disgrace. On the other hand, she could not tolerate competition from others. He would go the way of his mother. So how could she display her outrage without loss of face? He might not love her but she knew he was strongly attracted to her, and in time his infatuation might have turned to love. She bit her lip—yes, she ached for his love. Now that woman had cut the fragile thread holding Gerard and herself together.

She plunged the knife deeper in her wound as she wondered how many other rivals she possessed apart from Yvette.

Ramona tensed as she heard him bound up the steps, and returned to the pavilion to sit calmly on the bed. She gazed up as the drapes were drawn apart and Gerard entered. He looked drained. '*Ramona, chérie.*' He held out his hand in a plea for forgiveness.

She rose and backed away. 'Do not touch me, sir.'

His jaw hardened. 'Let me explain, *madame*. I finished with Yvette long before I met you. She means nothing to me. In fact, she has never set foot in this palace before.'

Lifting her chin proudly, she looked squarely at him. 'You have forgotten, sir, that I was unable to forgive my father's behaviour. How can I forgive yours?'

He sighed heavily. 'But there is nothing to forgive. I have not committed adultery with Yvette, for she is not married. She is a part of my past. I have not gone near another woman since we met as adults in Goa. Your father committed adultery. His case is different from mine. He left your mother for another woman.'

'Your mother, in fact.'

'*Oui*. But what are we arguing about? They too are a part of our past.'

She agreed with him, yet because of her hurt she wanted to needle him. 'How would you feel if a former lover of mine suddenly appeared, sir?'

A trace of a smile curved his beautiful mouth, which had given her so much pleasure. 'But I had proof that you have never had a lover, *chérie*.'

Ramona felt confused, wounded and on the verge of tears. I must not cry and let him enjoy my misery. 'Do not dare call me *chérie* ever again, *monsieur*,' she choked, furious that she had to resort to trite words that lacked the power of conviction. Words that had been and would be used by quarrelling lovers for evermore. She wondered if Yvette, with her wide experience of men, would have thought up something original.

He moved closer to her and she took a step back, but he caught her hand and tugged her towards him. 'You said you loved me.'

She tried to struggle out of his arms, afraid that she would succumb to his charms. 'That—that was before your mistress arrived to claim you, sir. Please let me go!'

His arms tightened. 'No. Yvette is not my mistress. What must I do to convince you? You are my wife and I want you, Ramona.'

'But I do not want you, Monsieur Fontaine. I no longer love you. I said those words in the heat of the moment. We agreed some time ago that we could separate if this marriage does not work.'

He caught her shoulders and shook her violently. She cringed as she saw the angry red of his face and the shards of rage sparking from his iridescent eyes. 'You haven't given the marriage a chance. We have our whole future together, and I swear there'll be no more affairs.'

With contempt she looked up at him through her eyelashes. 'Take your hands off me, sir. And show me the villa your good father willed to me. Therefore it is mine and it is there I wish to live till I can return to Madras and arrange for my passage to my mother's people in England.'

He laughed harshly. 'And what will you do there?'

'That, I fear, is my concern, sir. Now, if you please?'

'No!'

She detected despair in his voice, which surprised her; she could not believe that a man who had 'used' several women to pleasure him could be capable of feeling the noble emotion of love.

Gerard dragged her up against him and brought his mouth down hard on hers. It was a desperate kiss, trying to convey to her how deeply he cared, how much she had hurt him and how afraid he was of losing her.

Ramona sensed none of his emotions, as her own had undergone a battering; she believed she was too inexperienced to understand the workings of a male mind. Her pride came to the rescue, helping her to withhold her tears and resist his lovemaking.

She stiffened in his arms, till at last he let her go. 'I would be grateful if you would take me to the villa, Gerard.'

'Now?'

'Yes, please, now.'

His lip curled in a sneer. 'As you wish, *madame*.'

The villa was a short drive away, set in its own

garden, and though she could not see the roses distinctly she could smell their perfume. Gerard escorted her and informed her that he would be sending her horse and groom as soon as possible. Formally he showed her round the cosy little place with its front veranda backing on to two bedrooms, a small parlour and a lounge. He bowed over her hand. '*Bonne nuit, madame*,' he said coldly, and left.

The bedroom she chose had pretty chintz curtains that matched the counterpane. The bed felt comfortable enough for her to drop off to sleep at once when she stretched her body on it. But her waking hours were fraught with heartache, despite her occupying her mind in brushing up her skill by practising translations. She converted the parlour into a study, and heaped the three volumes she had brought with her at the corner of the table. Her heart sinking in despair, she hoped that once she arrived in England her services as a translator would be in demand.

Gerard had sent a few bolts of material, which she was about to return to him, but a woman servant, Motia, advised her to have a few dresses sewn by the local *durzi*, who would work on the veranda. 'Your clothes are threadbare, memsahib. When the dhobi was washing them they were tearing,' Motia complained. So Ramona agreed to have her measurements taken and let the tailor copy the designs of her old dresses.

She tried not to miss Gerard but she did, and prayed that he would come down to see her. After she had done a spot of work in the parlour she would take a stroll outside and watch the gardener tending the arbour of pink roses. They were Persian, and hardy in this climate, he informed her. 'The chief concubine of the Raja lived in your house, memsahib; she and his

wives were struck down with a disease, so in fear the
Raja left.'

'Oh, I thought he left owing to the lack of water and
because the palace is so far from the large towns.'

'It is so. There is water but not good to drink. That
tank there, near the roses, is for garden only. Do not
be tempted to drink it, memsahib.'

'No, of course not; I drink only the water from the
carafes.'

'*Ji*, that water is from the well.'

Ramona enjoyed chatting with the gardener about
the various flowers, and delighted in the pleasant
breeze; it helped to take her mind off Gerard and her
horse, still stabled at the palace. He needed exercise,
and suddenly she realised that here was an ideal excuse
to see Gerard.

But, even as the thought flashed through her
brain, Motia came to summon her indoors. 'Memsahib,
Fontaine Sahib is asking to speak with you.'

Ramona felt so happy that she said with abnormal
brightness to the servant, 'Thank you, thank you.' She
was pleased she had worn a newly sewn dress of
lavender muslin with frills at throat, sleeves and hem;
had even treated her versatile straw hat to a trailing
length of matching muslin.

With great difficulty she prevented herself from
rushing inside and throwing herself into Gerard's arms.
Instead she followed the servant sedately to the veranda, where he sat in a cane chair. He rose and, taking
her proffered hand, bowed over it.

'*Bonjour, madame.*'

She smiled at him. 'Good morning, Gerard.'

He returned her smile with a flash of strong teeth. 'I
see you have made yourself comfortable. Good.'

His affair with Yvette has made no difference to my

love for him, she confessed. If anything, I love him more than ever, perhaps because there was the fear that he could be attractive to other women. Who could blame them? He looked so handsome in his riding breeches, white shirt and wide-brimmed hat pushed to the back of his head.

'I came to return Midnight Grandeur to you. He needs exercise, so José gave him a run this morning.'

'Oh, where is my horse?'

He pointed to three of the animals tethered to a tall Simal tree growing a few yards from the house, alongside the front path.

Her heart slipped with disappointment. He did not really wish to see her, or be saddled with her horse and groom. 'I fear there is nowhere to stable him here.'

'Yes, there is. At the bottom of the back garden, behind a tall hedge, there is a disused stable and quarters for the groom. You are alone at night, with the exception of the female servant who sleeps in the veranda. And I feel sure she would rather return to her family at the servants' quarters at the palace. So José and Govind Lal have offered to stay here and guard you.'

Ramona glanced across at the tree and spotted the two men squatting by Midnight Grandeur, and the other steeds. 'Thank you. It's kind of you to think of my welfare.'

'But of course, you are my wife,' he said tetchily. 'Perhaps you would care to take a ride on Midnight Grandeur. I'll come with you. That is, if you have no objection?'

Her smile was so radiant that he felt his heart lurch with longing. But he warned himself not to be too hasty to win her back, or she would shy away like a frightened fawn.

'Yes, yes, I would, Gerard; I mean, I would like to ride with you. Just give me a short while to change into my riding things.'

'A pity; you look lovely in that dress. But run along. I'll be here.' He would wait for her till the end of time, he thought with an ache in his heart and a touch of amusement at the choice of his words.

In front of the villa lay a vast stretch of the plateau, with thorny shrubs growing sparsely—an ideal spot to ride. And it was here that Gerard and Ramona exercised their animals. But they could not keep up the pace too long because of the lack of water, which the horses needed after their ride. Gerard suggested that they dismount after half an hour's vigorous galloping.

They walked their horses and talked. 'Gerard, do you think you can sell Midnight Grandeur? It breaks my heart to let him go, but I need the money to buy my passage to England.'

He looked at her, astounded. 'But I thought you were comfortable at the villa. My father left enough for you to live on and I will give you the money for the Inca jewels. There is no need for you to sell Midnight Grandeur.'

'I am quite comfortable at the villa and it is beautiful.'

'Then why. . .?'

'However, I cannot live an idle life. I need to work at translations to keep my brain working, and the only way I can do this is by finding a job as translator. I fear I have earned my living for too long to accept charity. And, since we are to part. . .'

He became impatient. 'But you are not accepting charity. You are my wife! It makes no difference whether you live with me or not. The palace is your home and it is your right to occupy it with me. But I will not force you, Ramona. Come back when it suits you. If it makes you any happier then I have plenty of letters and documents you can translate, to say nothing of a whole library of scrolls the Raja left. You'll have enough to occupy you for the rest of your life.' He took off his hat and combed his fingers through his hair. 'And no more talk of leaving. We have to give this marriage a chance.'

What a heaven-sent excuse, and she took full advantage of it. 'Thank you, Gerard. When can I start?'

Inside, Gerard was shouting for joy. 'I'll send work over after lunch. How is that? You do not need to begin the translations till tomorrow morning. The library scrolls can wait for the moment. Now, shall we go?'

As promised, Gerard's documents arrived after the midday meal. Ramona felt tempted to start on them straight away, but the ride this morning had made her unusually tired, and she decided to take a short nap. But her sleep dragged on till late evening and, by the time she had bathed and dressed in another of her new gowns in the hope that Gerard would visit her, it was dark.

She took a short walk in the garden and noticed a new moon, complemented by winking stars on a backdrop of dark sapphire velvet. The perfume-drenched air came alive with sounds of insects and the sweet trill of a nightjar. Ramona strolled through her favourite arbour of roses, and for a while felt at peace. Even as she inhaled deeply, enjoying the balmy night, she was suddenly assailed with that all too familiar feeling of menace. Suddenly the moonlit garden took on the metallic gleam of a deadly sword, the perfume a heady poison. Those eyes pierced her back, and the evil presence seemed close enough to touch her. Ramona

knew that if she called out no one would answer. This
far from the house, Motia would not hear.

Without hesitation she turned and raced indoors to
her parlour-cum-study and collapsed on the chair in
front of the desk. Motia entered and said, 'I am going
home, memsahib. Is there anything you want before I
go?' she asked.

Ramona thought of confiding her fear to the servant
but, as she could not produce visible proof, decided
against it. 'Yes, Motia. Can I have some water, please?'

'*Ji*, memsahib.'

The water was a long time coming, but meanwhile
Ramona drew some paper towards her and began
writing a carefully worded letter to Gerard. She
explained that again a menacing presence plagued her,
and would be grateful if he could come and put her
mind at ease. It was also a plea for reunion with him.
As soon as Motia brought the water she would ask her
to take the note to the palace on her way home, and
make sure it was handed to Fontaine Sahib personally.

She heard the pad of bare feet and assumed that the
woman had brought the drink. Ramona stretched out
to take the tumbler while she read through the missive.
'Thank you, Motia. You can go now. Goodnight.'

Silence.

She took a long swallow of the cool liquid and looked
up. Her hand shook so violently that the tumbler
crashed to the floor.

'Govind Lal, what are you doing here at this time of
night?' A terrible awareness surfaced that here was the
embodiment of the menace she had suffered these long
months. It spread from him in terrifying waves.

Govind Lal was garbed in white, as usual, but now
he wore a sacred necklace of brown tulsi seeds, and on
his forehead was etched white horizontal lines, pro-

claiming him a devotee of Shiva, the god of procreation and destruction. He wore no turban, his grey hair scraped back and tied in a knot above his nape. The main source of the evil was the malice lancing from his black eyes.

'I have come to see that a holy rite is fulfilled, which my sister refused to honour,' he said in a voice calm and cruel. It filled her with chilling terror.

A growing dizziness afflicted Ramona and a haze began forming in front of her eyes. She shook her head to try to rid her head of the frightening sensation. 'Sister? W-what honour? I do not know. . . What are you trying to say?'

'Your ayah, a Princess of royal blood, disgraced herself by running away from her duty of burning on her dead husband's pyre.'

Though her senses were dimming, she realised that yes, now she spotted the resemblance of this man to her ayah. But she had not been able to connect the two because of their different sexes. 'What have I to do with it?'

'You are part of her, for did you not drink of her milk? No other relations of hers or mine survive. Thus, memsahib, in her stead, you must honour the rite of suttee.'

In her reeling state Ramona grabbed the topmost heavy volume on the table and threw it with all her might at the man. She watched it rising, floating slowly through the air, missing its target and slowly falling—falling into a hazy sea and finally blackness.

CHAPTER FIFTEEN

RAMONA regained consciousness with a heavy head and for the space of several seconds was disorientated, as if in the throes of a nightmare. Some time elapsed before she discovered that she lay in a high, dank room, its walls built of large squares of granite seeping with moisture and slime. She turned her head and spotted a dim oil lamp burning in front of an image of a Hindu god placed on a ledge. Her gaze travelled up to the dark ceiling, from which grey gossamer trailed. Ramona tried to swallow and in alarm found she was gagged. Struggling to sit up, she saw with added dismay that her wrists and ankles were bound.

As recollection surfaced, her heart hurtled in pure terror. She strained, listening for any human voices or footfalls, but not even the natural sounds of the night outside penetrated the stillness. She wondered vaguely whether she was underground. The place seemed to be deserted. Her eyes travelled round the walls, seeking an exit, and spotted a huge arched door with iron studs on it, like a prison—or dungeon. Oh, God save me, she prayed. Had Govind Lal left her here to die? She recalled his threat of forcing her to suffer the rite of suttee.

So dear Ayah was in fact a Princess! And Govind Lal considered Ramona royal too because she had drunk of his sister's milk. Irrelevantly she reflected that she could do with a drop of milk now to ease the dryness of her throat, parched by the gag. Above all, she must remain sane, stop herself from panicking.

Ramona's sensitive ears caught the pad of bare feet. Her body grew rigid with fear. A key twisted, the heavy door creaked open and a figure in white, whom she could just make out in the gloom, slipped in. Bolts slid shut. She recognised the person even at this distance. Govind Lal had come to collect his victim for sacrifice.

He squatted on the uneven, filthy flagstones beside Ramona's bound body and stared with victorious malevolence down at her. 'It is not the hour yet, memsahib. I must perform a sacred ceremony first. But I will tell why you have been chosen to die.' The situation had become bizarre, for he spoke amicably. Seating himself more comfortably in a cross-legged pose, he now enjoyed his role as narrator. 'The Princess Sushila, your ayah, ran away from Jansapur, the realm of her husband, the Raja. Because he had no male heir I was next in line for the throne. But my sister spoiled my chances by refusing to carry out the rite of suttee, and her shame fell on other members of her family. They are all gone but me. I was banished, and pledged to find and return her to the palace. After many moons I traced her to your house in Goa. Alas, I could not take her from there, as it is under the Raj of the Portuguese, and their punishment for suttee is harsh.' He paused and sighed. 'Also she was given to much cunning and guarded herself well, knowing that she would be hunted and taken home. But then she died. I was the sadhu your servants hired to give you the "blessing" on the eve of your leaving Goa. It was no blessing: it was my curse,' he hissed. 'And I followed you when you left with the sahib and the other foreigners.' He wagged his head gravely. Any number of questions swam in Ramona's tormented brain. If only he would remove her gag. 'At Mangalore I bribed one muleteer and took his place.'

Govind Lal extracted a small drawstring bag from his dhoti and pulled out a pan leaf, filling it with betel nut and lime paste. He folded it into a triangle and popped it in his mouth.

For a while he chewed thoughtfully, till the juice seeped out and coloured his thin lips blood-red, adding to his gruesomeness. Wagging his head, he went on, 'You are thinking that I am bad man to do this to you. But bad men do bad things for no reason. I am doing this for a reason: to honour the gods. They will restore my throne and you will enjoy eternal happiness. Thus is it written if you become sati, that is, a saint. I have tied your mouth not to stop you from screaming—who will hear you from this dungeon?—but to stop your curses. A sati's curse is much feared; you are knowing this?'

Ramona could not move, her eyes staring at him in horror; she knew he meant every word he spoke.

He nodded to the stone image on the ledge. 'Shiva knows I act well. There are many forms of suttee. The common way is for the widow to burn with her dead husband. But the rite can be performed without the body of the spouse. She can die in other ways. Some are drowned, some are buried alive. But over here a pyre will draw attention, so might drowning, and it will take me too long to dig a grave. Your sahib will have plenty of time to find and rescue you. So I have thought of an easy way for you, memsahib.' Govind Lal smiled in evil satisfaction. 'You want to know?'

Ramona nodded. She had to find out what this mad fiend planned for her. That it would be horrible she had no doubt. Yet if she knew his method of killing she would become accustomed to her fate; moreover, might conceive an idea to save herself.

He pointed to a spot high up. 'See that skylight, memsahib?' His voice deepened with reverence; as if he did consider her a saint. It made the situation all the more harrowing.

Her gaze followed his finger and saw the window, wide enough for a slim person to wriggle through. It seemed rather a useless fixture, since no natural light penetrated. 'It is from that opening that the cobras on the other side are fed.' Ramona felt her blood drain away in her chilling fear. 'In the vault the sahib keeps his gems. That used to be a temple. Even now the golden image of the Goddess Kali with her many jewelled arms sits cross-legged on her gold lotus. I have planned for your death, memsahib, by lowering you through the skylight and leaving your fate to the snakes.'

Cold sweat covered her body. She shivered violently, her scalp crawling, her stomach heaving. No! How long did it take to die from cobra bite? And how many of the creatures were there?

'Now you know, memsahib, it was I who tried to take you from your bed in the jungle. But when that failed I put a krait in your shoe.' Govind Lal rose and glared down at her. He looked sinister in the feeble illumination of the lamp. Light and shadow honed the sharpness of his gaunt face. Bitter derision slanted his gore-red lips. 'On account of my sister, I lost a kingdom. Therefore it is just that another woman she has blood ties with—she was like your mother—must die. That woman is you!'

'Sahib! Sahib!'

The urgency in the voice had Gerard bounding out

of bed. He threw a robe over his naked body as he
called out. 'What's wrong?'

'Sahib,' more soberly, 'the syce, José, would have
talk with you at once. He is saying it is about the
memsahib.'

Foreboding set Gerard's skin atingle. 'Send him in.'

'*Ji*, sahib,' the servant said and disappeared. He was
back in a short while with a greatly agitated José.

Gerard beckoned the skinny, dark groom into his
opulent bedchamber, dismissed the servant who had
woken him and closed the door. 'Now calm down,
José, and tell me what the trouble is. And start from
the beginning.'

The small Goan gulped in a few breaths and began.
'The memsahib's servant, Motia, has been beaten.
And—and, sahib, the memsahib is not in the villa!'

Tears appeared in the groom's eyes, but Gerard
wasted no time on sympathy; he felt stunned. *Mon
Dieu*! She had ignored caution and, in all foolhardiness,
set off for Madras, probably travelled all night on her
own. And yet on second thoughts he knew her well
enough to believe that she was not given to acts of
violence. No way could she have attacked Motia. 'Has
she taken the horse and her things?'

'No, sahib, I think it is that someone has taken her!'

Gerard frowned at José. 'What are you trying to say?
Someone broke into the villa and kidnapped Madame
Fontaine?'

'Yes, sahib. There are signs that this is so.'

Fear such as he had not known before in his life
enveloped Gerard. 'Where is Govind Lal? He was
supposed to be guarding her.'

'I do not know, sahib. He is very devout and perhaps
left the memsahib's veranda before dawn to find a quiet
place to pray. The gardener says he often does puja by

the tank in the rose garden. I will look when I get back.'

'Did you ride here?'

'I did, sahib. I came on the memsahib's horse. He is fast.'

'All right, José, see that my mount is saddled and brought to the forecourt. I'll be there as soon as I can.'

The sun was peeping over the horizon when the two men reached the villa, to see Motia sitting with her legs outstretched on the veranda. She rocked herself, wailing.

'Stop your howling, Motia,' Gerard commanded sharply. 'Tell me, what makes you think the memsahib has been kidnapped?'

She dried her eyes on the corner of her sari and moaned, 'I have bump on back of head, sahib.' Her rows of silver bangles jangled as she lifted her hand to pinpoint the spot. 'My legs hurt where they were beaten.'

'I'm sorry, Motia. Tell me what happened,' Gerard said gently.

'I was pouring water from goblet in pantry to give the memsahib last night before I left for my quarters, and I felt as if elephant kicked me. Then when my sense returned I tried to get up, but my legs hurt. I screamed to Govind Lal and José, but none heard. I managed t-to crawl out on veranda, but my mind kept going black. Even now I sometimes see two of everything. And the pain.' She touched her crown and groaned. 'Then José found me and he searched for memsahib but could not find her.'

'I'll have your hurt seen to, Motia,' Gerard said kindly. He turned to José. 'Stay with her.' He made for the parlour.

Gerard inspected the room. One of Ramona's leather volumes lay open, face down, in the middle of the floor, as if she had thrown the book at someone. Also the inkwell, quill and a sheet of paper lay in a spread of spilt ink on the glazed tiles, and beside them a smashed glass. But there appeared to be no signs of a violent struggle. The chairs were in place. He came to the conclusion that the water she had drunk had been drugged and as it had begun to take effect she had attempted to save herself by slinging the volume at her kidnapper, but the opiate had overcome her and she had sprawled across the table, upsetting everything on it. The tumbler must have knocked the corner of the table, or slipped from her hand in her fright.

Gerard swore bitterly, berating himself for not paying more attention to the fears she had expressed, and for allowing her to leave the palace. Now where was she? *Bon Dieu* save her.

'Leave everything as it is. I'm going back to the palace,' he told José. 'There's nothing we can do here. We must also find out who, besides my wife, is missing.' To Motia he said softly, 'José will arrange for a cart to take you back to your quarters. We'll arrange for a hakim to examine your hurt.'

Gerard kept up the tradition maintained by the previous ruler of holding a meeting for an hour every morning, attended by all his employees in the durbar pavilion known as the Hall of Public Audience. It was an ideal way of keeping in touch with the few people on the estate and listening to their complaints, queries, suggestions and praises.

At the appointed hour of eight o'clock he arrived at the marble many-pillared building of scalloped arches, decorated with arabesques of semi-precious stones. He mounted the steps leading up the back of the pavilion and through a trellised gilt door to a high jewelled throne laid with bolsters. From here Gerard announced, 'My wife is missing from her villa. Today you will all cease your regular work and hunt for her. A thousand pagodas will be awarded to anyone who discovers her. I also wish to have details of all persons missing on this estate. I do not believe that an outsider kidnapped my wife, and any moment now I expect a ransom will be issued. For your co-operation all of you will receive double wages.'

Before the meeting ended, Gerard learned that three people were missing. Two men had taken carts to collect stores from Colveram. The third missing person who should have been at the villa was Govind Lal. José had not found him at the garden tank, nor had the gardener seen him. Gerard's suspicions grew. The north Indian and José were the only two here who had accompanied them on the journey from Goa. It was true, Govind Lal had joined the column at Mangalore and it was from that port, Gerard recalled, that Ramona had felt uneasy. So that exonerated José from blame, for the time being. He could not clear the groom of guilt till he found Ramona.

After the assembly he left for the record office, also a library with scrolls in coops along the walls, which he had mentioned to Ramona. They contained the history of the ancient palace and its kings. The Raja, however, had not wished to be lumbered with them. He no doubt was anxious to save himself, his children and his zenana from the disease prevailing at that time. In this building, Gerard resumed his thoughts. But why would Govind Lal wish to harm Ramona? Why? Why? Why? All useless whys! Gerard stalked about the chamber, which he normally used to organise work on affairs of the state and do the accounts. He banged his fists down on an ornate desk. 'Ramona, *chérie*, where are you?'

* * *

After issuing his horrendous sentence of death, Govind Lal took a brass bowl near the idol. Sprinkling water from the vessel on Ramona, he began circling her, intoning the funeral chant, '*Ram. . . Ram. . . Ram nam sat hai. . . Ram. . . Ram.*' It seemed to go on for ages till her mind absorbed the chant and she silently intoned it with him. At last the ceremony came to an end. 'I must leave and find rope. I know where it is.'

She lay for what seemed hours in the ill-lit chamber, her body cramped, chilled, her mind very afraid, her ears attuned for any sound coming from the adjoining vault. Gerard was the only one who entered it; hence the only person who could save her—if the cobras had not killed her before then. She squirmed in horror. No, I must not dwell on the reptiles but think of how I can attract someone's attention. She remembered Gerard's mentioning that a man was employed to feed the cobras by lowering their food in a basket. Would Govind Lal bribe the man to allow him to do the chore? Yes, it made sense. So no matter how much she banged her heavy heels on the floor. . .

Her heavy shoes! Govind Lal had not thought to remove them. If Gerard entered the vault wearing snake boots, she should be able to hear him and attract his attention.

A key grated. She turned her head anxiously towards the door and stiffened as Govind Lal entered. On his left shoulder he carried a coil of rope. He threw it down at the side of her. Ramona noticed that he looked disturbed, and, unless she was deceived, even frightened. It gave her a little hope.

He glowered at her. 'They are searching for you as well as me. Your sahib is offering a reward of a thousand pagodas for your safe return. I had to kill that fool who feeds the cobras to take the key for this dungeon off him.' Here Govind Lal hawked and spat. 'His body I should have hidden. He would not take payment and began making too much noise. It is as well that he lives alone. As soon as I have put you in the vault I must make my escape.'

He ignored the terrified entreaty in Ramona's eyes and began coiling one end of the rope round her waist. Absurdly he told her, 'I will lower you gently, memsahib, so you will not fall and get hurt. Now let me bring ladder.' Testing the knot of the rope round her waist for firmness, he left a long length with which to lower her into the nest of cobras. Ramona struggled in terror. Silent screams hurt her throat.

Govind Lal rose and peered into the dark corners of the dungeon till he found the long ladder. He placed it against the skylight and began climbing up, perhaps to make sure that its rungs were intact.

Ramona saw her chance.

She inched towards the ladder, moving her body like a caterpillar: heels down, then pulling herself towards them, stretching her legs again and repeating the whole process. Silently, painfully she worked. By the time she reached the bottom of the ladder Govind Lal was halfway up it. On every rung he bounced up and down, obviously testing its strength to withstand his and Ramona's combined weight. She tensed, aware of the grave risk she was about to take; the tall ladder could well fall on her. Even so, she lifted her bound legs and, with all her might, thrust.

Gerard had announced at the assembly that he would be at the record office if anyone came up with any news. Now he wished he had joined the hunt himself. He stiffened as memory surfaced. Leaving a note in Tamil on the desk, he made for the stables. If anyone wanted him they could go to the villa, where he was heading.

On arrival he tethered the horse, and strode straight to the parlour. His excitement grew. He might find a clue to her whereabouts. Moreover, he needed to satisfy his curiosity.

Every item in the parlour remained exactly as it was when he had last seen it. He lowered himself on his haunches near the patch of ink where the paper lay, now almost entirely covered in dried ink. When he had first seen it he had thought it to be blank, a stray sheet fallen off the desk as she had sprawled over it.

With his hand shaking, he lifted the paper. Slowly he stood up and turned it over. He knew deep disappointment when he discovered that the ink had penetrated almost the entire area of her writing. There was just one clear line at the end of the letter, and as Gerard read it he experienced heartbreaking joy. It consisted of only four words, but they had the power to rock his very soul: 'I love you, Gerard,' he read at least a dozen times. His eyes misted. 'Ramona, *chérie*,' he muttered to himself, '*je t'aime*. I love you too.' What did it matter what their parents had done? He and Ramona had been blessed with deep love for each other. That was all that mattered. *Dieu*! He must find her.

The sound of a horse's hoofs distracted him. He stuffed the letter into his sash and strode out on to the veranda.

José dismounted, came loping across and bounded up the steps to where Gerard stood.

'You have some news, José?'

'I have, sahib,' the groom began breathlessly.

Gerard grabbed the small man's shoulders and shook them in his excitement. 'You have found the memsahib?'

José wagged his head sadly and Gerard dropped his hands. He did not want to hear what José had to say, but he was glad he did.

'I came to tell that the Brahmin priest who feeds the cobras has been murdered.'

'*What*?'

José nodded, feeling daunted; he had never seen the good Gerard Sahib's face so white, nor his eyes so ferocious.

Gerard beckoned the groom. They both ran to their horses and galloped back at full speed to the little pavilion in the palace gardens where the Brahmin lived alone. A group of people surrounded the area and both men and women were wailing. The moment Gerard appeared a path was cleared for him. The palace doctor knelt beside the prone body of the dead priest, its head covered with a cloth.

'How did Swamiji die, *Hakim*?' Gerard asked.

The white-clad doctor looked gravely at Gerard. 'He was attacked with a club, sahib. His head was battered. This is very bad. Why would men want to kill him? He has little money and his wisdom has been a great help to all on the estate. He was kind, holy man. He cared for the sacred cobras in your temple vault, sahib.'

'Was he alive when you arrived, *Hakim*?'

The doctor nodded sadly. 'He said one word, then died.'

'What word?'

'It makes no sense to me, sahib. He said, "Key".'

Gerard pondered. Key! It might in some way connect up with Ramona. 'Swamiji had one to the chamber adjoining the temple vault. He usually kept it on his person. That's the only key he possessed, I think.'

The *hakim* nodded in understanding. 'I will take look, sahib.' But there were no keys on the corpse.

Gerard made a thorough search of the Brahmin's
meagre possessions, but, apart from scrolls of the
Sanskrit scriptures and images of the God Krishna and
the Goddess Durga, there were only a couple of lengths
of cotton, which served the unfortunate Swamiji as
dhotis. Gerard felt a grieving anger that so kindly a
man had suffered a cruel death for the sake of a key.
Somebody needed the key to the dungeon attached to
the vault. He admitted that this could be guesswork on
his part. All the same, why would the dying man place
so much importance in a key? He must have been
murdered for it. 'All right, *Hakim*, I have finished
here.'

As Gerard strode out he absently heard the doctor
call to the surrounding women to prepare the body for
the burning grounds. Gerard's mind leaped with opti-
mism. Ramona might be a prisoner in the dungeon,
and he prayed he would be in time to save her.

Ramona watched in trepidation as the ladder toppled
away from her. Govind Lal yelled as he fell to the
grimy floor on the far side of the room. Mercilessly she
hoped that he had injured himself enough to prevent
him from hauling her up the ladder. She heard him
swear and then painstakingly shuffle towards her.

She cringed as she beheld his face, contorted with
rage, and apart from a limp he seemed to be unhurt
enough to complete his grim task of lowering her into
the nest of cobras. 'You thought to kill me, memsahib,
hey?' He caught the loose end of the rope and began
dragging her across the room, far from where he had
to prop the ladder against the skylight. Her body
scraped painfully over the uneven flagstones. 'But the
gods ruined your evil plans and saved me, memsahib.'

Faith and charity! The man did not know what evil

meant. The long hours without food and water, the effort she had exerted to pull herself to the bottom of the ladder and the recent pain inflicted by this man's dragging her body over the rough floor had depleted Ramona's strength. Numb despair entered her brain; she did not bother to watch Govind Lal erect the ladder again, but closed her eyes. Even the loud hammering on the door failed to stir her. She ascribed the sound to a dream; who would find her here?

'Open this door!'

It was Gerard's voice. All in her mind, of course, Ramona reflected, her body relaxed, seeming to float. The pain had left her. Perhaps she had died.

'Ramona, are you there, *chérie*?'

Her eyes flew open. She found that she had been hoisted over Govind Lal's shoulder. But he was finding great difficulty ascending the ladder. As he stood on the first rung it wobbled. Moreover, he had to grasp her legs to stop her from sliding off and had only one hand to manoeuvre with. She could hear his laboured breath, smell his oiled body. She decided to make it harder for him by wriggling with all the feeble strength she could summon.

Govind Lal dug his nails into her legs and swore, but she could not hear him because axes were being used to break the door down. The Indian had not only turned the key in the lock but also shot the bolts. He had somehow collected sufficient strength to hoist her further up the ladder and was now struggling to reach the skylight.

The door crashed open.

She felt herself falling, falling.

She heard Govind Lal screaming, screaming.

CHAPTER SIXTEEN

'*CHÉRIE*! How do you feel?'

Oh, that beloved voice! Ramona did not wish to wake up from this dream where her body, once bruised and aching, rested on piles of softness, like reclining on clouds. To open her eyes would be to destroy that glorious illusion.

She sighed and stretched. 'Mm.'

'*Ramona, chérie.*'

It was real! She opened her peacock-blue eyes to slits and gradually widened them to stare into Gerard's iridescent black ones. He was seated on a brocaded chair not far from where she lay. The chamber was bright and airy, full of the scent of roses. She spotted a bowl of them on a brass stand in the corner of the room. From outside wafted the sounds of squabbling mynahs and caws of crows. Raising her head a little, she found that she reclined on a silken divan propped with numerous cushions and bolsters. Her clothes had been exchanged for a lavishly embroidered lilac robe.

'You are in the palace lounge, *chérie*. It's mid-afternoon.'

Ramona smiled slowly. 'Oh, Gerard!'

He caught her hand and kissed it. 'Would you like something to eat, my love?'

She laughed unsteadily. 'Yes, please; I'm quite famished.'

His eyes softened as he tenderly touched her cheek, and rose. She leaned forward and clasped his strong fingers. 'Gerard, don't be long.'

246

'It's over there, *chérie*,' he said, pointing to a salver on a table not far off. Helping her to sit up, he placed the tray across her lap and resumed his seat. 'It's good and nourishing.'

She was halfway through the meal when she looked up at him. 'Gerard, what. . .?'

'Shush, my love; finish eating and we'll talk as much as you want. And do not feel afraid; you are safe now.'

After consuming every morsel, Ramona sighed and pushed the tray away.

He deposited it on the floor and leaned back in his chair. 'All right, *chérie*, ask your questions.'

'How did you know Govind Lal had abducted me?'

'I didn't at first,' he began, and told her concisely about his suspicions without disclosing how riddled with anxiety and desperation he had been on hearing of her disappearance, which had forced him to confirm his love for her.

'I don't remember what happened after he carried me part-way up the ladder,' Ramona said, frowning.

'When we broke into the dungeon,' Gerard explained, 'Govind Lal tossed you off his shoulder and I happened to be in the right place to cushion your fall. He continued his climb to the skylight, sat on the sill and kicked the ladder away to prevent us from pursuing him. It dropped harmlessly to the floor, but the exertion caused him to lose his balance and fall backwards into the vault.'

She shuddered. 'I suppose he's dead?'

'Yes. I managed to get him out, but his arms and legs were broken and he had been bitten several times: there was no hope for him. He died in agony. What I find puzzling is why he chose to kill you, *chérie*. You did not seem to know him.'

'I did not. But he knew all about me.' She gripped

her forehead at the temples and shook her head. 'It's unbelievable.'

He took her hand between his palms and smoothed it gently. 'You do not have to tell me yet, *chérie*. It can wait.'

She sent him a tremulous smile. 'I think it's best to get it over with.'

Shrugging his broad shoulders, he gestured her to continue, adding with a word of warning, 'But do not distress yourself, my love. You need not give details.'

'Gerard, Govind Lal was insane. . .' She gave him a brief outline of what had occurred. While she spoke she studied his beloved face, saw the expressions change from mild surprise to utter amazement. She felt immensely relieved, exhausted when the tale came to an end; as if she had just competed in an uphill race.

'I think, my love, that you need a healing nap. I'll leave you, as I have work to do, including attending the burning of the Brahmin priest. He was a wise and popular person, much beloved of the people on this estate. I too liked him and often took his advice. It would be improper if I were not present at his funeral.'

'Of course, you must go. Do not concern yourself about me. One last favour I wish to ask of you, Gerard.'

'Ask, *chérie*.'

'I would like to return to the villa. Despite the happenings there, I have grown fond of it. There is an aura of peace. And the rose garden! I have not seen its like before.'

At first Gerard hesitated; then he smiled easily. 'The fear has gone. By all means return. My father spent most of his last days there. He loved the garden and perhaps pictured you in it. That's why he left the villa to you and your mother.'

'Oh, yes, Mama too loved flowers.'

'José and a woman servant will see you are comfortable and safe. I'll join you for dinner tonight.' He said the last sentence in a low voice full of allure and romantic promise.

'But I thought you were going to the priest's cremation, Gerard.'

'It should be over by sundown, and I do not have to stay till the end.'

Back in the villa, Ramona woke from a restful sleep in her comfortable bed. She saw a servant girl hovering around, spreading a garment on a low sofa against the wall. Ramona glanced through the window and gazed at the sun, low in the sky. 'How is Motia?'

The servant girl turned. 'She is getting well, memsahib.'

Ramona smiled. 'Good. Do you think I can have a cup of tea before I dress?'

'Ji, memsahib, you assuredly can. The cook has boiled the water and I will bring char at once.'

As promised, the girl returned with a tray carrying the welcome brew. Ramona donned her robe, sat on the edge of her bed and drank thirstily. With idle amusement she listened to the girl playfully bullying a male servant to fill the copper bath.

The tea seemed to put new life into Ramona. She remembered Gerard's promise to dine with her, and decided to wear something special. Most of the dresses the palace tailor had sewn were for day wear. Perhaps the gown she had worn at the serai in Mangalore would be most suitable. As she crossed to fetch it from the cupboard she spotted a breathtaking gown spread on the sofa, over which the servant had been hovering.

She was still exchanging banter with the water carrier when Ramona called to her.

Saying a loud, '*Ji*, memsahib,' she bustled into the chamber.

Ramona stared in awe at the gorgeous creation. 'Whose is that?'

'It is yours, memsahib. Fontaine Sahib had it sewn for you. He asked that you wear it tonight.'

'Mine?' Ramona squeaked in astonishment 'But— but——'

'Memsahib, if you do not wear it the sahib will assuredly be very angry with me. He said, "See that the memsahib wears that gown." And I told him, "Very good, Fontaine Sahib, I will coax the memsahib to wear it!"'

Ramona laughed. 'If the sahib had it made for me then it would be most ungracious if I did not put it on to please him.'

'It is so, memsahib. Now let me help you to bathe.'

'No, no, I'm not used to being pampered. I will not be long. Perhaps you can help me put the gown on. It laces at the back and has very wide skirts, which need smoothing down with your aid.'

'*Ji*, memsahib.'

It was an excited servant girl who ushered Gerard into the drawing-room. She stayed long enough to see the stunned pleasure on both their faces before she withdrew.

When Gerard finally recovered from beholding Ramona in all her glory he sauntered to where she sat smiling up at him and caught her hand, kissed it and raised her from the chair. '*Mon Dieu*! I never knew ivory would suit you so well, though I chose it. It's the exact colour of your hair and it enhances the apricot blush of your skin. I did not see the finished dress, but I notice the *durzi* has created a masterpiece.'

'Thank you, Gerard; I love it. All this lace on the bodice and skirts and the full sleeves. But. . .but. . .'

'What, *chérie*?'

'The neckline is too low. It drops off my shoulders.'

He traced his finger along the edge, lingering at the deep valley between her breasts. 'No, it's just right—for me.'

Her skin prickled with pleasure. At this rate they would never eat. 'Dinner is ready. Shall we go?'

His white teeth flashed in a stunning smile and he offered her his arm. '*Mais oui*, Madame Fontaine.'

The cook had surpassed himself with a tasty menu, but Ramona could not manage a dessert. She watched Gerard eat with gusto. The light from the candelabrum cast shadows on the immaculate lace tablecloth and set the silver, cut glass and French wine sparkling. It also brought out the reddish glints in his dark hair and the iridescent gleam in his black eyes. He had discarded his lilac shot silk coat with her permission. The whiteness of his full-sleeved shirt and lace cravat complemented his mahogany tan. She was happy to see that he ate with complete ease, tucking the snowy napkin into the neckline of his embroidered lilac waistcoat.

At last he lifted his wine glass and saluted her. 'Excellent, *chérie*. But I fear I have overeaten, thanks to the good cook, Ali. Shall we stroll in the garden? Father and I often relaxed there and exchanged ideas.'

'Of course,' she said agreeably. But Ramona knew uneasiness; Gerard had not once spoken to her of love. She was hopelessly in love with him, but was he in love with her? How could she live with a man who did not love her? Attraction and infatuation were not the same thing; they did not last. And if that French coquette arrived again, would he turn to her? All these doubts she had to erase; else she must leave for Madras as soon as possible.

When they reached the arbour it was dusk, but bright enough to see the colours of the delicate pink roses that climbed the framework and also blossomed in carefully dug beds. Perfume from the blooms permeated the balmy evening.

Gerard turned her to face him. 'Now tell me what's troubling you, *chérie*. I cannot bear to see your lovely face marred by a frown. Tell me.'

Her deep blue gaze roamed his face hungrily. I must treasure this moment to remember and dream about when I am old and alone.

He shook her gently, 'Tell me, Ramona.'

'Could you take me to Madras, Gerard?'

She saw the anger creep in a dull red spread from his neck to his face. He tightened his grip on her bare shoulders. 'Why? Why, for God's sake? You and I are married. Our place is with each other.'

She nodded agreement.

'Then why?' And now she detected despair in his voice.

'It's the scandal I fear. At the slightest irritation, we'll be throwing our erring parents' infidelities at each other. It will not make for a happy life.'

'But we're both in the same boat. Neither of us is in a position to accuse the other. Besides, I cannot let you go.'

'Why, Gerard?'

His grip on her shoulders slackened to a caress that caused her body to tingle with pleasure. 'I love you, Ramona.'

She could not speak; happiness had rendered her dumb, but the rest of her came alive, like an animal after hibernation. Her eyes glowed like deep sapphires in the gathering gloom. She lifted her arms to encircle his neck and moved his head down to her lips, parting in invitation. 'I love you, Gerard,' she murmured in English.

Against her mouth he whispered, 'Say it in French, *chérie*.'

'*Je t'aime, Gerard*.'

The kiss was long and filled with love. At last he lifted his mouth and pressed her head protectively against his chest. 'This love we feel for each other we inherited from our wayward parents. For them it was wrong; for us it is right.'

'It might have been wrong for them, but at least now we understand how they felt.'

'Yes, and perhaps forgive them.' He lifted her left hand and eased off her mother's wedding-ring.

Ramona watched him in growing anxiety. 'What are you doing, Gerard?'

'This.' He hurled the ring into the tank and drew from his waistcoat pocket a circlet of wide gold. 'See the inside.'

She saw the letters G and R entwined. 'It's beautiful,' she said on a soft sigh.

He slipped the ring on her finger, caught her round the waist, and, hugging her close, said, 'Let's go to bed, *chérie*. I want to make love to you.' Lifting her chin, he raised one brow. 'Well?'

Happiness bubbled up in Ramona. 'And I, sir, shall not raise the least objection.'

The other exciting

MASQUERADE
Historical

available this month is:

HEIR APPARENT
Petra Nash

The unexpected and peculiar death of her brother Giles
was only the beginning for Mary Hadfield of a series of
odd events which looked likely to end in her losing her
home, after her father died of grief and shame shortly
afterwards. Her cousin, Jason Hadfield, never met
before because of a family feud, seemed to offer
succour, but Mary wasn't sure, particularly after meeting
the mysterious stranger, John Smith. He always seemed
to appear when he was most needed, like the Lazarus he
called himself, but knowing so little about him, how
could Mary truly rely on him?

TWO HISTORICAL ROMANCES & TWO FREE GIFTS!

MASQUERADE *Historical*

Masquerade historical romance bring the past alive with splendou excitement and romance. We wi also send you a cuddly teddy bear an a special mystery gift. Then, if yo choose, you can go on to enjoy more exciting Masquerades every months, for just £2.25 each! Ser the coupon below at once to – Read Service, FREEPOST, PO Box 23 Croydon, Surrey CR9 9EL.